PRAISE FOR THAT WHICH CANNOT BE UNDONE

"Who knew Ohio was so ominous! With desolate roads, abandoned buildings, beguiling pastures, submerged towns, and even haunted drains, it's little wonder the state is home to some of horror's most macabre storytellers. Conjured from such strange and fertile imaginations, and curated by the mistress of darkness, Jess Landry, That Which Cannot Be Undone, is a frightening addition to the folk horror genre and your perfect late-night treat." —*Lee Murray, four-time Bram Stoker Award®-winner and author of Grotesque: Monster Stories*

"I have been a longtime reader and friend of many of the writers gathered to tell horror stories in this book, but never had it struck me before: what a collection of dark talent we have in Ohio! Don't be fooled by their gentle midwestern charms -- this book shows just how dark it is inside their skulls, and just how imaginative these macabre minds can be! This title rivals any horror anthology you might have read before, and -- kind of like when you're binge watching episodes of the Twilight Zone -- I bet you won't be able to stop gobbling every story up. These tales of twisted fate, dark destiny and cunning consequence are page turners, written by superstars in the horror genre, and they are all so very good." —*Michael Arnzen, Bram Stoker Award-winning author of Grave Markings and Play Dead*

"From the cities of Cleveland and Columbus, to an old prison, a drowned town, an abandoned winery, and many other natural and notable locations, these stories place Ohio front and centre on the map of horror landscapes. A frightening anthology that has ensured if I ever visit Ohio, I will be very afraid." —*Iseult Murphy, author of All of Me*

THAT WHICH CANNOT BE UNDONE

An Ohio Horror Anthology

Edited by

JESS LANDRY

CRACKED SKULL PRESS

First Edition

10 9 8 7 6 5 4 3 2 1

Cover art by Greg Chapman

Cover design by Greg Chapman

Print ISBN: 979-8-218-05223-2

Printed in the United States of America

ACKNOWLEDGEMENT OF COPYRIGHT

CONTENTS

IN THE CLEARING

Megan E. Hart

W hite siding. Black shutters. Red front door. Green grass in a tidy yard with flowers blooming in beds beneath the windows. The people who lived in this house took care of it, Becka thought. If they took care of a house, they'd take care of a baby. Wouldn't they?

That's what the man had promised her, anyway. They'd take care of the baby, and until it was born, they'd take care of Becka, too. Anything she needed. Anything she *wanted*.

"It's a simple contract," the man said.

His name was Roger. He looked like an accountant. Small, bristly brown mustache. Thinning hair the color of sand. Rabbity front teeth that poked out even when his mouth was supposed to be closed. He'd found her sitting outside Vito's Pizza, where she'd been hanging around hoping to see someone she knew but had not yet pissed off too much to hit up for a few bucks.

"Arlene's inside," Roger said now.

The wife. None of this mattered until and unless Arlene approved. Becka knew how it worked with women. If Arlene didn't like her, there'd be no place to stay. No money. Roger would turn around and drop her back in downtown Dayton, quick as a rat could shit.

"Let's go in," Roger said in a low voice almost like a coo.

Becka straightened her shoulders. The drive had taken a couple of hours. They'd passed signs for Hocking Hills State Park, but she still had no real idea where they'd ended up, only that it would be a long walk back. There didn't seem much point in standing in the driveway. She'd agree to have a baby for these people, or she would not. She had about two bucks in her wallet. She'd lost her phone service months ago. Her back teeth were hurting again, rotten to the root. Her skin prickled and itched, and her guts ached deep inside with the heat of craving.

She was fucked, as the old saying goes.

"Come meet my wife," Roger said.

Well, it looked like she was going to get fucked again.

"Your room." Arlene pushed open the creaking door with her fingertips. She stepped aside to let Becka go first.

White walls. White furniture. Dark wood floors gleamed without dirt or stains. A fluffy white rug.

At the window, Becka looked out to the backyard and beyond, into the trees. She looked at Arlene. "You have woods."

"Our property backs up to park lands. Miles and miles. You could hike to the Devil's Bathtub from here if you had enough time."

Arlene's lip twitched. The two women stared at each other in silence through the doorway. Arlene finally stepped into the room. "We want you to be comfortable. After all, it'll be your home for the next year or so. Assuming you sign the contract, of course."

Startled, Becka stepped back. "A *year*?"

Arlene's gaze, steady but interrupted every few seconds with a series of hard, rapid blinks, reminded Becka of a bird's. She tilted her head like one, too. "Even if you catch right away, it would still be nearly ten months until the baby is born. And, of course, we don't intend to toss you out into the streets the moment the cord is cut. We'll want you to...feed it."

A small warmth rose in Becka's chest. Hope. Something she hadn't allowed herself in a long time.

"I love everything. It's all so clean." She sounded young and earnest and just the sort of girl a childless couple could trust to provide them with a baby.

Not like a homeless junkie-sex-addict-alcoholic-stoner who'd squandered and ruined every good thing that had ever happened to her.

"I'm glad," Arlene said. It was the first time she'd smiled, and it transformed her. "Your bathroom is through there. It's fully stocked with whatever you could possibly need, but if it's missing something, *anything*, you let me know."

"I'm sure it will all be great." How else could she answer?

If this was a fairy tale, then Becka was certainly the dirty little cinderseat who'd been given the chance to go to the ball. If she'd ever wanted anything more in her life than she did right now, she couldn't remember it. She wasn't going to fuck this up. With Arlene watching in silence, Becka moved around the room.

Inside the closet hung a couple dozen dresses, all of them in muted blues and grays and all in the same basic style. Scoop-necked, sack-like, meant to be pulled on over the head. No buttons, zippers or strings. They hung in order of size, small-to-large. Not to accommodate any size girl they might have brought home, Becka realized, but to fit her as she grew with her intended pregnancy. The dresser held unopened packages of clean white panties and matching bras. Soft white socks, everything fresh and pristine and unused. Brand new. She looked down at her faded jeans with the holes in the knees. She'd been wearing the same clothes for the past few days. Her battered sneakers had worn through at the toes.

Movement from outside caught her attention, and Becka looked out the window. Night was still a few hours off, but the trees at the far edge of the yard were already dark. She shaded her eyes.

"You have Bigfoots out there?" When Arlene didn't answer, Becka looked over her shoulder. "Sorry. Bigfeet."

"Where are you from? Originally, I mean."

Becka cleared her throat. "I was born in Connecticut. Came out here to Ohio for school."

"But you didn't finish."

"No," Becka said. "I didn't finish."

"What do you think about Ohio?"

"I miss the East Coast," Becka said after a second, risking the truth. "The pizza's a lot better. And it's closer to the ocean."

Arlene stepped closer. "Is that why you're so sad? You miss the ocean?"

"I'm not sad," Becka said, but she was.

"Do you have anyone you need to notify?"

"What do you mean?"

"Will anyone come looking for you?" Arlene's voice was like the rasp of knuckles on a cheese grater.

For a moment, Becka allowed herself to think of Vito. She owed him money, a lot of it. One more reason for her to hide away here for a year or longer, right? Hours from Dayton, in the middle of Bigfeet country, how would he ever find her?

"Nobody will come looking for me." Fresh sadness curdled inside her, twisting in the space below her heart.

"I'll leave you to get settled." Arlene ducked out of the room.

From downstairs wafted a smell of something delicious, and thick spittle squirted into Becka's mouth. She clutched at her belly, so flat it was almost concave. Her last meal had been half a burger and some fries taken off a toddler's plate in a diner while the parents were busy with something else. That had been days ago. A hot worm of hunger twisted inside her, nudging that earlier rise of craving that had also gone unfulfilled for way too long. She was hungry for so, so many things.

Becka plucked one of the dresses from the hanger to take with her into the bathroom. That's when everything went sideways. Not because of the toothbrush laid out for her, along with floss, mouthwash, and toothpaste. Nor the fluffy towels and washcloths or the simple cotton robe hung on the back of the door.

It was the drugs.

Lots of drugs.

This was no Alice in Wonderland deal—no little tags read *Eat Me* or *Drink Me*, but it was obvious that the vials and baggies, the special vape pen, were all meant for her. A chilly finger of unease played a tune down the washboard of her spine. Roger approaching her in front of the pizza shop hadn't scared her. Agreeing to go to his house and meet his wife also hadn't. She'd done worse in the past, for the promise of less. Now, a full-body shiver wracked her from head to toe. What kind of people mowed their lawn and weeded their flowers, but gave drugs to the woman they wanted to carry their baby?

Ultimately...did she care?

Powders and pills and potables, she thought. Anything she'd ever wanted, and some she'd never tried. The glint of a needle next to a small, clear vial of liquid set her back a step, one hand pressing the inside of her elbow. She fancied she could feel the pulse of her heart in the vein.

She'd start slow, she thought. A couple tokes. She wasn't preggers yet. No harm in that, right?

No harm at all.

"There, now, everything is fine. It's all just fine."

The man poised between Becka's legs had rough hands and the blood-shot eyes of a drinker. Arlene had introduced him as Dr. Tone, but Becka didn't believe he was a doctor. Instead of a white lab coat, he wore a camo jacket. Fingerprints smudged the lenses of his dark-framed glasses. He stood, patting Becka's thigh so she could sit up and let her dress fall back around her calves. The exam had been painless, quick, embarrassing.

"The contract." Arlene pulled a piece of paper from her pocket and unfolded it onto the table. "You'll sign?"

Becka's head spun. The weed was very good. She was famished. "Sure."

"In blood, as required," the not-quite-a-doctor said.

"I have my period," Arlene said.

Dr. Tone grinned, high color showing up in his cheeks above the sandy brown beard. "I'll be the witness."

The pen, a quill dripping red, shook in Becka's hand. She scrawled her name along the bottom of the paper. Arlene added hers. So did Dr. Tone.

The world was still a little fuzzy around the edges as Becka drew in a deep breath of the delicious scents coming out of the kitchen. She pressed on her empty belly, which would soon be full. It was difficult to worry about much of anything right now other than filling it.

Dinner.

Plates, a table, a bottle of wine, two men and the woman with smiles and words that drifted all around through the air before finally settling into Becka's ears. She was high. Then drunk. She was hungry, and she ate. A plate of spaghetti, then another. Garlic bread. Salad. More wine. Her belly bulged with it.

"How does it happen?" The words dripped out of her lips like honey or syrup or blood. "Turkey baster or...?"

"It will happen the natural way," Arlene said.

Becka looked at Roger. "You mean I'm supposed to fuck him."

"You'll lie together. As many times as it takes. Until you get with child."

"What happens if I don't?"

"You will," Dr. Tone said.

This was some serious *Handmaid's Tale* shit, but did Becka really care? The answer, boys and girls, was no. The food was good. The drugs were better.

The sex was okay, too.

Roger on top of her. Inside her. Arlene and the doctor watched. Coaching? Guiding? Becka didn't care. It was over soon enough, and she slept.

Becka's sheets were dirty.

Dark swaths of mud stained what had been crisp and white and clean when she went to bed. At least, she thought they'd been clean. Last night was hazy.

She swung her aching legs over the side of the bed. Everything hurt. Dirt splashed up her calves. Bruises marked the insides of her thighs. She staggered to the bathroom and into a scalding shower, and she scrubbed herself until she'd removed all traces of filth. A snaking scratch meandered from the inside of one thigh, down the back of her knee, and ended at the bump of her ankle. Fainter but similar scratches feathered her belly and side. A few of them had dug deeply enough to scab. The tips of her toes were raw.

She remembered being weightless.

What had she done last night? Where had she gone? Her last memory was of Roger pumping away on top of her, Arlene and Dr. Tone in the background shouting encouragement.

Puke surged up her throat. She didn't even make it to the toilet, just barfed right there in the shower. The vomit swirled around her scraped-open toes before going down the drain, but before it vanished completely, Becka thought she saw something wriggling in it.

She was no stranger to after-binge morning pukes, but this felt different. Another wave of nausea overtook her, and she heaved and heaved with nothing but bitter drool to show for it. Until, at last, one final gut-wrenching retch brought up what looked like a tangle of fine, wiry black hairs. The mess slipped into the drain before Becka could stop it.

In the mirror, her eyes looked red. Her lips slightly swollen. Her mousy brown hair hung lank and wet, but smooth, against her cheeks. She'd never been a pretty girl, but this morning, especially considering the night she'd had and the way she'd just hurled, she ought to have looked worse.

Something squirmed in her left eye. Black and wiry, like the stuff she'd puked in the shower. It was gone in an instant, leaving behind a faint blur that disappeared as soon as she'd blinked a few times.

When she brushed her teeth, blood swirled in the white foam she spit into the sink. When she ran her tongue over her gums, she tasted the richness of blood. She spat again. No blood this time, only the echo of it, like the memory of floating she was trying hard to forget. She probed a tooth in the back. It came out smoothly, no resistance, and very little pain. She flushed it down the toilet and hovered over the bowl, expecting to puke again, but she didn't.

Becka had never been much of a wake-n-baker. Weed was for night-time, so she could get her beauty rest. Pills were for the morning. Cool little white round pills that slipped down her throat without effort. Her stomach settled in minutes.

She combed her hair and put on the fresh white cotton panties and bra. Tugging one of those shapeless dresses over her head, Becka slipped her bare feet into brilliant white sneakers. Her toes stung. She went downstairs, hoping for breakfast. The house was quiet. She peeked out the front window. Roger's car wasn't in the driveway.

Arlene was in the kitchen. "Good morning, Becka. I've made you breakfast."

"You're not eating?" Becka asked from around the mouthful of scrambled eggs and wheat toast thickly laid with butter and jam that she shoveled in her mouth as fast as she could.

Arlene put a lit cigarette to her lips and drew in the smoke, letting it seep out from her nostrils in silence while watching Becka dig in. She ashed delicately into a crystal bowl. Her smile revealed straight but yellowed teeth.

"No."

Becka swallowed hot coffee. "Did something happen last night?"

"I surely hope so."

"I mean...did I go anywhere last night?" Becka looked through the windows to the yard and the trees beyond. "Did I go into the forest?"

"Do you remember going into the forest?"

"My sheets were dirty when I woke up this morning. I thought..." Becka shook her head. With the food and coffee settling into her stomach and the pills working their magic, it was hard to get worked up about anything.

"You must have dreamed it," Arlene said.

"I didn't dream the dirty sheets. Or the scratches." Becka said sharply.

She'd hated a lot of things in her life, but being called a liar was top of the list, mostly because she *was* a liar. And a thief, and an addict, and a lot of the other things she'd been accused of being, but being called a liar when she was telling the *truth* wasn't fair.

Becka followed Arlene's gaze with her own, back to the tall, dark trees swaying in a breeze that didn't so much as ruffle a blade of grass in the yard. Inside her sneakers, her excoriated toe-tips burned. Briefly, Becka closed her eyes.

Something squirmed inside her, low, deep in her belly.

"Is something wrong?" Arlene's voice drifted to her.

Becka opened her eyes. "I think I'm pregnant."

Black trees. Black sky. A flash of ivory through the branches overhead. The moon.

Becka grabbed at a bush full of briars that pierced her palm. She drew it back against the front of her billowing gray nightgown. Blood dotted the fabric.

Her toes whispered over the dirt and stones and fallen pinecones.

A humming thrum surrounded her. She entered a clearing. A circle of coals in the center glowed until a breeze came and kicked up the flames. They rose, red-gold-orange-yellow, flaring, and in the shadows, a multitude of eyes shone.

In the morning, every morning, her sheets were dirty, but the bottoms of her feet were clean.

Pills in the morning. Powders during midday. Weed at night.

The days passed while Becka got high. Or did they? Maybe she was living one endless day. She woke, dress, ate, drank. She watched television with Arlene, who knitted blankets, booties, bonnets.

Becka's belly grew. She moved into the next size of gowns. Dr. Tone came to examine her, happily announcing how well it was going.

Five months along, late in the afternoon, Becka went to the fridge for a snack. Arlene was napping, as she often did in the lazy hours before dinner when the summer sun had turned the house into an oven. Becka preferred it when Arlene was sleeping. It gave her the illusion she was alone in the house. As she bent to pull out a package of deli meat and some cheese, a tickling touch made her jump.

She knew who it was before she turned around. Knew what he

wanted. Other than that first night, Roger hadn't done so much as brush her sleeve as she passed him. Every night he stared at her across the dinner table with the look of a starving man, but he never touched her.

Roger's clumsy embrace ignited an inferno inside her. Legs shaking, Becka hiked up her dress to offer him access. He fumbled with his belt, glancing over his shoulder, muttering a string of words she couldn't understand.

"Hurry," Becka said.

He fumbled. She caught a flash of pink in his fist, framed by wiry black threads. Tension lurched inside her. Did something twitch in her eye? Her stomach roiled. It was just hair, she thought, backing up against the kitchen table as Roger approached her.

"Roger!" Arlene's voice rang through the kitchen, although she hadn't shouted. "What do you think you're doing?"

He froze, fingers wrapped around his rapidly deflating member. Becka put her hands on the mound of her belly and let the dress fall down to her shins again. Arlene's lip curled.

"If you won't let me," Roger said, "why can't I, with her?"

Arlene strode across the kitchen and slapped him across the face. His head rocked back. Roger didn't make a sound, not even as the pale imprint of her hand filled in with red. Without looking at Becka, he zipped his pants and left the room.

Becka waited for Arlene to say something, but the other woman only stared at her, arms crossed over her chest. Finally, Becka said, "Are you going to kick me out?"

"Of course not."

"Because you want the baby."

"We all want it," Arlene said.

Another curling twist of something unfurled in Becka's guts. "Who's we?"

"The ones who wait."

"What are they waiting for?" Becka asked.

"The coming of the new god."

"And then what?"

"A new god means a new world," Arlene said.

"What does that mean? What will happen then?"

"That," Arlene said, "is what we are waiting to find out."

She pushed Becka aside and assembled an enormous sandwich, which she set in front of Becka at the table. She added a syringe. A spoon. A packet of brown powder. A lighter.

Hunger growled in Becka's belly. "Why are you giving all of this to me?"

"Why aren't you resisting it?"

Becka put both her hands flat on the table. She couldn't sit very close anymore because of the bump of her belly. Inside her, the baby threshed and writhed.

"Because I can't help myself," she said, not for the first time ashamed to admit it. "But I know it's not good for the baby. Why do you keep giving this shit to me? You're going to make it come out wrong."

Arlene's lips skinned back over her teeth, yellow and long and prominent. She leaned so close that Becka could smell the acrid odor of her skin under the cloying stink of scented soap. Arlene stroked a hand down Becka's hair; it had grown from shoulder-length all the way down to her waist. Arlene's nails tangled in it. Becka's scalp stung at the tug.

"Of course we are," she said.

When young Becka had imagined her life, it had sometimes included a vague idea of children. A husband. A house much like Arlene and Roger's. She had never imagined herself *pregnant* except as a nightmare, something to be feared, avoided. Terminated.

Her teeth fell out, one by one, but she could not bring herself to care.

"This will help with the stretch marks." Arlene, sitting on the edge of Becka's bed, tugged up the gray nightgown to expose the mountain of Becka's stomach. She cupped a palmful of oil that she began rubbing into the flesh.

Becka, propped up on a pile of pillows, shook her head. "Those are scratches. Anyway, what do you care if I get stretch marks?"

Arlene rubbed more oil into Becka's skin. Slowly. Becka arched under the pleasure of that touch. Everything ached, it seemed. The closer she got to the end, the bigger and more swollen her body became. Also, it had been months without any sort of contact, sensual or otherwise, and although she could glut herself on food and drugs as much as she wanted, she'd been sorely missing human touch.

"You might not think I care about you, Becka, but I do. You are the vessel that will provide the child who will change the world."

Rub. Rub. Rub.

"Are you going to kill me after it's born?"

Rub.

Rub.

Rub.

"Of course not," Arlene said. "I told you, we'll need you to feed it."

"Is it going to eat me?"

Rub.

Pause.

Rub.

"If we're lucky," Arlene said, "it will eat everything."

With Roger gone, banished and never spoken of again, Arlene had to leave Becka alone while she went to the store. Becka didn't mind. Arlene would bring back whatever Becka put on the shopping list. There would be bowls of gooey chocolate pudding. Ice cream. Creamy macaroni and cheese, the good kind, not that four-for-a-dollar powdered cheese crap Becka had survived on for weeks at a time. No matter how much she ate, she was never sated.

There would be new intoxicants to try, too.

Her toes remained raw at the tips, but no longer hurt. Nothing much could hurt, not with everything she took coursing through her veins, digesting in her guts, dissolving through the thin, fine membranes of her sinuses.

In the kitchen, she opened a bottle of vodka and glugged enough to choke her for a moment. Her eyes watered, so at first she thought the shadow that appeared in the doorway in front of her was a hallucination.

"Holy shit," said the man with the pizza box in his hands.

"I didn't order a pizza," she said.

"It's me, you dumb whore." Vito tossed the pizza box onto the table and grabbed her by the upper arms so she couldn't get away. He looked at the immensity of her belly between them. "The fuck?"

It never mattered to Arlene if Becka couldn't manage to form coherent sentences, but Vito looked appalled at the babble that fell from her lips, words like stones. Or frogs, like in that fairy tale that had always freaked her out when she was a kid. He shook her hard enough to rattle her bones, then stepped back.

"Disgusting," he said.

Becka shrugged and lifted the bottle to her mouth again. She swallowed long and hard. Held the bottle out to him. There was something strange about Vito being there in Arlene's clean, bright kitchen, but Becka couldn't think of what it was.

"What did they do to you? Bruno said he saw you go off in a car with some dude. It took me forever to track you down." Vito looked around the kitchen.

"How'd you...?"

"The guy who picked you up came back to the shop. Bruno pointed him out to me. Turns out a little talk with Fuck Around," Vito showed off his left hand, then the right, "and Find Out were enough to convince him to tell me where you were."

Becka's toes throbbed. "You cared about me?"

"I care about the money," Vito said.

"...havin' a baby..."

His lip curled in the bush of his gray and black beard. "They paying you? I didn't come all the way out here to Bumfuck not to get *something*."

"Pizza?" The word slurred as Becka's focus swung to the box on the table. The smell of sauce and pepperoni woke the baby. It kicked. Becka's mouth watered. Vito's pizza was shit, but people were too afraid of him to ever say so.

Vito sneered. "That was just an excuse to get in the house. Fuck, you're dumb."

"Not dumb. Drunk." Unsteadily, Becka lumbered to tug the pizza cutter off the magnetic strip holding it in place next to the steak knives. The metal blade tore through the imperfectly square-cut pizza, hours cold, and into the cardboard beneath. She tossed the cutter onto the kitchen table to lift one slice to her mouth. She'd have to gum it.

"And pregnant. You still using? Never mind, you're using. Bring it to me. We can work out a little arrangement—"

Vito's voice cut off into a gurgle. Something hot and wet, stinking of meat, sprayed across the room. Becka, pizza slice drooping in her fingers, turned to see that Arlene had returned. The older woman wielded the pizza cutter with deft grace, slashing again at Vito's throat.

He staggered forward, arms pinwheeling. Becka couldn't move fast enough to get out of the way. One flailing fist caught her belly. Becka fell away, clutching it protectively. The baby kicked, angry, but at least Vito's punch didn't seem to have hurt it.

The pizza box had fallen onto the floor. Vito toppled, face down, next to the spatter of sauce and cheese. Blood spread out from beneath him in a slowly widening puddle. The slice in Becka's hand plopped next to his head.

"His pizza sucks," Becka said.

———

"Not long now." Arlene's eyes glowed.

"And she's been given—" Dr. Tone said.

"She's been given everything," Arlene interrupted.

Both of them turned to look at Becka, who had at last managed to sit upright. She swung her legs over the edge of the bed. She ran her tongue over the dents in her gums where her teeth had once been; sharp nubs were forming underneath the skin. She heaved herself to her feet so she could waddle to the bathroom, where she opened her mouth to study herself in the mirror. She pressed a fingertip to her bottom gums, and when she withdrew it, pinpricks of blood appeared as though she'd been stuck with tiny needles.

Becka put her hands over the slowly turning lump inside her. In the mirror behind her, she caught sight of Arlene's mouth stretching into a grin, revealing those big teeth. They were fake, Becka realized now, and ran her tongue once more over the bumps in her own gums. But hers would be real, when they came in.

And they would be sharp.

"Is Roger ever coming back?"

Arlene ladled a portion of meat and potatoes onto Becka's plate. "Roger is no longer one who waits."

"A baby should have a father."

"Roger is not the child's true father, Becka. I thought you'd have figured that out by now. He was only the vessel. The way you are only the vessel, not the child's true mother."

Becka shredded tender meat between her new teeth. Chewed. Swallowed.

They'd see about that.

Again, dark trees. Black sky. White moon.

Red blood.

Becka didn't remember leaving the house to enter the forest, but she never did. For the first time, her feet pressed the earth, taking all of her weight. She stood with her legs wide apart. Hot fluid trickled down the insides of her thighs. It spattered on the leaves and dirt beneath her bare feet. Her belly tensed, and she pressed her palms flat to it.

Five figures in white-hooded robes surrounded her, chanting in a language she didn't understand. Arlene was there, too, her hood hanging down in the back to expose her face. Becka suspected one of the others was the not-quite-a-doctor, but she had no clue who any of the rest of them might be.

Becka had never seen a baby being born. Hell, she hadn't understood how babies were *made* until she was a junior in high school, and then she'd barely believed it. She'd known, though, that there would be pain and blood.

She squatted, and the white-robed attendants flocked around her on either side to hold her upright. Her body strained, pushing down. She couldn't stop it. All she could do was scream through every pain and wait for her body to split in half.

With each ripple of contractions, she bit her lower lip until her new teeth snapped together, an open slice of wounded flesh between them, and she gulped the thick, metallic fluid as eagerly as she'd ever guzzled wine.

"Leave her, now." Arlene gestured at the white-robed attendants. "You've finished the rituals. She has to do the rest of this alone."

"Alone? Wait, what?" Becka put her hands on the taut, straining flesh of her belly. "How am I supposed to do this all by myself?"

"Hey, c'mon, this isn't right. We can't really just leave her here *alone*." One of the figures pushed its hood back. Dr. Tone. Firelight glinted off his glasses.

"Women have been giving birth without assistance since time immemorial. She'll be fine."

Tone shook his head. "No. I'm a part of this—"

"You're a part of nothing!"

The attendants holding onto her all let go. Stepped back. Tone moved toward Arlene, his face grim in the dancing shadows from the fire.

Without their support, Becka fell forward, both hands on the ground. Deep inside, she felt a stretching, sharp with electric zaps. More fluid spattered, forming a glistening puddle beneath her.

"The whole point of this was the baby, and after every fucked up thing you've done to it so far, the chances of something going wrong in childbirth—"

"I COMMAND YOU TO GO!"

Arlene's grimace twisted her lips until her mouth gaped from ear to ear, a toothless cavern. Becka swayed, blinking, as the ground tried to rush up and punch her in the face. That had to be an illusion. Arlene's mouth was not that wide.

In seconds, the white robes scattered, fleeing, pushing and shoving each other to be the first out of the clearing. One fell and was trampled without heed by the rest of them. It staggered upright and fell again. Moaning, it didn't get back up. Crimson bloomed on the white fabric.

Dr. Tone hadn't moved. He unzipped the front of the robe and tossed it aside. He backhanded Arlene hard enough to spin her around. Her robe tangled around her ankles, and she staggered before falling down next to the fire. Tone bent to put his hands in Becka's armpits, lifting her. He muttered words in her ear in that same language...but now she did understand it, because the baby did.

Her baby.

It kicked hard enough to show the imprint of a tiny foot against the swollen skin of her belly. Tone's noxious breath gusted over Becka's face until she gagged. "If anyone should be here with you, it's me," he said. "I *deserve* the honor!"

"I don't want my baby to die! I don't want to die!"

"Breathe," Tone said, right before his face disappeared in a burst of flame.

Arlene hit him again with the flaming chunk of wood. A tooth hit Becka in the face. She screamed, bearing down again. The pain inside her centered. Deepened.

The child stretched her, crowning, and she put a hand there to feel the soft, slick down of its head. Its pulse beat beneath her fingertips. Her body strained again. Everything inside her tightened. Pushing. She could not have held back any more than she could have kept a river from rushing over a cliff.

Becka screamed, an endless primal howl that tasted of ash and lightning and tore at her throat while she guided the baby from her body. Slick with blood, the solid weight slipped out of her, fell squalling in her hands, and then to the forest floor.

She snatched the infant against the front of her nightgown seconds before Arlene could lift it. The older woman's fingernails scratched the dirt where the baby had been only seconds ago.

"Get away," Becka said.

"The child's mother stays—"

"I," Becka's voice was low and dangerous and full of power, "am the child's mother."

Arlene stumbled back, a hand to her gaping mouth. "You signed the contract. You agreed to this, to give it to me—"

Becka clutched the infant, ominously silent, to her breast. A long, silver strand of drool dripped from the corner of her split lips. She heaved a breath. Then another. Everything inside her pulsed and throbbed. More pushing. Blood gushed from her, followed by the splatter of something thicker. Larger. It hit the floor with squelch.

She bit the cord to sever it.

The pain no longer mattered. She was no longer cumbersome and graceless. With ease, the child still cradled against her, Becka got to her feet.

Arlene stumbled back. "This is not what I was promised!"

"When you trust in a deceiver, you should expect to be deceived."

At her breast, the baby rooted to latch onto the nipple. A sharp sting pierced Becka, but she didn't wince. This was a mother's love, she thought. Pain and blood.

"Please." Arlene dropped to her knees, hands up. Without teeth, her words lisped. "I did everything I was supposed to do! I sacrificed! *I* deserve to be the mother of the new god!"

"As it is, it shall ever be, it cannot be undone," Becka said.

The child's head turned. Trickles of blood ran from the corners of its mouth. It reached its small claws toward her and let out a mewl.

"See? It wants me! Come here, my sweet darling." Arlene reached for it.

The child lunged from Becka's arms and into Arlene's eager embrace, but the older woman's cry of triumph was cut off sharply when the baby tore out her throat. It fell to consuming her rapidly, flesh and sinew and bone. It left nothing behind, not so much as a scrap.

The others had been lucky to run when they did, but it didn't matter in the end. Becka would find each one of them and give them what they'd been waiting for. They would be consumed.

So would everyone else.

So would every *thing*.

For months, Becka's mind had been nothing but a blur, but everything had clarified for her. Moments ago she'd been filled with the infant. Now, in its place, she was filled with knowledge.

And power.

After all, who was more powerful than a new god except the one who gave birth to it?

"Come on, little one," she said to the child, who had already doubled in size after its first meal. "Let's eat."

THOSE WHO TRESPASS

Tim McWhorter

The remains of the limestone building towered over them like a mausoleum for giants. Having once housed Kelleys Island Wine Company, the nearly century-old pile of rubble hadn't seen fresh grapes in decades, the cellar no barrels. Green moss and tentacle-like vines scaled the crumbling white façade, threatening to pull it asunder. Slender, arched windows lined the walls where glass once kept out the rain. The absence of a roof, claimed by fire for the final time in 1933, allowed all manner of nature to infiltrate. On the surrounding grounds, where workers once ate boxed lunches under the northern Ohio sun, trees now stood, hiding the ruins from the wandering gaze of passersby.

It all proved irresistible for three adventure-minded students from nearby Tiffin University. Private property or not. Posted and verbal warnings be damned.

"She's got to be down there." Heather spoke the words as if pleading her case. Their elusive friend had pulled one of her infamous disappearing acts, even though they'd all sworn to stay together. Approaching the main section of ruins, Heather had seen Hagin putting her earbuds in, slipping into her own little world. She should have kept closer tabs on her. "Pretty sure I heard her singing that damn song again."

Jill crouched at the opening to the defunct winery's cellar, aiming the flashlight from her cell phone down the stairwell into the subterranean darkness. "I can't see shit. Wait...no. I can't see shit."

"Ha-gin!"

Dusk was falling when they'd snuck onto the restricted property. In the half hour since, their lengthy shadows had succumbed to nightfall. A light mist, fresh off Lake Erie, had crept across the island, and little brown bats had emerged from their slumber to crisscross through the autumn sky. The condensation collected on tree limbs before dripping onto the blanket of leaves below. The bats hunted in silence.

Leaves crunched in the dark. A twig snapped.

Heather turned and shined her cell phone's light behind them.

"Shit," Jill muttered, fighting off nerves. Then, much louder, "Hagin, get out here! Let's go!"

"It's probably just a squirrel," Heather said. "Or a deer." She turned back and joined her light with Jill's, peering down the narrow stone stairwell.

"Okay, so..." Jill started, ignoring Heather's use of the word "probably" and the tales she'd recently heard about the place. Not to mention the queasiness in her stomach since discovering they'd lost cell service the moment they crossed onto the property. "Devil's advocate. What if she can't just *get out here*? What if she's hurt or lost or...?"

"Then we need to find her," Heather said, remembering their freshman year when Hagin would go MIA at a party, and Heather would spend half the evening tracking her down to make sure she wasn't being cornered by some douchebag with a pocket full of roofies.

A shiver shook Jill's shoulders. She took her bottom lip between her teeth and illuminated the path before them. "Those steps look like a broken neck waiting to happen. Think there's another way in?"

Heather shined her light along the foundation of what remained of the building's north wall, then brought it back to the open stairwell. "If Hagin went in this way," she replied, "then we should, too."

"Great." Jill toed a small rock down the stairs, watched it tumble and disappear into the void. She adjusted her glasses farther up her nose, took a deep breath, then the first step. The old, broken slabs were host to scattered leaves, slick with the encroaching mist. She cursed under her breath as she used the damp walls to steady herself. The soggier the leaves became, the more treacherous the going would be. Luckily, the amount of debris decreased with each step. Soon, dry, bare stone greeted her. She ducked under the archway and left the moonlight behind.

The temperature change was immediate. While the air above ground was only moderately cool, the air in the wine cellar sprouted bumps on her arms. The old joke about a witch's tit crossed her mind, but Jill let it go. Why steal Heather's thunder? She anticipated a stench to accompany the cold air, but surprisingly, detected only the faint odor of nature and old earth.

Jill swung her light up the stairs. "You coming?"

"Right behind you."

Comforted by the sound of Heather's footfalls, Jill turned back and navigated the last two uneven steps. At the bottom, she waited until Heather had pulled up beside her before once again calling out their friend's name.

Once the echo of Jill's voice had died out, Heather said, "Damn. Colder than a witch's tit down here."

Jill smiled and rubbed her free hand over her arm with the cell phone. "Hagin!"

"Ha-gin!"

Only the echo of their voices answered, accompanied by water dripping somewhere in the ruin's bowels.

"Really hope she's okay," Jill said.

Heather reeled in her imagination before it could run away. "I'm sure she is."

They stood at the edge of a room the size of a large workshop, chasing away shadows with their lights. The limestone floor was cracked, littered with collapsed sections of stone walls that had given up trying to remain in place. Weeds grew in the fissures and water puddled in the low points. Errant tree branches trespassed about, having infiltrated through holes in the weakened ceiling. Two dark passageways beckoned from opposite sides of the cellar. One led to the right. The other to the left.

"So?" Heather asked. "Which way?"

"I don't know, but..." Jill pursed her lips and shook her head. "This sure as hell isn't what I signed up for. I mean...fuck me, this place is creepy."

A noticeable breeze blew through the room. Somewhere beyond the limestone walls, a barn owl's hoot disturbed the night.

"I can go look for her if you wanna stay here."

"Oh, hell, no." Jill said. "We're staying together."

"But—"

"We're *not* splitting up."

"Fine." Heather sidestepped the rising tension in Jill's voice and scanned one passageway after the other. "Eenie, meenie—"

"We should've listened to him."

Heather stopped. "Who?"

"Mike," Jill said, avoiding Heather's gaze. "That weird guy on the ferry earlier."

Heather thought back. It had been such a long day, the ferry ride to the island seemed forever ago. "Oh, him? I don't know. I thought he was kinda cute."

"He told us to stay away from here."

"Okay, but seriously, Jill. You actually believe those stories of his? Occult ceremonies? Curses? Witchcraft? The less seriously we took him, the more elaborate his stories became. Not to mention the fact that it was only ten o'clock in the morning and the guy was already lit. How reliable a narrator could he be?"

Jill shook her head. "It doesn't matter if I believe him or not. We shouldn't..." She threw up her hands. "I mean...we're only gonna check it out, you said. Take photos from the road, you said."

Heather clenched her lips, fighting back both a cold shiver and the urge to lash out. Within the battle, she found a compromise. "Yeah, well, I didn't hear you yelling stop as your skinny ass climbed through the fence."

Jill opened her mouth to rebut, then closed it. Why was she starting an argument? Now, of all times? She focused her energy instead on inspecting a large moss-covered stone near her feet.

Heather took an audible breath, then exhaled just as deep.

"Look," she said, the pause in action allowing her voice to calm, "more than likely, those corridors join back up somewhere. Probably the other side of the building."

Jill adjusted her glasses and took her own resetting breath. "And if that's the case..."

"We'll either meet up with Hagin," Heather said, "or end up back here."

Jill nodded, then gestured with her hand. "Then lead the way." The light mist off the lake had followed them in and now swirled around their feet. "But be careful. Wouldn't take much to snap an ankle down here."

"Okay, Mom." Heather smiled before turning away. "Here's hoping this corridor is just one big roundabout." She trained her light on the floor as she ducked her head into the opening on the right. Rocks the size of skulls littered the edges of the tunnel. Some even took on the appearance as such. Heather scanned the walls. In enough places to spark discomfort, vacant, gaping holes stared back.

"I'd say this place isn't exactly stable." Jill shined her light around.

"Yeah." Scanning the ceiling above, Heather found it in similar condition as the walls. "Probably a hardhat zone, if we're honest. Let's not be down here too long."

They took ginger steps, conscious of the rough terrain and anything that might be hidden by the mist. Just ahead, a rotted wooden doorframe lured them on.

Approaching, Heather turned to Jill and raised her eyebrows.

Jill shrugged. "Might as well."

Heather poked her head and cell phone through the opening. "Hagin?" This time she spoke just above a hush. When no response came, she stepped through the doorway and into the next section of corridor.

They had taken only a few steps into the new passageway when Heather noticed the changing environment.

"Geez," she said, waving away the cloud of moisture that now hovered around her waist. Thankfully, the mist was fine and allowed her light to penetrate its ghostly presence. She could still see her feet, but barely. "How spooky is that?"

"Crazy," Jill said. "And it's making things more dangerous down here. Really need to watch our steps now."

They both turned their lights forward.

"Come on," Jill said, her voice unsteady. "Let's find our girl and get the hell out of here."

Their footsteps echoed off their surroundings as they walked further ahead, occasionally kicking small rocks they could hardly see, much less avoid. They soon came across a tiny room, no larger than a janitor's closet. It was doorless and held no sign of Hagin.

Heather walked on.

Jill was about to call for their friend, when something caught her attention. She jumped and drew back, before leaning in once she realized what she was seeing. "How the..."

Heather turned back and joined her light with Jill's. "Is that..."

Jill knelt in the mist to get a closer look. "Looks like it."

An abandoned tennis ball, covered in dirt and grime, had been stripped of most of its yellow fuzz. The ball's damp, bare skin resembled that of raw chicken. Puncture holes, like those created by long sharp teeth, peppered one half of the ball while the other was caved in and flat.

"Not sure how it got down here," Jill said, "but it looks like it's been here awhile."

"Um, Jill?" Heather tapped her friend on the shoulder. "Think I know how it got here."

Jill rose, joining her light with Heather's. "Aw," she said. "Poor fella."

Leaving the crusty old tennis ball behind, they approached a carcass lying under the blanket of condensation. Decomposition made the animal's tenure in the corridor difficult to determine. Dark matted hair blanketed the skin as stiffened legs jutted outward. Its hide clung to bone with no muscle in between. A hollow cavity, where its stomach had once been, housed cobwebs and the shells of dead beetles.

A smattering of large rocks surrounded the animal.

"What do you think?" Heather asked. "German Shepard? Lab?"

"I don't know, but..." Jill swallowed hard. "I don't think its head is supposed to be facing that way."

Heather waved away the mist and knelt closer.

Jill was right. The dog's neck appeared broken. Its muzzle and hollow eyes faced backward, as if the dog had died looking over its shoulder.

"What's in its mouth?"

Heather leaned over the carcass. The dog's teeth, bared in an eternal snarl, gleamed in the light, a contrast to its black decaying gums. "Looks like a stick."

"Ouch," Jill muttered. "Crammed down its throat like that?"

Jill knelt beside Heather. Leaning her cell against a nearby rock, she used both hands to pry the dog's jaws apart. The sound of bones breaking filled the cellar. The tearing of petrified cartilage joined in.

"Pull it out."

Heather wrinkled her nose as she reached into the dog's mouth. Her first attempt at pulling out the stick resulted in it snagging the dog's teeth.

"Strange," she said. "It's not just one stick. Looks like several sticks tied together with twine." Wiggling it back and forth, Heather worked the collection of sticks free. Small feathers—dry-rotted and crumpled—hung at several of the joints. The entire assembly created the crude illusion of a figure.

"Oh, my God." Jill dropped the dog's jaws and bolted upright. "You know what that is, right?"

Heather held the stick figure at arm's length. "Not sure. I've seen things like this in—"

"It's a totem, Heather." Jill slapped the object out of Heather's hand. Retrieving her cell, she swung its light around, eyes widening the more she processed. "Occultist's use them. Like for curses and shit."

Heather rose, wiping her hand on her pant leg. She shined her light farther up the corridor. At the end of the beam, yet another rough doorway awaited them. "Why do you think it's here?"

Jill brought her trembling light back to the dog, then Heather. "I don't know, but it's nothing good. Purely evil." Using her light, she zeroed in on the dog's broken neck. "We need to get out of here. Like now."

Jill turned and started back the way they'd come.

"Ow, shit!" Heather shouted, accompanied by the tumbling of rocks.

Jill spun, her light finding Heather crumpled on the floor, nestled within the fog. "Shit, Heather! I told you to be careful."

Heather massaged her ankle. Sarcasm tinged her voice as she spoke. "I was as careful as I could be given the circumstances." She kicked at a lone, softball-sized stone with her uninjured foot. "Besides, pretty sure that fucking thing rolled out and planted itself right where I was gonna step. Almost like..."

Jill brought her light from a nearby pile of rocks back to Heather, still vulnerable on the ground. "Yeah?"

"Almost like it was *trying* to trip—"

A low rumble rattled the building's remains.

They shot their gazes and lights skyward. Dust drifted down as small rocks broke loose from the patchwork of stone above Heather's head.

"Come on." Jill extended her hand. "You gotta move!"

Heather grasped Jill's hand and, favoring her ankle, got to her feet. They'd hobbled only a few steps when several large rocks fell from the ceiling. Debris plunged through the mist as it crashed to the ground, forming a small mountain on the spot where Heather had been sitting.

"Holy shit," she said, eyes wide. She raised her light to the gaping hole in the ceiling. Jill's soon followed. Moonlit treetops stared back, silhouetted against the night sky.

"You okay?" Jill turned her light on her friend. "I mean...any one of those would've..."

"I'm all right," Heather answered. "Just a little—"

A football-sized boulder careened from above, catching Heather above the ear, caving in her skull. Her neck folded awkwardly under the weight. Her throat released a guttural yelp. Her arms sailed outward like flags in the wind as the stone drove her to the ground with a heavy thump.

Jill screamed.

Blood flecked with gray matter seeped from the crater in Heather's ruined head, dyeing her hair a dark red. Her body twitched. Her legs scissor-kicked for several seconds. Eventually, her body, and the rest of the abandoned wine cellar, fell still.

The spreading pool of gore inched toward Jill's feet. Trembling from head to toe and with burgeoning tears blurring her vision, she took a step back. The spread continued. When she stepped back a second time, her foot caught a rock. Reaching out and grasping nothing but open space, Jill landed on her bottom. The impact jarred her teeth. It launched her glasses from her face and the cell from her hand. Shadows swallowed the glasses while the phone clattered across the floor, its light flaming out.

The only thing that saved her from being enveloped by pure, inky black was Heather's cell. It remained alight beside her still body, illuminating the ghostly haze.

Jill scrambled over to her friend. After a deep breath, she reached across Heather's prone body and retrieved the orphaned cell. Whispering "I love you," Jill pulled back and climbed to her feet.

A sound broke through the calm. Not just a voice, but a familiar voice, echoing from the large room where they'd begun their search.

Hagin.

Using the phone's light to cut through the condensation, Jill ran toward the voice.

Tripping, stumbling, and breathing only occasionally, she groped her way along the stone corridor. Within sight of the blurry doorway, a great force swept her feet out from under her. Rough, uneven limestone rose up to greet her. It scraped her hands. It slapped her face. It purged her lungs of their last bit of air.

Sprawled on her stomach, Jill gasped in an attempt to get the air back. None returned. She reared her head back and stretched her throat. Only a mouthful of damp mist was her reward. Desperate seconds passed before she could breathe again.

"Ha—"

A powerful grip took hold of her shoulders and bent her backward. Sharp pains slashed through her abdomen and lower back. Pressure mounted as her upper torso was forced farther in the wrong direction. The pain grew legs. Agony spread throughout her body. The scream she heard was weak and her own.

She flailed her arms, striking out at whatever force was at work. They failed to connect. There was no one there. Trauma forced her eyes and mouth wide as her body arced unnaturally against its design.

Something in her gut ruptured.

Muscles tore.

Her spine snapped.

Blood gurgled in her throat, stifling her cries.

With nothing left to hold it forward, Jill's body folded backward onto itself.

The last thing she heard was the sound of footsteps and a brief tumble of rock.

———

"Shit!" Hagin reached down and rubbed her throbbing ankle. She'd made it all the way back to the main room, navigated several rock-strewn corridors, without an awkward step. Until now. "That's gonna swell up."

She plucked the earbuds from her ears and slid them into the pouch of her hoodie. She tapped the screen on her cell to silence the music. Aided by its light, Hagin limped across the remaining ruins of the fog-laden wine cellar.

"Heather!" she called out. "Jill! You guys'll never believe what I found. There was this room. Really weird shit. Creepy shit. But I didn't dare mess with anything without you guys. And I'm sorry, I know we said we'd stay together."

At the foot of the flagstone steps, Hagin shined her light up the stairwell to the empty night sky beyond. "Guys?"

———

Dear Reader,

While researching the location for this story, I came across an interesting (not to mention, creepy) video where someone explored the winery's ruins both inside and out with a droid. I've watched the video numerous times, using it for both research and inspiration. If you would like to check it out for yourself, head over to YouTube and search "Mr. P Explores...Kelleys Island Winery Ruins." Hopefully you find the video and location as fascinating as I did.

– Tim McWhorter

I DREAM OF TEETH

Randall Drum

I want to close these eyes. Rest. Sleep deeply and dream like I used to. It doesn't happen very often anymore. I'm certain it won't happen tonight either, thanks to the young man I was with only an hour ago. The one I tracked for three weeks before killing him. The one like me. But different.

Perhaps it's just my brain doing what it does: keeping me awake and on the hunt until there's no more night left to hide any bodies and I'm forced back to my dark, fourth-floor apartment in the city. Thirty years of shitty neighbors and shittier view. Always exhausted and mind reeling. Full of all the things to see. All the things to feel—whether I really want any of it or not. But I don't have a choice anymore. That's the way it is.

I collapse onto my bed, roll over and kick off my shoes. The ceiling fan above me spins and I blink quickly a few times to wet the eyes, capturing the fan in brief moments, making it move in slow motion. The gentle *tickticktick* of the pull chain against the burned out lightbulb relaxes me and soon enough the blades recede into the flat gray light that washes the ceiling. I am ready.

The canvas is set.

A gentle pressure builds from the back of my brain, swelling in my head until it uncoils and crawls over and through my nerves. My chest grows heavy and my breaths come in quick, shallow bursts. Thighs tense and toes curl. I'm so close. Synapses howl in a ring of fire, and I can sense the confessions as they circle the periphery. Only the strongest will find a way through with their colors and sounds and experiences. I am so hungry for the joining. A liquid flutter turns electric and my veins become filaments. I am incandescent. A rolling spasm consumes me.

And they come.

The first is dull. Gray. Cold.

I paused after reaching the fifth peak of the morning. My gloved hands, soaked with sweat, stiffened from the snow and ice, and the bones in my fingers screamed. I thought about digging out another fortress as I had done atop the last four, but my arms still burned after the recent climb and were of no use. I was the only one who knew they were there, of course. They were just for me. Defense against no one, save for the occasional shopper.

From my high seat on the mountain, I ruled the shopping center parking lot. My kingdom was a dreary landscape dotted with tall lamp posts, each surrounded by mountains of snow and ice born from the efforts of plow trucks clearing space for those daring enough to brave the heavy winter storms. It wasn't much, but it was mine.

I looked at the next mountain and considered another climb. Not as high as the last two, but I was tired. Maybe hungry. I couldn't tell. My whole body throbbed and my thin winter coat was no match for the wind. I didn't know what time it was, but it was probably getting close enough to lunch that I should head back to my father's trailer, which lay on the other side of the service road behind the grocery store. I started my slide down the hill. And that's when I found you.

You hooked me with a fingertip, barely catching my hood as I reached the bottom. I don't think I would have noticed you if you hadn't. The nearest stores were dark and there were no cars nearby, so I started brushing away the snow, which became thicker and harder packed the deeper I tunneled. The ache in my fingers disappeared, replaced by curiosity.

I don't remember how long it took to dig out enough to see your face, but there you were with that big smile, so happy to see me. You looked cold. I mean, there was barely any pink at all, so you just *had* to be. There wasn't much else to your face, really, as crushed as it was. You were small and I wondered if you were nine like me. I remember looking into the space where your eyes should have been.

You and I were still alone, so I kept digging. You didn't even have a shirt on, but you didn't let it bother you. I remember my face flooding with warmth when I saw you were a girl. I stood back for a minute or two, not sure what to do next. Should I run back to the trailer and tell my dad? Should I cover you back up and keep you a secret? Would I get in trouble? Would someone think *I* put you inside the mountain?

My hands moved, having made the decision for me, and I pushed snow back into place. Hiding you. Keeping you to myself. We both knew I was doing the right thing. I took a glove off and stroked your teeth as I took one last look at your smile, my fingers nearly as white as yours. I had three holes where grownup teeth would never grow. A car accident a year ago saw to that. I was jealous.

They were so white.

So perfect.

So I took them.

That night, my father wrapped himself in his heaviest coat and together we crossed the vast parking lot, braving the cold, lured by the red and white glow of the Graceland Twin Cinema marquee. I don't think he noticed me eying the mountain that held my secret, its prize buried even deeper under a fresh coat of thick snow.

We saw a movie every weekend he had me for visitation and I don't think he ever saw more than the beginning and ending of any of them. He always fell asleep. It didn't bother me, especially if the movie had naked people. So I sat quietly with the handful of others scattered through the theater and watched the crazy man on the screen build a mud mountain in his living room so he could find aliens. My father never did anything like that.

Sitting low in my seat, I touched my pocket and felt the little lumps of treasure. I pulled one out and held it up. The roots poked my fingers as I turned it around and examined it by the light of the movie.

And then it happened. Like the dad on the screen who couldn't help himself, I took the tooth and put it in my mouth. I rubbed it on the tip of my tongue. It was so smooth.

Without warning, even to myself, my fingers pushed up. The tips of the roots pierced my gums with a gentle *pop* as I guided it into an empty space. Blood splashed onto my tongue and my mouth burned, but the pain decayed when I closed my eyes.

That's when I knew you.

When I joined you.

Your name was Angela, and you were ten years old. You were scared of horses and your dad dropped dead in front of you at his brother's birthday party three years ago. Seven days ago, you were throwing pennies into a fountain pool at the Northland Mall with your mom. She bought a new hat.

Four days ago, a teenager pushed you into the backseat of his car.

While I tripped through your life, pausing at random moments, something began happening to me. Something more than pictures. I *felt* you hit your head when you were forced down to the floor of the car. I could feel your arms as they were bound. As we were bound. My body tingled, like a foot falling asleep, and my heart swelled in my chest, pounding so loudly I just knew someone else in the theater would hear it. A warmth spread in my pants and I realized I peed, but I couldn't move. You had a hold of me.

Our shoulders ached from having our arms behind us, and our legs cramped. Cold. Dark outside the car on a road with no houses and wearing nothing but pain. A rag in our mouth. Pushed down by a boot that wouldn't stop. Our head hurt from the inside out and our eyes felt as though they were going to fall onto the pavement.

Then our body became weightless and we couldn't see anything and we were spinning in the air and wind rushed around making us go faster and faster. And then, just as quickly as we had joined, we separated, and I watched as you disappeared into the black, where no one would ever find you again.

My father woke me up. The movie was over and it was time to put on our coats and go back to the trailer. He pointed at my jeans and asked if I had an accident. "Scared of the aliens," I said.

Nearly eight years passed before I could feed again. It was senior day for concessions at Worthington High. I squeezed into the tightly packed snack booth with two other students. Refrigerator. Drink cooler. Microwave. Racks for chips and candy. A single electric burner and a cash drawer. All the comforts. On the other side of the counter was a gym full of wrestlers, coaches, and parents, all in a concert of motion and sound. Watching, cheering, all pushing their kid and teammates to fight hard as they rotated around the gym. Two rent-a-cops and four medics stood by the open, double wide doors, and waited for the inevitable. They usually only send one ambulance, but regional finals get two. I put more hot dogs in the water to boil.

With so much happening at once, it was hard to hear people ordering their snacks and drinks. But it got real quiet, real fast, when Donny Heinz smacked down on the mat for the last time. Only the people closest to him heard the clap of his skin on the mat and a *thud*, like a slab of meat on pavement, and they collectively gasped as Donny lay motionless in an impossible heap. The referee's whistle chirped, and a silence spread throughout the gym as he yelled for help.

Donny's father nearly tumbled down the narrow bleachers, his footsteps echoing off the walls as everyone else in the gym held their breath. One medic ran outside and returned moments later, pushing a gurney shouting, "Make a hole!" The other three already had hands on Donny. All two-hundred and thirty-eight pounds of his blubbering, monstrous opponent collapsed as his knees buckled. He covered his mouth with his giant hands, but vomit shot the gaps and splattered onto the mat.

I saw Donny's face as they rolled him onto his back. Bloodied. Eyes unmoving. His head didn't move with the rest of him. They lifted him up and started wheeling him away before they even strapped him down. A medic straddled Donny, pumping his chest as his father chased close behind. Everyone was so focused on the action that they didn't notice what I saw. There, just at the edge of the mat. Maybe it flew when

Donny's face hit the floor. Maybe it got kicked around when the medics swooped in. But there it was.

A tooth.

Donny Heinz's tooth.

They were wiping blood and puke off the mat while the cops and coaches helped clear the gym when I hopped the concession counter and swept up my prize. I slipped it into my pocket as fast as I could and followed everyone out to the parking lot.

I went straight home.

Mom was out for the night, still trying after all these years to find me a new dad. I dropped my clothes in a pile by my closet before laying down on the bed. Donny's tooth slipped into my mouth like it was meant to be there. Just a pinch as I squeezed my jaw tight and my body spun into his.

Donny's heart was bad. Turns out he was broken from birth.

We lived in a small house two blocks from the train museum. We lost our footing once and slipped to the bottom of a coal car. Had to beg our laughing friends to help us out.

We didn't want to wrestle next year.

We knew it was wrong the moment the big moose lifted and flipped us down to the floor. Bones splintered and shredded nerves. Our spinal cord never had a chance. It was over faster than we could feel the pain.

Lights out Donny boy.

We fly. We tumble and spin in the black.

Oh, and do we spin!

I asked her to be still. She didn't want to. I told her if she kept wiggling she might fall and we would have to start over. We met at a frat party. Friend of a friend of a friend.

She cried and I'm pretty sure she was trying to pray. It was hard to tell with the gag. The back of the chair was gone, but the seat was wide enough for her to stand on comfortably.

"I don't want to knock you down," I said.

She looked up to the rafters of the derelict warehouse. The light from the battery-powered camping lanterns dropped off around twenty feet or so, and the rope disappeared into the darkness above. I found out about this place when I overheard another grad student telling someone he knew where a junkie had died. Said the body was still there. My heart skipped, and I quickly found myself on the way to the far west side of the city.

Nothing.

No body. Not even a stain. I only found potential.

I don't think she appreciated how hard it was to get the rope up and over the iron beam the day before. I got lucky on the chair. Some poor asshole in the corner office probably sat in that chair for thirty years managing the day to day receiving and shipping crates of who the fuck knows what. I wonder if he used to look at the beams and think about a rope, too.

The tape around her wrists and calves held up well, especially considering how much she thrashed around in the trunk. I'll need to buy more.

"You know I can't understand what you're saying, Dawn." I reached into my backpack sitting on the floor next to the chair. "Pay attention. This is important."

The first two hurt more than the others. A brief flash of fire, a rush of endorphins. My mouth pulsed hard with my heart, a splendid wet rhythm. Dawn tried to look anywhere but at me and the blood that trickled down the pliers as they scraped and cracked and unseated my teeth. Rubber-wrapped handles helped me keep my grip. More blood than I expected, really.

"Look at me, Dawn," I said. She squeezed her eyes shut, whimpering.

"Look at me!" Blood flew past my lips and peppered her white T-shirt and fashionably distressed denim shorts. Pain ravished my tear- and blood-streaked face as it etched a path through my jaws and down onto my neck. We were in this together. The shining moment where I would finally embrace what I was.

"Good girl." She was quite beautiful in this light.

One by one, I placed each harvested tooth on the edge of the chair, surrounding her with them. Radiant. White glass marble washed in red.

After the fourteenth I couldn't feel my mouth at all. Two minutes later, all twenty-five sat worshiping at Dawn's feet. My shirt belonged on the floor of a trauma unit.

"Okay," I said. I had to choose my words carefully because now I sounded like I had a gag, too. "We can carry on."

I wrapped my arms around her legs and lifted her feet off the seat. I only needed a couple of inches. She shook, and I braced her tight with my head, leaning into her thigh.

"I don wan oo drop you." T's were impossible.

I nudged the chair just enough so I could push it about a foot away. Dawn had stopped praying and could only manage weak bleating. I didn't want her to break, so I bent at the knees until I could let her go without either of us falling. She stretched her toes toward to the floor but only found empty space.

I stepped close, only inches from her face, and listened to the surges of air screaming through her snot choked nose. Her spasms faded to a sporadic twitch and soon stopped altogether. I let her hang for three more minutes before I released the tension on the rope and lowered her to the floor.

There was still more to do.

Five minutes. It was always easier to pull teeth from someone else. I laid them out like the diagram I found online, each in their proper position. I wondered how long it would take for someone to find her. A college student dead in an abandoned warehouse. Hanged. Her mouth emptied. I collected my teeth from the chair and pushed them into my pocket. I could deal with them later.

One by one, I pushed Dawn's teeth into my swollen, bloody maw. Each a brushstroke of a painting that wasn't complete until all twenty-eight were in place. I dropped to my knees and closed my eyes.

And it began.

Just like all the others, her memories mingled with mine, danced, swirled, pollinated mine until we joined. She gave me nourishment that I desired. That I needed.

I drank each in as the black approached and the wind spun around us. We watched as we pulled our teeth. Set them at our feet. Our shirt soaked in the blood spilling from our grinning, toothless face.

We watched as we slowly lowered us off the chair. We tried and tried and tried to scream. Our mouth was so dry. Our toes couldn't find the ground. The rope tightened around our neck and our throat seized. We couldn't breathe. Edges blurred and colors separated until only an anemic orange tint lingered. Glorious!

The wind whipped us around even faster now and we twisted and knotted like a kite string in a hurricane. We saw ourself come closer, examining us, becoming just a shape standing near. Another shape appears to us. Behind us. We try to turn, but we can't.

We're in too deep.

A hand on our neck, gripping hard. We're on the floor, face driven into the dirt and dust. We're rolled, flipped on our back as the blurry shape sits on top of us. Strong. It's edgeless, fused to the void. Then pain. Sharp and slippery and pushing between our ribs. Our breath escapes and we can't draw more. Something wrenches inside and pushes up and our heart skips beat after beat. There's a scraping around one of our eyes.

Tugging.

Plucking.

Then the other.

Warmth spreads across our cheeks and down to our ears. Weak, and unable to scream, we're so very, very cold. We're swept up and we bend and stretch in the violent wind that carries us farther and farther away. We can't see past the black.

We are the wind.

His name was Jason. Only twenty-four, but well versed in his ways of feeding.

With our joining ended, the colors of his memories wane, and my canvas clears. I refocus on the ceiling fan, spinning just as I had done with Jason this evening. I can breathe deeply again and the fury that had overwhelmed my brain finally settles. The ringing in my ears remains, as always.

I roll over in the bed, away from the damp sheets. I've never fed on my kind before and doubt I'll need to feed again for quite some time. Morning light peeks around the edges of the heavy curtains as I close Jason's eyes and search for echoes of the joining that ricochet through my body. As sleep erodes the world around me, I realize I was wrong, and I dream.

SOMEONE FOR EVERYBODY

Marvin Brown

He'd won her heart by bringing her cold pizza, and broken it six years later on a crowded riverfront boardwalk, walking away on a path of brittle leaves. Arianna had thrown in the towel before meeting him, convinced at twenty-four that sustainable love, like college, wasn't for everyone. A strange man upended the notion when he tapped her shoulder and presented a huge slice of Italian sausage deep-dish. Barrett confessed he witnessed Arianna's disappointment at arriving too late to the Deep Dive food truck on the East Bank promenade. The vender had packed up his truck and kindly told her he'd be back tomorrow. Barrett recalled her furrowed-brow beauty as she replied, "Oh, yeah? Rats!" and he knew on the spot they had to meet. After Arianna walked away, Barrett told her he bribed the vendor, Max, to unpack the ingredients, reheat the oven, and bake up one more pie—which he'd pay for entirely —so he could have a big slice of it. By the time Barrett tracked her through a clot of festivalgoers and caught her on the boardwalk in front of Alley Cat Oyster Bar, the food was cold.

How aggressively weird, she thought, that a stranger would watch her closely enough to gauge her disappointment, coerce the vendor, and stalk her in public. But that was Barrett, she'd quickly learn, a man who didn't squander moments, big or small. The man was muscled chocolate and generated his own field of energy and swept her into it. To live and love in the now. That was Barrett, he of the juicy lips, superb cheekbones, big hands, and popped-out abs, who could pin her legs back and pound her until she travelled out of body to hover above and admired the choreography of his thrusts.

As they dallied around Greater Cleveland, Arianna watched the way he watched her, unnerved but flattered by how fiercely he studied her.

"I'm impervious to seduction," she warned. "Built walls around my walls."

"Walls keep the good out as well as the bad," he replied.

"Oh, yeah? Which are you?"

Barrett's plump bottom lip tightened from a grin. "Lady, I'm a wrecking ball!"

By the time they had dined in nearly every trendy restaurant in Cleveland, Arianna had already backpedaled on a self-made promise to not surrender to this man. She was his, no matter what.

"I love you," she told him two months into things. "Even though you never say it, I think you love me too."

"I love you too," he replied.

It was all she'd ever need to hear. "I love you too" wrapped her in comfort for years, and that distance eroded thoughts of it ever coming to an end.

After being adrift on a miracle current for nearly six years, Barrett pulled the plug. He couldn't make her understand, despite her rage and tears and promises to change whatever needed to be changed. He was eerily resolute, but that was Barrett. What was weird was she hadn't exhausted him—he had exhausted her. Defenses down, naked to the world, hollowed out by love, all she had left was Barrett. He'd taken her back to where they began and left Arianna like he'd found her, alone amongst a crowd, and with a cold gift of despair.

He'd only once before thought of ending things. You only need to have the notion once for it to forever remain a sprout in the deepest soil of the brain. A whispered thought was tucked away from light and water needed only a little of each for it to begin to stretch out.

He'd met Laurel when they were both in their early thirties. At the time, Trevor was in better shape and a better headspace than usual, which probably helped. Laurel came on strong, which definitely helped. Gorgeous and confident, head to feet. Her infectious laughter was big, like her sneezes, and her weighty cocoa breasts, and her kisses. Laurel inspired him to be the man she needed him to be, which was the man he always wanted to be.

They sat on the lawn surrounding the Lock 3 amphitheater in downtown Akron, their bare feet partially eaten away by the ryegrass. The Goodyear blimp buzzed above the Rubber City. "Tell me three things to help me push back my insecurities about this relationship," Trevor asked.

She tilted her head skyward, seeming to soak up the sun, then returned her gaze to his. "Um, first, I will love you as hard as I can for as long as we have together. Two—"

"You know what, honestly? That'll do," he said and pulled her up to his lips. Laurel was God-sent therapeutics for a man who needed to ward off lingering symptoms. She didn't seem to mind the way he tucked his insecurities into stupid quizzes, and wasn't put off by his sexual appetite. She needed it when he needed it. The woman had hips and thighs and knew how to use them. And, *mmmm*, her kisses tasted like...forever.

Relationships for him had always been rollercoasters, but not this one. When Trevor introduced her to Stricklands ice cream, Laurel said it was the best she ever had. Waiting to squeeze into Luigi's Restaurant, she let him drone on about noir films, which he'd loved ever since his father had taken him to the Civic Theater to see a revival of Hitchcock's *Shadow of a Doubt*.

She looked at and listened to Trevor like it was her mission. Day in and out, this woman built a better man. Six years as a couple had been a ridiculously smooth ride, healing, until their final week together. She'd been prickly that week, quiet. She drifted from his touch and conversation. Energy hissed from him like he was a punctured tire. Every insecurity crept back. He'd gone nearly deaf and blind when Laurel finally told him she was leaving.

"Please," he begged. He wanted to quiz her, to get the answers he needed.

Obscuring tears and throbbing ears distorted an explanation that might have been health related, or some issue of incompatibility. No answer could make it make sense. Trevor was weakened to his knees as the best thing to ever happen to him walked out. He stayed that way until daylight faded, vacillating between the minutia of what went wrong and a sad little idea flowering within his skull.

Their bare shins took the brunt of the chill from the foam Lake Erie pushed-pulled along the shoreline. These days when they haunted Cleveland, they'd spent more time on the Cuyahoga River, the West Bank, disappearing into the mass of flesh packed into the Flats—anywhere that was out of sight of the lake. There were nights, though, when the lake called them; daring or pleading or simply waiting, each ultimately bringing them back. They stood now safely on the shore, heels sunk into mud and algae, even as the water shoved and tugged at them mischievously. *A little farther, a little deeper*, it whispered.

Twice a year, the lake churned water from its depths. Water above swapped places with the water below. The turnover was necessary for all life in the lake to survive. The smell of the turnover, the reek of sulfur gases and displaced decaying matter, dissuaded tourists, but reminded monsters to come home.

They felt tired, in need of the companionship in abundant supply across this great city. Murky waters, up to their hips now, gently rocked them like they were in the hands of a playful lover. Survival depended upon coupling, and the men and women who came and went contributed to a lifecycle that seduced, energized, then drained.

Daylight began fading and they were shocked to realize they were in up to their chest. Waters had gone still; on the surface, shadows shimmered like ghosts, and in the distance, they heard the whine of Herring Gulls. They fought their way back to shore, resisting the call of the lake.

But they'd be back. Creatures from the water, as big as muskellunge and so small as to hardly be known to exist, all returned to its darkened depths and hushed center, and maybe—who knew?—swirled down there for the rest of their lives.

She'd known for years that marriage, children, and long-term commitment were not in the cards. Her condition had taken those from her, but maintaining the *life* in her existence was non-negotiable. For Regan, every day was a tick-down to a long slumber; each of those days was countered with determined lunges toward joy and pleasure.

Meeting Barrett, she'd known almost instantly that he dwelled, like she did, in the glorious moments of a relationship, not its ultimate trajectory. Laugh when something was funny, fuck when you were horny, ugly cry on days you couldn't take it, dance when the music hit just right.

She kissed Barrett just after meeting him. There was no way of knowing or caring how long it would last. When she broke away for air, the handsome black man with the luscious lips and perfect bright-white teeth stared into her like he was seeing something he'd never seen.

"Did I scare you?" she asked.

"I'm the opposite of scared."

This time he kissed her, holding her head in his big hands. Something passed between them, mouth to mouth. Energy? Fear? It didn't matter, both were life.

"Your hands are dry," he noted. "They need lotion."

Regan chuckled. "Your kiss sucked the moisture right outta me!"

She took him to her favorite spot in Ohio City: Mitchell's Ice Cream. They walked the blocks of West 25th down to the West Side Market, where they gorged on exquisite pastries and fresh fruit. By dinnertime they had ruined their appetites.

"You're always looking at me," she told him.

"You're something I've never encounter before," Barrett replied. "And those copper-colored eyes..."

"Look, Barrett, I'm not complicated," she told him, pulling him down a narrow aisle of discounted hardbacks in Horizontal Books. "I'm clingy enough to let you know I care, but I don't need all the details, the filler. Just the good stuff, the *right now* stuff."

"Right now," he replied, "I'll like to find a hidden alleyway and have my way with you!"

"Barrett, Cleveland alleys aren't going to be the naughty rendezvous you might hope."

"The dirtier the better, baby!"

This thing they had was a bit like leasing one fine car after another. Never worry about long-term care. Keep to the basic checkups. Never have to see it rust away. And yet, she and Barrett found ways to stretch glory past single perfect moments, and stitch them together into what was becoming a lasting tapestry. Long juicy kisses. Quickies on the kitchen table. Postcoital drydowns. Moisturizing massages. If she wasn't careful, she'd drift past her own boundaries of commitment. Was she being reckless? Fearless? Neither and both.

"We're burning hot, baby," Barrett liked to tell her.

"Problem is," she teased, "what burns bright, burns out fast."

"Let it burn, baby!" he replied.

And so they burned. He could use her up; a woman with a limited shelf life wouldn't sweat the annihilation. Then the time came, as it always had, for Regan to bring things to their conclusion. She sat Barrett down and her hesitancy caught him off guard. She crushed him an explanation that took them to the end of the road. They sat close. Eye to eye.

"I call it the lifelong sleep," she began, explaining the affliction that caused her to fall into a six-year coma. She had the disorder for most of her 36 years—six years of sleep, then six years of life—making long-term relationships impossible. They had burn as long as they could, she'd told him. She saw his tears, only now realizing those were something she'd never seen from him.

His big hands took hers. "Your hands need lotion."

She wiped his cheek. "It was the good stuff, Barrett. No filler. Thank you. For all of it."

He didn't ask for elaboration of her condition, didn't beg for more time. Even though he seemed to still burn with energy, while she flickered like a dying candle, he seemed fragile.

Barrett accepted her affliction unconditionally and told Regan, despite her protest, that she was worth the wait. He was at her bedside two days later. His face, his eyes, those teeth and smiling lips were the last things she saw.

They each lived in sad palaces. Only a merciful God could have brought them together.

Laurel crossed the sterile room to Regan. Amid the feeding tubes and bedsheets, nestled in the complex bed in the long shadows of technology beeping and buzzing around them, Laurel's lover was a slave to dreams. To live a life that way, abbreviated, was to live in a palace of misery and isolation that only Regan could reside. We too, Laurel thought, resided in a lonely palace.

They sat next to the bed. They were in their Laurel years, where they would remain for another two years. That would cap six years of delicious affairs and strategic dinners; relationships destined to fail. Cocktail dresses and yoga shorts. Pantsuits and comfy sweats. Eyeliner and lipstick. Menstrual cycles and heavy, tender boobs. Bra straps and bikini waxes. Mansplaining and objectification. Finally, it would be an end for Laurel. And then the turnover. *She* would spend a painful twelve hours in transition. Bones would make subtle adjustments with micro-snaps of agony. Hips would reposition, sending the report clanging throughout the spinal column. Things that shuffled at the quantum level echoed upward until they burned on surface nerve endings. Titties would deflate along the ribcage and tighten and solidify into pecs. Woman parts would seal, protrude, and its flesh elongate. Balls would drop down to their delicate cove above the thighs. Uterus shriveled away, drawn down to a walnut prostate. Cocoa skin would darken to a russet sheen. Voice would deepen to Barrett's soulful bass, and *his* Adam's apple would swell out of the throat. The life that had been on the bottom would shift to the top. Finally, naked, shivering, Barrett would wipe away the fresh water that dribbled from his ears and tear ducts and more that trickled down his inner thighs.

The bed was adjusting on its own, positioning Regan to prevent bedsores. Laurel thought of hand-in-hand strolls around the city, small talk that felt like comfort food, how things could be that good again. Beeping machinery broke the rhythm of their thoughts. They sluggishly drew the chair closer to the bed. This body knew its time was winding down. These final months, weeks, days increasingly bogged them down, submerged them in muffled and blurry existence. Eventually, not even the life energy they sucked from their companions could any longer offset the crushing depths. But they'd soon break the surface as Barrett. Renewed. And hungry.

The Barrett years loomed, as did Regan's awakening. The arrival of Barrett would be timed close enough to correspond with Regan's return from her six-year slumber. If she had been truthful about her condition, Regan's eyes would soon open to Barrett as they had closed to him, and they would begin again.

Laurel took one of Regan's dry hands and rubbed it with lotion from the small bottle from their purse. The lovers hadn't burned out; they were embers ready to be stoked back to flames. Laurel sighed. She and he, *they*, missed Regan's copper eyes, could hardly wait to look into them again. Another couple of years. Barrett will be waiting, right where they left her. They could feast off Regan for the rest of her days, and love her along the way. This time Barrett would energize her the way she had energized them. This time lovers would reside together in a gloriously sad palace.

SEVEN MYTHS THEY TELL YOU ABOUT THE TOWN BENEATH THE LAKE

Gwendolyn Kiste

1 *There are no ghosts in the lake. All the people got out long before the flood.*

It's your father that mentions it first. Or maybe your mother. Or even your aunt or your grandparents. Truth be told, you don't really remember, because you're no more than five years old when you hear about it, their words ringing like a warning in your mind.

"There's a whole town down there, waiting in the dark."

You're sitting on the beach, the grit and grime of the Ohio air settling in your lungs.

Everybody knows about what happened here. It's an urban legend that isn't a legend at all. It's the stone cold truth.

"This never used to be a lake." Your mom squints in the July sun, the noxious scent of SPF wafting through the air. "Then fifty years ago, the government came and flooded all the houses, so they could make this place."

"Why?" you ask, your heart tight in your chest.

"Just because," your dad says. "Everybody wanted a lake."

But you have to wonder if all those families who lost their homes really wanted any of this.

Together, you and your parents unpack your Lunchmate cooler and have a picnic on the beach, baloney and mayo sandwiches and fresh-squeezed lemonade. Giggling, you skip along the sand, as your mom tells you not to swim in the water.

"It's unclean," she says, and you're not sure if she's talking about the potential algae bloom or about the potential ghosts.

She doesn't scare you, though. When nobody's looking, you dip your toes in. Even though it's the middle of summer, the water feels ice cold. It also feels like home.

Soon, the sunset is glinting like diamonds off the water, and it's time to pack up. Your parents are driving back home when your mom motions to a tidepool along the state highway.

"There's a stone chimney poking out of the water over there," she says, and you peer out the window, but the car whizzes by too fast for you to see.

Only there's something else worth seeing. A dark-haired woman walking along the shoulder, arrayed in a pale pink dress, a long braid down her back.

"Who is she?" you ask, but your parents never notice her.

The ghost, however, notices you. Your eyes lock, and with your breath caught in your throat, you keep staring at her, even twisting around in your seat to watch her.

At the last moment before the car takes a sharp turn, she smiles at you.

You can't help but smile back.

2. *Nobody remembers the townspeople these days. Their names and faces were lost to time.*

The lake glistens before you, and you stand at the edge until your mother calls you back.

"Filthy water," she always says, and you're not one to argue. Not even when you hear the faint whispering, sweet as candy floss, eternal as time. Not even when you're sure you know who it is.

You're twelve now, on the precipice of adolescence, that final perilous slide toward being a grown-up. Whatever that means. Some days, you feel like you're strapped into a roller coaster, and you're almost at the top of the track, too far gone to stop now. You want to run, but you already know you can't escape yourself.

You can't escape this place either. At night, when you close your eyes, you dream of the water. And you dream of the ghost. You've seen her a hundred times now, walking along the road or rising up out of the darkness. Nobody else can see her. You stopped asking them years ago.

What you haven't stopped doing: talking about the town beneath the lake. Breathless, you babble on about it, even though nobody wants to listen.

"It's just a bunch of houses," your friends say. "What's the big deal?"

It's a question you can't quite answer.

That spring, your family goes out on the water, all of you huddled in a speedboat. With big, bright smiles, they chortle on about the shapes in the clouds, but you're looking in the opposite direction. You're looking into the dark of the water, until you're sure you see it. The whole town waiting to be rediscovered.

"What if she's lonely down there?" you ask, but no one answers.

3. *The people in the town had plenty of notice, and they all escaped, no problem.*

During study hall, you sneak away to the school library and search through the local books on a dusty back shelf, the ones with yellowed pages and bindings that crumble if you breathe too deep. You find an old volume on county history with a few grainy pictures of the town. You also find the name: Laceyville. A sweet little community with a post office and a baseball team and dozens of families who probably planned to stay for generations until there was no place left to stay.

But best of all, you find her, tucked away in a tintype photograph, wearing that same pink dress and long, beautiful braid. The book doesn't say much about her, not who she was or what she was called, but you can make your best guess. She wasn't like the others. She never married, never went along with the grain, and never wanted to leave either. Her home was her sanctuary, the one place in all the world where she felt safe. At least until the men with shiny suits and greasy smiles came and stole it away from her. They used towering stacks of paperwork and sour-faced judges, and that was more than enough to win their case.

You close your eyes and imagine what happened to her. When the day arrived and the floodgates opened, the government didn't take roll call. They didn't check every house to ensure it was empty. And why should they? The homeowners were all adults. They were responsible for themselves. They took their thirty pieces of silver, whether they wanted to or not, and they moved out their meager bits of furniture, and disappeared into the night.

All except for her. She isn't recorded on a death certificate, but you already know the truth: she wouldn't go. She opted to swallow mouthfuls of dark water, curled up in a bed that was hers, waiting patiently for the end to come. And come it did, burying her in a watery grave of the world's making.

You wish she would have run. You know if given the chance, you'd run, but for now, you're stuck here, so you'll have to make the best of it. You're sixteen with a dubious driver's license and the key to a beat-up Ford Aspire, the bright blue color of a robin's egg. It's just big enough for everyone to pile in, always headed for the same place—back out to the lake.

You want to talk about what you've learned to all your friends. About the ghost, about the houses in the water, about the way the Army Corps of Engineers came and stole so many lives away. But it's Saturday night, party night, and nobody cares a lick about those long ago families.

"They'd be dead by now anyways," your best friend says with a toss of her long blonde hair, as if to suggest that's that.

As everyone carouses on the beach, you wander alone to the edge of the water, that line where the sand ends and something else begins.

That's when you see her, no more than a dozen feet away. The ghost is watching you, her face just beneath the water. After all these years, you feel like you know her better than you know your own family, and somehow, she knows you better than your own best friend. A silent bond, a silent understanding.

But you tell yourself you're being ridiculous again. *Fanciful,* your mother would say. There's probably no ghost at all. You need to keep both feet on the ground. You need to do your best to build a life for yourself. A future. You need to get along with the rest of the world, the real world.

So you turn away from the ghost and have a piss-warm beer and laugh at all the jokes that aren't funny, and when a boy with bright blue hair kisses you hard on the lips, you close your eyes and pretend to enjoy it.

This is what's expected of you, so it's exactly what you'll do.

When you look again, the ghost is gone, and your heart aches a little, because you wonder if you've chased her away, if you've made her feel unwelcome. She never makes you feel unwelcome. She always makes this place feel like home.

At midnight, with a case of beer already gone, you can't help yourself. You shed your clothes like a useless skin and wade into the water. This inspires the others to follow, their shrill laughter echoing into the night, the moonlight glinting off your bodies.

They stay close to the beach, but you swim out a little farther. The hills of Harrison County seem to be closing in around you, the darkness of the lake ready to gobble you up, but you don't mind. You almost want to invite it in.

Then, all at once, you do invite it in. The water rushes up to greet you, and you're sinking fast. Sinking because you want to. Because it feels right.

Above you, your friends are calling out your name, and in spite of yourself, you look back, hesitating just once, just long enough for somebody's hand to hook around your arm. For an instant, hope blooms in your chest, and you tell yourself it's her, the ghost returned to you. But even in the depths, you see that flash of blue hair. It's only the boy who was kissing you earlier. He wrenches you to the surface of the dark water and drags you back to the pale sand like a ragdoll.

Your friends, or whoever they are, surround you in an instant.

"What the hell was that?" they ask, their mouths gaping, their eyes black and bottomless. "You could have died."

You could have gotten us into trouble is what they really mean. Because how would they have explained it to the cops when they found your body bobbing in the shadowy water? That's if they found your body at all.

You only shrug. "I just wanted to see the houses," you whisper, and they all guffaw at you, their high-pitched laughs like hungry hyenas.

"Try that again, and you'll end up stuck in that awful underwater town," your best friend says, and though it's supposed to be a warning, you can't help but think that might be better than this.

That maybe you'd feel safer among ghosts than among friends.

4. *The people got boatloads of money for their houses. That gave them a chance for a new life. And isn't that all anybody wants: a fresh start?*

It's the day before high school graduation, the whole world stretched out in front of you like a golden promise. You and your friends will soon be scattering like cockroaches, headed in the fall to Ohio State and Kent State and Oberlin, the future bright as the August sun.

"We'll keep in touch," they all promise, and you almost laugh aloud, because that's what everybody always says.

You bet the people in the town beneath the lake said it too. As they packed up their jalopies, fleeing like the Joads from Oklahoma, they probably promised to write each other, promised to stay in touch with the next-door neighbors who had practically been their kin. Neighbors who would soon be no more than strangers.

With the foothills of the Appalachians standing sentry around you, the others guzzle down bottles of Southern Comfort and Mad Dog 20/20, a blunt passed around like a precious artifact, the rank smoke rising up in the June air. You don't join them. Instead, you wait quietly by the edge of the water all night, but the ghost doesn't come to you this time, and though you don't want to admit it to yourself, there's a pang in your chest. You wish she'd been here. You wish she'd said goodbye or good luck or even asked you to stay.

Your friends vanish, one by one, until dawn arrives, and you're the only guest left at a deserted party. Until you've waited long enough, and you too have to bid the lake and the town beneath it farewell.

"See you around," you whisper, and for a moment, you're sure you hear it. A small sob, somewhere far off, somewhere deep beneath the water. The cry of a girl. The cry of a ghost.

But you tell yourself it's only a trick of the wind.

5. *Once the government decided to build the lake, there was no way to stop it. The people couldn't argue. They couldn't do anything about it at all.*

You're home for spring break, not that it's much of a break. It's your last year in grad school, the weight of your dissertation breaking your back and breaking your spirit. You can't sleep at night, the gentle call of the lake still boiling in your blood.

But you tell yourself not to listen. You've got a future, something you're building, something good. This is what you've been practicing for your whole life. This is what you want.

It's another lie you tell yourself.

On your last evening home, a few people from high school invite you out for a late-night party, and at first, you politely decline until they tell you it's at the lake. You flush a little, thinking of the town and the ghost you've done your best to forget.

"For old time's sake," you tell your friends and join them on the beach.

Everyone's drinking Milwaukee's Best, anything to save a buck, as they talk about another recession—how it's coming, how there's nothing you can do about it. You try not to listen. Instead, you break away from the others and pace along the sand. You expect to be alone until a shadow passes over your face, and you see her there.

Your own beautiful ghost, waiting for you.

"Hello," she whispers, and it's the first time you've ever heard her voice.

"Hi again," you say, your words wavering, everything in you wavering. Your feet firmly planted in the sand, you reach out for her, but it does no good.

You blink once, and she's gone, dissipated into the air like morning fog.

"What are you doing?" Your once-upon-a-time best friend is

standing beside you, her nose crinkled, a sneer on her lips. "And who are you talking to?"

"Nobody," you say, and you're starting to wonder if it's true.

6. *The town is long gone now, the houses in the water turned to rubble.*

You're alone on the beach, shivering in your faded Case Western hoodie, the sunrise creeping closer.

"Are you there?" you call out to the water, your voice splitting in two. "Can you hear me?"

You wait a long time, but even though you linger on the sand for hours, you get no reply.

You're thirty-nine now, firmly entrenched in middle age, and nothing's worked out the way you planned. You've got nowhere to go and no one to be.

Home—it turns out it's something you can't put a price on. You understand that more than most now, a stack of foreclosure papers tucked in the trunk of your car.

"It's just a house," your friends say. "What's the big deal?"

And you still can't quite answer that question except to say it does matter. It feels like the only thing that matters.

You've waited all night, but the ghost doesn't come to you this time. You're fading away from her, and she's fading from you. That's the way these things go. It's like a fairy tale, something you only get to believe in until you're old enough to know better.

There are other things you believed in too. Like the future, like your dreams. You adored your little house, the one you bought south of Cleveland, with its neat bay windows looking down on a tiny backyard. It was no mansion, no pristine embodiment of the American dream, but you loved it anyhow. You loved it because it was yours. That is, until the bank came along and told you otherwise.

You did everything right, everything the world told you to do. Get a degree, get a job, get a life. You did your best to build a future. Except your future didn't hold. That recession they all talked about materialized after all, and it gobbled up your existence, never even bothering to spit out the bones.

The people who lived beneath the lake know what that feels like. They know what it's like to have their best intentions stolen from them.

The houses are still down there. Everybody knows that. You wonder if their walls remain upright, if there are still floral curtains on the windows and silverware in the kitchen drawers.

But then you remind yourself it's been almost a hundred years now, and you can't imagine there's anything left.

Soon, you can't imagine there will be much left of you either.

7. *The ghosts don't care about the living. They don't even know you're there. And they'll never remember you. You're nothing to them now.*

You're back in your childhood bedroom, a fortysomething receding into yourself, tallying the days like a prisoner with a life sentence. You've tried to find your own way. You've tried to get it right. But sometimes, right isn't within your reach.

Tonight, there's an impromptu class reunion that ends up at the lake. Because everything ends at the lake. You say hello to all the people you used to know. The boy with the bright blue hair isn't a boy anymore, and your former best friend's blond tresses have turned to gray. Everyone around you keeps getting older.

As you gaze out over the water, you think how it could be your sanctuary too. It's what you've always wanted. You sense it deep in your marrow, the way this is it, your last chance. The ghost hasn't returned for years, and you know why. After everything, you stopped searching for her, stopped dreaming the way you used to.

But you can change that. In this moment, it feels like the only thing you can still do.

Nobody else notices as you wander right up to the water's edge. They don't see when you kick off your shoes or when you take a deep breath and dive down into the water.

It's warmer than you remember and more inviting than before.

It takes a moment, but the splash of your figure must get someone's attention, because you hear them now, your friends' voices behind you, calling out your name. But this time, you don't look back. Instead, you keep sinking, as fast as you can, your body an anchor, vanishing into the dark, into the places that no one will ever be able to find you.

No one except her.

Your eyes adjusting in the murk, she emerges slowly at first. You shouldn't be able to see her clearly, she shouldn't exist at all, but there are things in this world you can't quite fathom. Like the way she's always stayed the same, even after all these years. Stasis is her kingdom, her sanctuary.

"Hello again," she says, and something flashes in her eyes, like she's surprised to see you. As though she was sure you'd forgotten her, an urban legend, a silly myth from childhood. Only you've never let her go, not really, and now she'll never let you go either. Through the dark, she reaches out and entwines her hand with yours.

"I've missed you," you say, and she exhales a deep, throaty laugh, and you do the same, the water slipping into your lungs, not slowing you down for a moment.

The town materializes beneath you, all the houses still standing, their walls upright, their roofs intact, as if they've been waiting for you. This is it. Home. You're finally home. A place the world tried to destroy —for you and for her. But you've found it together, and nobody will take it away now.

With the ghost at your side, you drift down the road among all the empty houses, your feet barely touching the floor of the lake, everything turned to mud and darkness. Neither of you minds. At least you're together. No matter what, you'll always have each other.

Somewhere above you, there are voices still calling out your name, but they're fading now, and soon, you'll never have to hear them again.

"Welcome," the ghost whispers, and with the water shimmering around you, she leads you up the stairs to the last house. Her house. The house that belongs to both of you now. Her hand steady, her eyes gleaming, she reaches out and opens the front door.

Smiling, you grip her hand tighter and step across the threshold, just as the darkness devours you whole.

EVERY GOOD DEED...

Weston Kincade

Luis Gomez sat in thought at the base of a thicket of trees. He had spent the night there, watching the stars through the branches. As he ruminated, he tossed a hand grenade above his head, then caught it, higher and higher each time. Although it was 2021, mentally Luis could have been dressed in fatigues, sitting in a Vietnam forest on lookout for the Viet Cong. His mind returned there often. Only the flaking paint from continued use betrayed the forty-five years the grenade spent in Luis's hands. His age would surprise most, with thick, dark hair that didn't betray his sixty-three years of life. Luis tossed the souvenir up once more and glanced at the apartment complex around him. This cloistered park was surrounded by brick buildings built around the same time as the war.

Thankfully, people tended to give Luis a wide berth if they noticed him. The few close enough to make out his juggling toy sometimes panicked, but that was rare. While Cleveland, Ohio was a fairly friendly city, it was still a city, full of people with their own minds and motivations. They wouldn't notice an atomic detonation overhead so long as it didn't affect their cell reception. As society adapted to the Covid pandemic, more people were out. The sun struggled to reach through the trees. Luis pocketed the hand grenade in his jacket and took a deep breath of crisp morning air.

"Today will be a good day," he told himself, a plea more than a prediction.

Zipping his ancient WWII bomber jacket against the wind and masking up, Luis set forth on what had become his daily routine. He boarded the local bus, watched crumbling asphalt, decrepit buildings, and colorful graffiti pass by, then switched to bus 51. Gardens and mansions swept past. Areas of construction and renovation dotted the streets. A short while later, Luis stepped onto the sidewalk at the hospital, a towering building covered in tinted glass with a heliport on the roof. It was massive, making Luis feel even more insignificant. Dora would be waiting inside, opposite a plastic barrier, struggling to breathe. Thankfully, ventilators had saved her life. Luis kept her company for over a week, as he had the last twenty-two years of marriage. Ten days ago, Dora was happy, jubilant, and the overwhelming reason Luis had made it since the war. He spent years homeless, living on the streets, until he met Dora.

She was the lighthouse in his stormy life. He had come back from the war and found himself hopping from building site to building site, wherever construction took him. Luis spent nights at the local watering holes until the habit upended his life. It's a fragile balance that must be maintained, so he'd move on to the next site again and again, until one night he found himself face-up on a cold concrete floor staring into Dora's deep, brown eyes.

"Luis, you can't sleep here," she said ever so pleasantly, her southern accent evident.

Luis struggled to piece together recent memories, but he drew a blank. "I...where am I?"

"You're in the middle of the dining room."

Luis pulled himself together and sat up. The room around him shifted slightly with the rays of sunlight streaming through the windows. He wondered how long he'd been asleep. Somehow, no one in the food kitchen had seen fit to wake him.

Dora motioned from the table nearest him, smacking the bench.

"Come on, darlin'. Have a seat and I'll fill you up. Ray's got brisket going for tonight."

Luis followed her instructions, his stomach growling. "Thank you. What was your name?"

Dora smiled and brought a tray of steaming brisket and stewed vegetables. "It's Dora, honey. You looked like you had a long night, so we just left you be for a bit. You're looking a little skinny, so put this down your gullet."

He followed her instructions from then on...for years to come. It was a simple meeting, one filled with empathy and compassion, and it changed the direction of Luis's life. It gave him direction and someone to care for in turn as their passion for one another grew. Luis shivered as he stared at the intimidating building. He hated dealing with people, especially recently. This was more interaction than Luis had seen in decades. Disability checks had their advantages. The words of the doctor who recommended his discharge echoed through his mind, "Not mentally capable." Luis brushed it aside and strode toward the glass building. Passing through revolving doors, his fingers tightened around the grenade in his pocket. "On edge does not mean mentally incapable," he grumbled, signing in.

At the check-in desk, the receptionist said, "Oh, Mr. Gomez, your wife's nurse asked me to watch for you. Could you take a seat in the waiting room? She'll be right with you."

Luis nodded and did as she asked. It was spacious, with chairs and calm paintings lining the walls. Bare coffee tables were scattered across the room.

Scanning by nature, he eyed the occupants of the room. Luis's paranoia had diminished over the years since Vietnam, but not by much. A land mine six months into his first tour changed his life in a second. One moment he was leading a scouting patrol through the jungle, the next he was mopping blood from his eyes and staring up at the chopper ceiling, en route to Firebase Betty. Since then he'd always walked with a slight shuffle.

People bustled by, but most maintained their distance. Patients and their guests fiddled on phones, laptops, or read, while children played at a lower table. Luis's hand stiffened around the old grenade when a uniformed police officer stepped through the revolving doors. A leash dangled from his hand, connected to a perky German Shepherd with its tongue hanging out. The officer joined the check-in line, dog in tow. He perused the room casually and waved at a hospital staffer who evidently knew him. She smiled back and strolled over for a chat. Luis watched it all like a movie. Distracted, the dog casually sniffed around, pulling the leash through his partner's fingers. The officer noticed with a glance but did not react, preferring the current conversation.

Any who noticed their arrival or the dog's free reign did not seem to care. The stiffness in Luis's hand slowly spread through his body as the dog inched closer, sniffing plastic plants, tile, carpet, and even a few pant legs. Ten feet fell to eight, then six, until Luis was sitting stock still, forming himself to the back of the chair, wishing he were invisible. To his surprise, the canine did not alert, at least so far as he knew. Luis could not claim to know any of the commands or signals, but the way the dog's tongue lolled did not signal aggression. Instead the dog inched closer for a sniff, then sat down, gazing into Luis's eyes. A small, silver dog tag in the shape of a police badge advertised his name as Ranger.

After a moment of wary hesitation glancing from the dog to the distracted officer and back, Luis's muscles eased a fraction. He carefully lifted his free hand to the dog, palm up. Two sniffs led to subsequent licks. Before Luis knew what was happening, Ranger's chin settled in his palm, dark eyes staring at him with concern. He scratched the dog's chin in pleasant surprise.

"Too jumpy," Luis told himself. "I'm too jumpy. Cómo estás? How are you?"

The only indication that Ranger heard was a twitch of the ear, but his gaze did not waver.

"Aren't you a friendly one? So your name is Ranger. Good boy. I'm Lou."

He continued scratching.

"You been working hard?" Luis asked. "Ahhhh...si, yes. All that breathing hard, you must have been." Taking a closer look at the dog, Luis spotted two healed-over scars. "You've seen some shit, haven't you, boy?" Ranger's eyes answered knowingly. "Ohhh, porque eres un viejo soldado."

With so few visitors over the years, his conversational company had been limited to Dora. It was just too difficult to predict strangers' actions, and that made every interaction like walking a razor's edge. Any second they could say or do something, and there were too many triggers that could set him off. He knew it. That was why he avoided them, but Ranger was different. He listened. He didn't judge. Luis had never had a dog—not really by choice. The opportunity had just never arisen, and he never had the desire, but now he wondered if there was something he had missed. His hand drifted to the dog's ear, massaging it little by little. Ranger leaned into it.

"You're a fellow soldier like me, a frontliner. Infantry to the core, hooah," he whispered. It lacked enthusiasm. "For whatever it's worth, it doesn't matter. None of it matters. Nada importa. The only thing that matters are the ones you love." He nodded as though the dog had heard and agreed.

To Luis's surprise, a nurse he had seen on previous visits approached, her face calm and collected. She looked tired, but her gaze told him something was different today. It was direct, unflinching, and set on him.

"Uh oh," Luis muttered. He glanced around, thinking maybe she meant someone else, but social-distancing protocols had left the seats on either side vacant. "Please pass by," he mumbled. "Pass by. Ay, Dios mio. Just pass by."

Unfortunately, Luis's pleas fell on deaf ears as the woman in blue scrubs stopped a few feet away. "Mr. Gomez, will you come with me?"

Luis's gaze rose past a name tag that read Alaysia to a dark-skinned woman with a short afro. Her face was emotionless. *This can't be good,* was all that came to mind. His darkest fears played through his head. Luis had seen that look before. His fingers clutched the grenade within his pocket, but he followed her to a windowed alcove further away from other patients. She stopped and turned to face him. That stony gaze found Luis again, halting him.

"Mr. Gomez..." she took a deep breath, then continued, "I'm sorry to have to tell you, but Dora didn't make it through the night."

Luis had no response. It did not make sense. He had just seen her the day before, and she was getting better. *On the mend*, were the words Dr. Stodges used. "But...but...but..."

"I know, Mr. Gomez. She was responding well, but you know how hard it was for her at night. We tried calling you but got no answer."

"I...I slept outside." Luis's lower lip quivered. "I missed it. I missed her." He nodded to no one in particular and took a deep breath. "But the ventilator. It was helping."

"Yes. Unfortunately, last night she had an acute asthma attack while intubated."

"What does that mean?"

The nurse flipped open the medical file she brought and scanned the first few pages. "She experienced increasing bronchospasms and respiratory failure," Alaysia read aloud, "leading to an unexpected cardiac arrest. At 2:59 this morning, she was pronounced dead." She closed the file and returned her attention to Luis. The emotionless look was replaced with compassion. "I'm sorry, Mr. Gomez. The ventilator just wasn't enough." She tried to grab his hand, but Luis shied away. "Asthma and Covid don't mix. She fought hard, you saw it, but it was just too much this time. I'm sorry for your loss."

"I...I...this can't happen," he muttered simply. His gaze slid over the nurse's shoulder, through double doors into the clinical area. Mobile stretchers lined the hallway. Each was occupied and covered with a white sheet. It occurred to Luis that Dora could be lying on any of them. Tears etched their way down his face. He fingered the hand grenade's pin longingly. *It would only take a small jerk, pequeño,* he mentally considered for the first time in years.

Alaysia tried to steer Luis away. He lingered for a moment, then allowed himself to be led to his seat, where he slumped into the chair.

She asked, "Do you need someone? I can call a family member or a friend, or we can get a counselor?"

Her questions took a moment to sink in, but Luis shook his head no. She said more, but he did not hear. Luis could not form the words he wanted to say, but it was enough. The nurse left the waiting room.

His thoughts were of the wonderful woman he'd come to love, whose heart was only eclipsed by her compassion for the downtrodden. He wasn't the first underdog she had helped, not even the first veteran.

She was a weekly volunteer at the shelter he frequented and even ran weekly game nights of chess and checkers, supplying the boards herself. Luis had just never noticed her, or anyone for that matter.

However, she'd seen something in him he didn't see in himself. She saw the strength that would help carry him through civilian life. It just needed redirected. He needed her help, but he was blind to anything outside of his known world. The war had forced him into a life counter to the values held by civilians, one of murder in a tortured land, and now he was floundering. War is murder for those at the brunt of the fighting, no matter how you wrap it. Rage and his Kabar had been all that stood between life and death in two ambushes he vividly remembered. Now his salvation, his shining light, was relegated to a number—another death in the Covid pandemic, one more tally in the virtual record.

Rage grew in Luis—rage at the medical staff who hadn't reached him, rage at the doctor who dismissed him years ago, rage at the people sitting in the waiting room who looked so comfortable and content in this world of chaos. But his rage simmered and turned to shame when Luis realized he was as guilty as them.

Dora's words came to him. "Don't you go blaming those people for what ain't their fault. Take responsibility." She had been stern but supportive.

He fingered the grenade in his pocket. Just then, Luis felt a slight pressure on his knee. Opening his eyes, he found Ranger's head sitting atop it. The dog's coffee-brown orbs held more compassion than any human's he had ever seen, as if to say, "I know you're sad. I'm here with you."

Luis's free hand drifted to Ranger's head, petting the canine unconsciously as thoughts spun and tears ran. Nurses at the check-in counter glanced his way periodically, concerned.

Minutes passed. Patients of all ages wandered about. Beneath his fingers, Luis noticed the edges of the grenade had been worn smooth over the years. He caressed it within his pocket, again contemplating suicide...*But the collateral damage,* Luis concluded. He could not be responsible for that. Ranger nudged his free hand. Unconsciously, Luis had stopped petting the gentle creature. Ranger whined. A smile returned to Luis's lips, and he scratched the dog's ear. It thumped a leg gratefully. His smile widened, but it did not last.

A moment later Alaysia returned with a plastic bag full of Dora's belongings: folded clothes, jewelry, and more. The nurse set it on the seat next to him. She said something about not having enough room, but Luis could only stare at the bag. The pink floral dress Dora wore to the hospital peeked out. He gazed, entranced as though it were the most exotic of venomous vipers. As such, he did not hear what the nurse said, nor did Luis notice when she left.

He lost track of time as his thoughts wandered to Dora, the last time he had seen her and the most beautiful moments they shared, until Ranger brought him back with another nudge. This time he had not stopped scratching the animal. Instead, Ranger's head turned in the direction of a girl in a bedraggled Sunday dress sitting next to her mother. She was small, quiet, and went unnoticed while her mother's nose was stuck in a fashion magazine. At first Luis was not sure what had garnered the dog's attention, but an extended moment later, he did. Old training kicked in, and Luis was alert.

Glancing around, he took in his surroundings, everything that passed his notice over the last half hour. Down the hall, ambulances were unloading patient after patient, some already covered by sheets. A door opened and Luis spotted filled body bags stacked in one room. Some of Alaysia's words returned, "We don't have beds, and the morgue is full." Evidently he had heard, just not processed. Emergency medical employees bustled about. The hospital was inundated with Covid cases. His gaze returned to the little girl. The dog was right. Her face was blue, and she was hardly conscious.

Leaping to his feet, Luis ran across the room and reached for her, shouting, "Señora, your daughter! She cannot breathe." He grabbed the girl's shoulders and stared into her downturned face, giving her a shake.

She did not respond.

The girl's mother jumped from fright but quickly turned her attention to the child. "Doctor!" she shouted. "Help! Help! My baby can't breathe."

White coats and blue scrubs split from the bustle and descended on the child. They moved her to the floor, tilted her head back, and began

CPR, while another nurse ran for a stretcher. It all happened so quickly. Stepping back, there was a moment of pride before something different caught Luis's attention. What he did not expect was the one thing he felt around his finger, the pin to the grenade.

A frantic memory of something rolling from his pocket as he jumped forward brought his gaze to the floor six feet away. In the middle of the hallway sat his freed hand grenade. *Hello friend*, was all that came to Luis's mind, but a half-second later the grenade seemed to tick in his head, marking the seconds. *No time. Ahora.* "Move!" he shouted.

Before Luis could cross the distance, Ranger sprang into action. Clutching the hand grenade in his jaws, the dog sprinted through the room, dodging people and bolting through the revolving doors as though he knew the danger.

"Nooooo!" Luis made it two feet before crumpling to the floor, aching at what would come and counting the seconds. He made it to three before an explosion resounded, shattering the glass walls lining the front. Shouts and screams echoed from outside, while blood and gore dripped down the glass.

Patients who sat or stood watching the events unfold screamed and ran, while others turned cell phones on the spectacle. Suddenly Luis felt something cold and hard against the back of his head. He instantly knew the officer was behind him and placed his hands on the floor. He waited, eyes closed, for the blessing and punishment. He deserved as much if not more, or so his guilt told him.

The gun barrel shook, then vanished after a drawn-out moment. The shouts changed. They were angry now and directed at him. Luis's hands were soon cuffed behind his back, and the officer searched his pockets. The only thing he found, beyond a battered wallet and keys, was the pin still clutched in Luis's fingers.

While sitting in his jail cell two weeks later, a letter came in the mail. Luis was surprised when the security officer handed it to him. The last couple of weeks had been filled with guilt over his part in Ranger's death and depression over the loss of his beloved Dora. She was the only thing keeping him together. How long he would be stuck here, he did not know or care. Arraignment would come later. What he did know was that he would never be free of the guilt and shame of Ranger's loss. It consumed him. Ranger had lost his life, the officer had lost a partner, he had lost his one true love and his only friend. Luis never had many friends. Now there was nothing driving him forward. However, what made him sit on the bottom bunk and stare was the name on the return address, Elaine Bradford.

Quién? I never met her, I'm sure of it.

The envelope had already been unsealed and checked, so Luis unfolded the handwritten letter inside. In neat, scrawled cursive, Elaine penned:

Mr. Gomez,

I read about you in the news. The Times even called you a terrorist. I know that's not right. I am so sorry for your loss. God knows what you must have been going through that day after losing your wife, but I can only think he puts people on Earth to do what is necessary. It may not always work the way we think it should, and we make mistakes, but I wanted to thank you so much for saving my daughter's life. I couldn't let it go unsaid. I didn't...if not for you, I don't want to think what would have happened.

Thank you. From the bottom of my heart, thank you. I know the future must look dark, but you will forever be in my thoughts and prayers.

Elaine Bradford

Luis sat in thought, and for the third time in his life, silent tears fell. He remembered the first. They were happy tears, at his wedding seeing Dora in that beautiful white dress, smiling down a rose-lined path. The second had been two weeks ago. This time, he could not tell if they were happy tears or tears of sadness, but they would not stop.

RECLAMATION

Kealan Patrick Burke

I t was a little over an hour's drive from Maggie's house in Columbus to The Wren's Nest Cabins in Hocking Hills. As always, she set out early, allowing extra time for traffic, and as soon as she turned east onto US-33, she thanked her good sense. It was not yet ten a.m. on a Tuesday morning, a time of day usually light on traffic, and yet the highway was choked with vehicles, few of them moving.

"What's this about?" Maggie asked Charlie, the ghost of her deceased cat. Feline leukemia had robbed her of her beloved polydactyl Maine Coon six months before, but she refused to forget him, opting instead to imagine him sitting next to her, staring raptly out the passenger side window. She'd even hung one of his little jingly toys from the rearview mirror, and every time the little bell tinkled, tears pricked her eyes. Sometimes she allowed herself to believe the bell was his way of assuring her he was still around, but knew it was just the jolts and vibrations from the road.

In the absence of an explanation from Charlie, she jabbed the radio on and fussed until she found the traffic report, but it told her nothing she didn't already know. There was an unusual flow of traffic in the northbound lane headed toward Columbus, but the reporter was optimistic that the congestion would clear soon. *Soon* was a little too vague for Maggie's liking. She could not be late. She was never late, but now that Wren's Nest had been bought out by some faceless tech group, she was more anxious than ever to give a good impression. She'd miss Des and Sue Alderton, the cabins' former owners, a kindly elderly couple who'd always treated her well and never tried to micromanage her, but even though Lancorp Inc. was less personable and undoubtedly less relaxed about things, the pay was much, much better, and that was a trade she could handle. She was just glad they'd kept her on, a development she hadn't expected. With all the money they'd put into renovating the six cabins scattered around the perimeter of Hocking Hills State Park, she'd assumed they'd hire some hip young cleaning service and not an independent contractor looking down the barrel of her fifty-fifth birthday. Perhaps they'd been impressed by the guest reviews and her flawless record of attendance. Maybe the Aldertons put in a good word. Whatever the reason, with Kylie starting high school in the fall, the ten dollars an hour bump in pay was nothing to be sniffed at.

"In this economy, we'll take what we can get, right Charlie?"

She imagined the cat meowing in agreement and wished she could reach over and scratch behind his ears.

She eyed the time on the dashboard display, and nervously drummed her fingers on the steering wheel. "C'mon, people." For now, she was stuck, her battered old Mazda idling behind a GMC pickup truck, the fumes from which she could smell even with the windows up.

Fifteen minutes later, the cars began to move, but not before Maggie looked once more at the chaos of cars in the northbound lane. Nothing but blank faces stared back at her.

She reached the first cabin—The Love Shack—with twelve minutes to spare, hardly a new record, but *good enough for government work* as her dear departed father used to say. Of course, she had worked for the government and after twenty-six years of service, they'd deemed *her* not good enough for *them*, so maybe that old saying needed an update.

When she'd left home the sun had been shining, but by the time she reached the cabin, the sky had turned grey, and rain speckled her windshield. A light greenish mist made an unfinished watercolor of the small log cabin and the overhanging sycamores.

Though she'd had much more fulfilling jobs in her life, Maggie couldn't say she'd ever worked anywhere quite so pretty, and as often as she complained about the work, it was preferable to being sequestered in a cubicle for ten hours a day. She liked Hocking Hills and had visited the State Park and Old Man's Caves several times when Kylie was young enough to appreciate their splendor. Now, as with so many young people of her generation, her daughter was unlikely to ever see Hocking Hills again unless someone posted pictures of them on Instachat or Snapface, or whatever those apps were called.

She parked the Mazda in the gravel driveway and gathered her bucket of cleaning supplies from the trunk, depositing them on the stoop of the small bungalow before returning to fetch the vacuum and mop. Armed for war, she knocked three times on the door and, satisfied that the cabin was empty, punched in the keycode and let herself into the house.

"Housekeeping!" she announced, remembering the day two summers ago when she'd knocked, announced herself, and entered only to find a woman standing stark-naked before her at the kitchen island, hair wild, red-eyed from liquor, mouth agape with shock, a coffee cup raised and frozen before her hungover face. iPod earbuds were nestled in her ears and from where Maggie stood, she could hear the tinny sounds of music. "Oh shit," the woman said and quickly ducked down behind the island while Maggie retreated to her car until the woman and her partner could compose themselves enough to make their apologies. In retrospect it had been funny, and the compensatory cash tip had been more than worth it, but Maggie wasn't someone who enjoyed intruding on people's privacy. Situations reversed, she'd probably have died of mortification, so now she was more vigilant in giving people time to realize she was among them.

"Housekeeping!" she said again, and cocked an ear, listening for the frantic sounds typical of guests who've overslept and were just now realizing their mistake. But she heard nothing, which didn't always mean she was alone. In Maggie's experience, couples who came to The Love Shack tended to drink a lot and sleep heavily, so she edged her way carefully down the hall and poked her head into the kitchen. It was deserted but for the debris of overindulgence: four empty bottles of wine, dirty dishes smeared with what looked like pasta sauce, and two empty packs of cigarettes. Some of the wine had spilled and dried on the bare wood floor, but that wouldn't be a chore. There was a lingering smell of incense, and the burnt-rope stink of the marijuana it had been used to hide.

Maggie set her bucket down. There was a time, not so long ago either, when she and Teddy would have left similar evidence in their wake, but neither of them had the constitution for such revelry anymore. These days more than one bottle of wine—always white because red curdled her stomach—gave her a headache that lasted days, and pot just made her sleepy. While she felt a nostalgic pang for the wildness of her younger self, she cherished more her calm and cozy Friday nights with Teddy watching documentaries on Netflix.

Maggie had always been a hard worker, and mostly she didn't mind the chaos guests left behind them. There were exceptions of course, because people tended to do things in other places they wouldn't do at home, like defecating on the bedroom floor or leaving a puddle of vomit in the linen closet. And there was the recurring guest who, for reasons that would forever remain a mystery, liked to wash his underwear in the Mr. Coffee machine. (Nobody was happier than Maggie when they replaced the old coffee makers with single-serve Keurigs.)

As disgusting as all that was, Maggie had learned quickly to separate herself from it. There were, after all, people out there who got up every morning and went to work scraping brains and other gory ejecta off the walls at crime scenes, a job that required a level of detachment Maggie knew was beyond her. Thankfully, today, and in the kitchen at least, the celebratory fallout was minimal. She threw open the sliding doors to air out the room, wishing as she so often did that their guests took the no-smoking policy more seriously because she hated to be a tattletale, but was duty-bound to report the violation to avoid being blamed for it herself. She made a note of it on the checklist tacked to her clipboard and went further into the house.

There were four rooms in The Love Shack: the kitchen, with a tidy little breakfast nook in the corner by the big window which looked out onto the woods and the small creek beyond, one medium sized bathroom, a small living space that doubled as the entryway, and one large bedroom. The living space looked untouched. The welcome manual, takeout menus, and brochures for Conkle's Hollow Nature Preserve and Cedar Falls on the small glass coffee table had either been ignored or replaced exactly as they'd been arranged prior to the guests' arrival. The stuffed deer head mounted above the stone fireplace looked dumbly at her as she nodded her satisfaction. One less room to worry about. She'd give it a light dusting of course because people didn't always need to occupy rooms to leave traces of themselves behind, but this was light work.

She moved onto the bathroom and inspected it from the doorway: damp towels crumpled on the floor, guest soaps unwrapped and left on the sink to bathe in their own slimy foam, a pile of cotton disks smudged with orange-colored makeup on the counter, trashcan full of plastic wrapping, wadded up balls of toilet paper, and used floss. The water spots on the mirror held her attention until reflected movement in the shower behind her made her gasp, body jolting as she quickly sidled out of the room, leaving the door ajar so whomever was in there could still hear her.

"Hi, housekeeping. I'm so sorry. I didn't realize anyone was still here."

And how *could* she have known? She'd been here almost ten minutes already and had repeatedly announced herself. She might have thought the guest simply didn't hear her over the running water, but the shower was off. Whoever was in there was just standing in the stall. This realization summoned an ugly thought: What if she'd walked in on a robbery and the thief was in there hiding? It had happened before. Not to her, but Carl the maintenance man had entered another of the cabins to tend to a backed up sink only to find two sickly young men trying to make off with the flatscreen TV. Lucky for Carl, they'd fled at the sight of him. As in many rural areas, opioid addiction had taken its toll on the people of Hocking Hills and the crime rate was getting worse by the day. Secluded cabins were easy targets for the desperate and damaged.

The most likely scenario was that she'd walked in just as someone *finished* showering, but anyone with a lick of sense would have called out to her. Besides, she didn't hear the telltale dripping of a recently hushed faucet, and, because her mother, God rest her soul, hadn't raised a fool for a daughter, Maggie hustled back to the car without waiting for an answer from the person in the stall. The cell signal out here in the mountains wasn't stellar, but it worked, and in short order, she was in her car with the doors locked, the phone to her ear as it tried to connect to the cabin. Through the rain on the windshield glass, she watched for any sign of movement but saw nothing. At the rear of the cabin was a back door leading out onto a deck and a hot tub and the woods beyond. Maybe whoever she'd caught hiding in there had decided to use it. She imagined Charlie purring as he rubbed against her arm, comforting her, like he always did when he sensed she was upset.

But why *was* she upset? This kind of thing happened all the time. What was different about this instance? She hadn't even had a chance to check the bedroom. Maybe the guests' bags were still there, and maybe someone was still asleep in the bed. Maybe despite her best efforts, they simply hadn't heard her come in. So what had made her guts tighten and the hair on the back of her neck stand on end when she saw that figure, mottled by the pebbled shower glass door, move in the mirror?

She concluded it was several things:

Firstly, there were many places to hide inside the cabin. Behind the transparent door of a shower was easily the worst of them.

Secondly, when she replayed what she saw in the mirror, she realized the figure hadn't been crouching or hunkered down, as anyone would to make themselves smaller and therefore less likely to be discovered. The figure had been standing there, watching her, and the movement that had caught her attention had been a spasm, a flinch as of involuntary pain, or need, perfectly befitting the expected behavior of an addict. No, she did not think it a late guest. Everything suggested she'd walked in on something unsavory, and she was not going back inside until she knew the place was vacant.

Then there was the smell: the faint stink of rotting vegetables.

And lastly, if the guests were still inside, where was their car? The parking lot was empty but for Maggie's Mazda, which had reinforced the impression that the cabin was deserted when she'd pulled up.

She hung up the phone, unanswered, and put her hands atop the steering wheel. There was no doubt she was doing the right thing, the smart thing, but economic realities cared little for logic, and every minute spent sitting here was money lost. She could call someone at Lancorp and report the situation, she could even call the police, but the inevitable hubbub would mean a day out of her paycheck. Somehow, she didn't think the company charitable enough to renumerate her for time spent dithering over nothing. Still, it wasn't like she could go back inside that house, not without knowing what was going on in there.

But now that she'd considered the implications of her good sense, doubt began to creep in. What had she *really* seen? Could she be sure it hadn't been a woman hiding in there, perhaps somebody else's victim, flinching from the aftershock of some unspeakable hell? She imagined driving home and turning on the TV to news that a rape or assault victim had been rescued from the cabin, imagined the guilt that would follow with the realization that she had done nothing to help. Frustrated, she picked up her cell phone again and scrolled through the numbers until she found Carl Christian, the maintenance man, who, like Maggie, had been kept on when the property changed hands. There was no guarantee he was on site today, but it was worth a shot. Whatever happened next, she'd feel better having Carl and his toolbox for backup.

"'Allo, love!" he said, answering on the first ring. As always, she cringed at his terrible attempt at a British accent (which was, despite its awfulness, still marginally better than his Irish one), but was relieved to hear his voice.

"Hey Carl. Are you around today?"

"Over at The Swan. Busted floor tile where someone dropped a bowling ball. Don't ask me what they were doing with it. Why? Everything okay?"

"Not sure. The guests in The Love Shack were supposed to check out at nine, but somebody's still in there. Hiding in the shower. It's probably nothing, but I want to be careful. Something feels hinky. There's no car here."

"Could have parked at the welcome center and hiked it up there."

"With their bags?"

"All hipsters love a fitness challenge. You spooked?"

"A little." *A lot*, and she couldn't even say why.

"Okay. Just finishing up here and then I'll head over to you. Where are you now?"

"Parked outside the cabin."

"Doors locked?"

"Of course."

"Good. Be there in ten. Hang tight."

Now that she knew he was coming, she felt mildly ridiculous. If he showed up and there was nobody inside the house, he'd be a good sport about it, but she'd also have cost him time out of his day, and like her own situation, there was too much to do and not enough hours to get it done. The Love Shack was only one of the cabins she had to clean today, and who knew what Carl's workload was like. Distractions were not welcome, and here she was becoming one. Still, she was thankful when she saw his truck in the rearview, and watched as he hopped out with a spryness that belied his age, cigarette clamped between his lips.

She rolled down her window, and Carl dropped to his haunches so he was face-to-face with her. "What have we got, Maggie?" His feathery silver hair danced in the burgeoning breeze.

"Honestly? I don't know. I thought I saw someone in there, but the more I think of it, the more I think maybe I'm just being a chicken."

"Chickens live longer," he said. The smirk on his face told her this was a clumsy nugget of wisdom he'd made up on the spot, and she couldn't help but smile.

"Do they?"

He shrugged and chuckled around his cigarette. "Probably not." She was glad she'd called him. Carl was at least ten years her senior and possessed of a perpetual optimism she envied. She had never seen him without a smile on his wizened face. The deep wrinkles at the corners of his eyes and mouth testified to a life spent finding the upside in everything.

He nodded toward the cabin. "Want me to take a look?"

"If you wouldn't mind."

"Not at all. I'll roust them varmints for ya, little lady," he said, in a drawl she could only assume was supposed to be John Wayne but sounded more like someone remembering how to speak after a stroke.

"Thanks Carl, you're a star."

He rose and took a hurried final puff on his smoke before tossing it in the dirt. Then he winked. "Make some more of those vanilla sugar cookies you gave me at Christmas and we'll call it square."

"Deal," she said.

He slapped a palm on the roof of her car and then sauntered back to his truck, where she watched him rummage in his toolbox. He returned armed with a hammer.

"Do you want me to go with you?" she asked, as he drew abreast of the Mazda, bound for the cabin.

"Naw, I got this. You just lock the doors and sit tight and if I'm not back in ten minutes..." He paused for dramatic effect, "...call the President."

Then he grinned and made his way to the cabin.

Though comforted by his presence, it didn't sit right with her to just wait in the car. What if something happened to him in there? What if she'd just sentenced him to death? She put a hand on the door handle, ready to join Carl in his investigation, but he'd already disappeared inside. She stared at the open door to the cabin, the rain falling hard enough now that she had to turn on the windshield wipers. Their rubbery honk grated on her nerves and for the hundredth time so far this year, she vowed to do something about them.

I need a vacation, she thought, knowing it would be a while before she took one. Teddy was so busy with work that she hardly saw him anymore. Sometimes it seemed as if life outside of their jobs had become an afterthought, that their lives *were* work and little else, though she cherished the rare nights and lazy Sundays in which she and Teddy did nothing together. For years, poor little Charlie had been part of that equation, but Charlie was gone now.

It made her antsy that she couldn't hear anything from the cabin, so she rolled down her window, the rain bouncing off the door and speckling her arm, summoning gooseflesh. She heard nothing over the flatulent honk of the windshield wipers except the rumble of distant thunder.

Around the car, the trees hissed and swayed in the wind. Quiet lightning flickered through the boughs. She waited, five minutes, ten, and when there was no sign of Carl emerging, his smile telling her that everything was fine, she called his number, felt her apprehension rise a few notches when it went to voicemail. To allay her mounting panic, she turned on the radio, and caught a news story in progress:

"—to his Democratic rival's comments this morning, Republican senator of Ohio, Mike McGee, says Kestrel's agenda is to incite panic with little evidence to back it up. He claims Kestrel's opposition to the recent fracking efforts in Hocking Hills, which have been a bone of contention among climate groups since the beginning, are purely political, and that his so-called 'Pandora's Box Theory' is the worst kind of fearmongering. Kestrel's statements were in response to the leaked documents about toxic chemicals seeping into the groundwater, which has yet to be confirmed by the—" Irritated, she turned the radio off again and looked at Charlie for support, but Charlie wasn't there.

She couldn't just sit here anymore, but what were her options? Drive away and leave Carl, or go inside and risk involving herself in a potentially dangerous situation? She gripped the steering wheel hard as if she might throttle from it the best course of action, then shook her head. She'd told Carl she had called him because she was chicken, but that was not true and never had been. Her whole life had been a fight. This right here, whatever it was, was just the latest one.

Bracing herself, she cracked the door and stepped out of the car, but not before fishing a can of Mace from the glovebox, because she was brave, not stupid.

Despite the new chill in the air, she did not hurry to the cabin. Instead, she walked slowly, head cocked, ears attuned to any sound from inside, but over the wind, she heard nothing.

At the threshold, she was struck once more by the heady smell of vegetation, stronger now than it had been before. The foul air roiled toward her from inside the cabin as if someone had left vegetables to rot in the heat.

"Carl?"

She waited a beat, willing him to answer, thereby assuring her that her sense that something was terribly wrong was misplaced. When he didn't, she looked longingly back at her car, her escape, her last chance to flee before she involved herself further in whatever was happening here. Would anyone blame her if she left? Instinct demanded it, and yet here she was, knowing she'd never be able to live with the guilt if she abandoned Carl, who had come only to help.

"Damn it," she told the wind, and entered the cabin.

Inside, it was much as she'd left it, albeit with Carl's muddy footprints on the floor, something which might have annoyed her at any other time, but now served as a track for her to follow to find out what had become of him.

They led her to the bathroom, which she was only partially relieved to find empty. Whomever had been lurking inside the shower—assuming she hadn't imagined them—was gone now, but she noted the floor of the stall was filthy, mud and leaves clotting the drain. She followed Carl's tracks down the hall to the bedroom, the only room she hadn't inspected since her arrival.

Here the stink of spoiled vegetation was strongest. It offended her nose and made her eyes water, and she brought a hand up before her face to shield herself from the worst of it.

"Carl?"

No sound from inside the bedroom, only the squeak of hinges in need of oiling as she used her free hand to open the door.

The floral-print curtains were partially drawn, limiting the amount of murky daylight allowed to filter into the bedroom, but not enough to keep her from seeing what was there to be seen. She saw that her earlier supposition was correct: the guests' bags were on the floor, partially packed, and there was still someone here, a figure lying in the bed amid tousled sheets. She'd also been correct in her feeling that something was terribly awry inside the cabin. She just couldn't have imagined the extent of it. Instinct was a hand on her back, pulling her out of the room, but confusion stalled her because it was difficult to process the scene before her.

The sheets covering the figure had been kicked off or stripped away leaving him lying on his back, arms by his sides and feet together atop a mattress stained green and yellow. It was as if he'd been doused with something while he'd slept. But that wasn't the worst of it. Her initial impression was that the man had been burned alive, even though the bed and the room around him seemed untouched by fire. Harder to explain were the pulsating, gelatinous yellow lights that stippled his body. Those pustulant orbs illuminated the warping of his flesh, leaving him looking more like something sculpted from tree branches than anything human, a latticework of wood and vines and blackened skin. She might have thought him an elaborate woodland sculpture if not for the slight rise and fall of his chest and the putrescent boils stippled across it.

Run, she advised herself, *figure it all out later, if that's even possible, but for now, just run.*

A strange soupy green mist curdled up from the floor, rose in tendrils from the body on the bed, and her mind flooded with desperate, ill-formed theories, her mind's insistence on divining sense from a scenario that seemed to have abandoned it entirely. Two words resounded in her skull, recalled from the radio report: *toxic chemicals*. But what kind of chemicals turned a person into a husk? She didn't know, because she'd never seen the effects of such things on the human body, and didn't want to be seeing it now, particularly if it meant that by coming in here, she might have exposed herself to it.

For one moment more, she stared at the thing on the bed and thought it might have shuddered, though she couldn't be sure that wasn't just her pulse thundering behind her eyes.

And then it spoke, the voice like someone dragging a rusted knife over concrete and her body took over and she was hurrying, staggering, stumbling back into the hall, the front door suddenly much too far away. Any moment now she expected that thing with its horrible earthy smell to grab the back of her neck, to infect her with whatever it had succumbed to, and was relieved when she made it past the threshold unmolested. She paused for a breath, the words from that awful thing's mouth still echoing in her ears: "it knows you, maggie..." And now she knew her imagination was in hyperdrive, because there was no way that man, that thing, knew her name.

She was at the car door, heart beating furiously and painfully against her ribcage, when she remembered why she'd gone inside the cabin in the first place.

Carl.

Hand still on the car door, she cried out for him, competing with the angry roar of thunder to be heard. The wind howled around her, eager to mute her. She called out again and thought she heard a voice. But whose?

No, she counseled herself. *Just go. Report this. If he's here, they'll find him, but this is not something you know how to handle, and nobody in their right mind can blame you for that. Now get your ass in the goddamn car.*

She did, had her seatbelt on, and her fingers on the keys, when Carl appeared, seemingly from somewhere behind the cabin. Her breath caught as she looked at him, and then he started to blur from the rain and the tears in her eyes. But not before she saw the dark veins writhing beneath his skin and the pulsating sickly yellow orbs which had once been his eyes. He was mouthing something at her, his face slack and mournful, skin the color of old flour. His shirt was torn and stained yellow in several places. He did not move to intercept her, and she made no move to go to him. It was too late for that. Carl was gone, taken by whatever biochemical madness had found the cabin. He raised an arm and pointed at something to her right but she dared not look.

"I'm sorry," she said aloud, hoping whatever was left of the man she knew—if anything—understood and forgave her, and then she keyed the ignition and put the gearshift in reverse. Before her foot had a chance to hit the pedal, she heard the tinkling of Charlie's bell, dangling from the rearview mirror. She looked at it, just briefly, wanting to believe it was her beloved cat sending her a sign that everything was going to be fine.

But then a curious rustling, creaking sound drew her attention to her right, to where Carl had been pointing. The windshield wipers gave a rubbery honk. The wind buffeted the car. Maggie couldn't breathe. And in the passenger seat, her dear departed Charlie, now made of vines and bark and twigs and leaves, eyes swollen yellow boils threatening to burst, purred as he dug his claws into her wrist.

A CURE FOR LIVING

Rob E. Boley

It wasn't bereavement that brought Kaley to the cemetery that night. No, it was adventure. Rather, a microadventure.

From her apartment in downtown Dayton, Ohio, she could bike to over a dozen graveyards. These places offered sanctuary from the shambles of her life—the empty space Chris left behind. She could sleep under stars and dream among ghosts, if such a thing existed.

It wasn't a ghost that woke her up, though, but a man's distant whisper, "That's it. Easy."

The words dragged across her consciousness like a lover's caress. Kaley opened her eyes. A half moon hung crooked in the sky amongst a sprinkle of stars. She lay in her sleeping bag which was nestled inside her waterproof bivvy bag. The taste of wine had soured on her tongue. Her blood felt thick, her head stuffed with cotton.

The man's voice whispered again, "Almost there," followed by sounds of exertion.

Her heart flailed in her chest. Sleeping in cemeteries often led to close calls, like the morning she woke up before sunrise to a pickup rumbling past. This was closer, almost right on top of her. Fuck. The last thing she needed was legal trouble on top of everything else.

She'd bedded beside a large monument—in memory of Michael and

Vanessa Brasty. According to their tombstone, *Their love will live forever in our hearts*. A surprisingly detailed picture of the couple was etched into the granite, their heads cocked together as if silently judging the empty cabernet bottle beside their grave or perhaps listening, like Kaley, for more whispers.

"That's it," urged the voice.

The words were but steps away. Maybe she was hearing people having sex? This cemetery was near a semi-rural village several miles south of downtown, accessed by the Great Miami River Trail. Out here, spots for a late-night rendezvous were surely limited. Okay, so maybe this wasn't so bad. Maybe the voices were just as guilty as her.

She needed to investigate but the bivvy bag cocooned her. Flexing her core like a worm, she scooted forward and peered around the monument. Michael and Vanessa stared down, offering little comfort.

In the next row, a thin man dressed in black stood over a fresh hole. Another man stood shoulders-deep in the hole. Black ski masks covered their faces.

Graverobbers? The fuck?

Her hands shook. Her pulse pounded between her ears. This was way worse than late-night screwing. These people were stealing a damn corpse. Who knows what they'd do to her if they realized she was witnessing their crime.

She could either stay hidden from sight yet totally vulnerable, or she could wiggle out of her bivvy bag and escape. If being with Chris had taught her anything, it was that doing nothing rarely made a bad situation better. She chose escape.

Kaley strained against the ground to pivot ninety degrees. With her feet facing the Brasty monument, she'd be out of the graverobbers' sight. She moved in painfully small increments to minimize the squelching of the bivvy bag's waterproof fabric. Getting out of the bag wasn't especially difficult, but doing it quietly was a long labor. Adrenaline flooded her body.

Almost there. She pushed with her legs, accidentally nudging the empty bottle. It tipped, prefacing the immense noise of glass clonking stone. Loud as a gunshot out here. She froze.

Everything went still as though someone hit the pause button. Even her heart surely skipped a few beats.

A shift of motion from the open grave prompted her to move. She tried desperately to yank herself free of the bag. The thin man lurched into view. Heart rattling, she thrashed. Another man approached, impossibly large.

They were on her before she could birth herself from the waterproof womb. She screamed. Something sharp jabbed her shoulder. Her limbs grew heavy. Darkness oozed into the emptiness inside her like coffee filling a mug.

Kaley woke later from a syrupy, dreamless sleep as a muscular woman cradling her like a baby lowered her into what felt like an adult-sized bassinette. On the ceiling, a terrified woman wearing a gag slowly came into focus. No, the ceiling was a mirror, in which she saw herself lying in what resembled a cross between a casket and a tanning bed, only high-tech with assorted tubes and wires connecting it to a control station manned by a thin man, likely the same thin man from the cemetery. More wires ran from there to an identical empty casket, its door open.

Her vision wobbled. This was more than a wine hangover. They'd drugged her. Her reflection wasn't wearing her favorite microadventure outfit—her grey mesh pants and breathable black long-sleeve top. Instead, she sported a cream-colored onesie fitted with various wires, receptors, and plugs. It was thicker than spandex but every bit as form-fitting. Her cheeks smoldered. Someone had undressed her. She wanted more than anything to get out of this fucking box and lunge at the thin man. When she reached up a trembling fist, the muscular woman grabbed it. She fastened straps around Kaley's ankles and wrists.

"The mirror's a nice touch, right?" said the man, now standing over her. He wore a lab coat and a blue surgical mask. "This used to be a sex club. It closed years ago, but it's perfect for us. Discreet location. Ample parking. Tastefully decorated." He pointed up. "Mirrors on the ceilings."

Kaley strained against the straps while the man connected several wires from the inside of her casket to her onesie. Some were standard plug receptacles. Others were thin floppy needles that he slid into ports on her suit, tiny pinpricks of pain that made her bladder quiver. Next, he removed her gag and forced a rubber bit attached to a hose between her teeth.

The muscular woman wore standard white polyester scrubs, her biceps straining the fabric. A black athletic training mask with valves on either side covered her face. She must've been the one digging the grave at the cemetery. Kaley had mistaken her for a man. The woman walked to a gurney upon which sat an ominous black bag. She unzipped it and scooped out a body.

A fucking body. She placed it into the other casket, and now Kaley could see it clearly in the mirror above.

The body was of a man with dark hair, nearly buzzed. Bruises and scrapes covered his misshapen skin, the limbs distorted like an old rag doll. The legs were crushed, the broken flesh exposing cracked bone. The stink of death assaulted Kaley's nose.

"Once I close your lid, the vessel will fill partially with salt water," said the man. "Don't be alarmed. *Your body* is perfectly safe."

She thrashed futilely against the straps while he checked the connections once more and shut the lid. Everything went dark. The only sound was her own breathing, her quivering heart. Warm salt water oozed around her. She floated in formlessness. The air from the hose tasted like lemons.

Inside of the casket's lid, lights flickered impossibly out of reach— stars on a moonless light. The world fell away. She was no longer in a casket, in a room, in a building. Nothing mattered. Not the aches in her body, the worries in her mind, the Chris-shaped emptiness in her heart. Sweet serenity filled her.

Darkness. Peace.

The man's voice stabbed through the void, "Your name is Daniel Gogul. You're a 40-year-old man from Georgia."

Birds chirp relentlessly this bright spring morning. You're back in Ashtabula, Ohio, visiting family. To work off last night's pizza, you stroll around town scrolling through emails on your phone. No word yet about the bid for the government contract.

Eventually, you end up on Bridge Street with its various shops and restaurants. Lake Erie is close enough you can smell it in the air.

After taking a side street, you hear tires squealing followed by a murderous yowling. You round the corner in time to see a station wagon accelerating away from a cat lying dazed in the road—a grey tiger with pale yellow eyes. It looks nothing like your cat back home, Ellie, yet you're instantly drawn to it. The scrawny thing must've been hit. It limps to the curb—one rear leg bloodied—and settles under a car, eyeing you warily. You step closer, and the cat remains still. It has matted fur, torn ears. It's young, no longer a kitten but not full-grown either. Closer yet. Almost there.

Knock. Knock.

That's when the knocking starts. The rhythmic pounding jars your senses. It comes from a nearby house. Apparently, the noise rattles the cat too. It dashes awkwardly across the yard of a grey two-story with a small porch barely big enough for two chairs and a pitcher of tea. The historic home must be undergoing renovations, because the cat slips inside a piece of plastic covering a basement window.

You don't know why you follow. Maybe because you miss Ellie. Maybe you feel a bond with the injured feline. Whatever the reason, you crouch beside the plastic-covered basement window.

Knock. Knock.

The knocking comes from next door. Must be someone doing a home improvement project. No way are you leaving this kitten to hide fearfully in the dark plagued by such an awful sound. You despise loud knocking.

Knock. Knock.

Using your phone as a flashlight, you slip through the window and into an unfinished basement. No, unfinished doesn't quite cover it. This is undone. Bits of rubble crunch underfoot. The walls are bare concrete. A stack of torn wooden paneling lies in the corner next to a rolled-up mess of carpet. The ceiling is all beams and pipes and the skeleton of a drop ceiling. Much of the piping is incomplete. Possibly in process of repair.

Knock. Knock.

Kitty paw prints in the dust lead you to a hole in the wall. No, more than a hole. You pull aside a piece of plywood to discover a tunnel at level with the floor. The curved passage is about knee-high. You aim your phone down it. Far in the distance, two glowing yellow eyes stare back.

Knock. Knock.

"Son of a gun," you say. "Come on, kitty."

It doesn't budge. You crawl into the passage. Maybe it was once part of the Underground Railroad. After all, Ashtabula's placement on Lake Erie made it a key part of former slave's passage north. Or maybe the tunnel dates to Prohibition and the smuggling of illegal booze.

Knock. Knock.

You drag yourself into the darkness, which stinks of mildew. The little cat watches you inch closer and closer. You're nearly within reach when the tunnel shifts around you. Bits of sediment sprinkle down onto your head and back. You crane your neck to look upward. The passage's ceiling is a patchwork quilt of moldy bricks and brittle mortar.

Knock. Knock.

More debris rains down into your eyes. You curse and wipe your eyes. It's not too late to turn back, but you're almost there. Whatever's happening next door must have weakened this structure.

Knock. Knock.

For a moment, everything goes still. Your heart shrivels in your chest. You've made a terrible mistake. The kitten mews. You lunge for it but the little shit dodges. Your shoulder crashes into a support beam. The passage rumbles in response. Paws pad over your back. Turning on your side, you aim the cellphone light behind you. The last thing you see is a flash of stripes.

Knock. Knock.

The passage collapses atop you. Tons of concrete, rock, and debris pummel your body. Horrible wetness coats your face. You try to move, but your limbs are a mess of shredded meat stuffed with broken twigs. Such agony. You can't even scream, because whatever miracle of anatomical engineering once existed in your throat has been demolished. All you can do is listen.

Knock. Knock.

And hurt.

Knock. Knock.

And suffer.

Knock.

Kaley woke with a start on a surprisingly comfortable bed in a clean room lit only by a floor lamp aimed at the tile floor. A bed pan sat on a nearby corner table. Her head ached.

What the fuck just happened? She remembered that strange casket, darkness, and that damn cat. Knocking. Basement. Collapse. It was more than a dream. In that casket, she'd died. Daniel had died. And with him, all his dreams, fears, and ambitions.

Death visions aside, her new grim reality sunk in. She'd been kidnapped. How long would it be before anyone noticed? With Chris gone, possibly quite a while. Her job as a recruiter for an academic executive search firm was entirely virtual. There wasn't a team meeting scheduled for another two weeks. She was supposed to meet her parents and brother tomorrow—or maybe today?—to celebrate Mom's birthday. Her being a no-show would be a point of concern, but likely no great surprise. She hadn't been the most reliable sister or daughter lately.

In the distance, vague noises. Something metallic. A voice. Car horns. She could only listen. Sometimes footsteps passed in the hall. She also heard other things—things that couldn't possibly be there like a kitten mewing or repetitive knocking.

Knock. Knock.

She swore she smelled Lake Erie.

Growing more frantic, she searched the room for anything she could use to escape, but found nothing. The bed frame was solid metal. The air vent, too small to fit through. She paced the room's length but quickly grew dizzy. When she tried pulling off the onesie, an electric current jolted her from within the suit. With a yelp and a curse, she punched the wall.

She examined the fibers and ports of her suit. Its function and design made more sense than it should have—thanks to a drone armoring project Daniel had worked on last year. The dead man's knowledge and memories sat unseemly in her mind, like the foreign debris from a discourteous houseguest. Except she couldn't tidy up her brain. She couldn't sweep or wipe his ideas away.

Knock. Knock.

The thin man entered wearing his lab coat and mask, stylish pants, and a swanky pair of vintage oxblood monk strap leather shoes. He carried a folding chair which he erected in front of her.

Next came the muscular woman. Arms like tree trunks. Chest like a gorilla. She wore matching black athletic pants and a top with her sports mask. With light steps for one so large, she placed a tray with a covered dish and coffee on the corner table.

The man sat and crossed his legs as if to show off his footwear. "My apologies for the accommodations. To be honest, we weren't ready for a, uh, long-term client, but when opportunity arises..." He cleared his throat as if embarrassed. "You can call me Dr. Graves."

"What'd you do to me?" Kaley asked.

"I'd thought to begin with an orientation of sorts—I even made a PowerPoint—but Ms. Wells..." He gestured toward the woman-shaped gorilla. "...convinced me that letting you experience the Demiser first was better."

"What'd you do to me?" Kaley asked again.

"We allowed you to experience death."

"Allowed?"

He shrugged. "We gave you for free what others pay dearly for. You'd be surprised how...therapeutic death can be for the average person. Rather, for the average person with extraordinary wealth. We go our whole lives immersed in our insecurities and obsessions—only to discover ultimately that none of it matters. By then, it's too late." He held up a finger. "Unless we can experience death's liberation without losing our bodies."

"That's what that machine does?" Kaley asked.

"We call it the Demiser."

Knock. Knock.

She watched her captors to see if they acknowledged the noise. When they didn't, she asked, "Don't you hear it?"

Graves shook his head. "What?"

"The knocking."

"The Demiser sometimes causes echoes of the deceased's final passing. That's why—"

She cut in. "That horrible death I experienced really happened?"

He nodded. "Each corpse has a story—a singular tale of the last moments of consciousness. That intimacy can be shared only once with only one lucky individual."

"Lucky? People really pay for this?"

"Indeed. A surprising number of people and a shocking amount of money. For the most part, they pay to experience peaceful deaths. Dying in their sleep. Or surrounded by loved ones. Pleasant heart attacks, and the like."

"How does it work?"

He shrugged. "My father invented it. We've only been operating barely a year and we're still figuring some things out. Some of our clients have experienced unexpected complications. That's why you're here. The more...vigorous deaths allow us to better monitor the Demiser's workings and understand its, uh, side effects."

"Side effects?"

"Yes, like whatever you're hearing."

"What other side effects are there?"

He waved her question away. "Pardon the expression but we're dying to know—why were you sleeping in the cemetery?"

She saw no point lying. "It was a microadventure."

"Micro-what-now?"

"Microadventures were made popular by a Brit named Alastair Humphreys. They're outdoor mini-excursions that almost anyone— even people living in cities—can achieve in the context of a regular life."

Kaley had first read about microadventures in an outdoor magazine at her dermatologist's office. She'd been hungover and heartbroken—distraught by how things ended with Chris. Microadventures gave her something to strive for—to escape the brutal loneliness in her heart.

She continued, "Adventure is a state of mind. Having adventures doesn't necessarily mean hiking for days in wilderness. It can be as simple as sleeping under the stars in a field."

"Or a cemetery?"

"They're surprisingly peaceful places," she said. "Usually."

Later, Ms. Wells pushed Kaley in a wheelchair down a hallway. Light grey walls. Framed artwork, not too modern. Vinyl tile that looked like marble. Vintage light fixtures. Art deco trim.

Wells parked the chair outside a room with a sign identifying it as Room Number Six. When she lifted Kaley, she expected Wells to stink of death but she smelled of creamy citrus. Her hands were calloused. Her well-manicured nails were coated in a two-tone polish. Black and yellow. She carried Kaley into Room Number Six, which appeared to be the same room as before. Mirrored ceiling. Two high-tech caskets. Wells placed her into one of the caskets. Then Kaley watched in the ceiling mirror as Wells deposited a corpse into the neighboring casket.

This body was of a tall man with brown hair and slight beer belly. Bloated, waxy flesh. A gash in his side was sewn shut with black thread. His knuckles and arms were shredded as if with a cheese grater. Dark blotches covered his freckled skin so that it resembled old cheese. His swollen lips were discolored, as if smeared with goth lipstick.

The casket lid lowered.

Darkness. Peace.

Dr. Graves' voice announced, "Your name is Hugh Newton. You're a 43-year-old man from Seongnam City, South Korea."

Raindrops rage from the night sky. You're driving a rental car, one blackened dirty hand clenching the wheel. Dried blood covers your knuckles. On the rearview mirror, your badge from the Society for Film and Media Studies Conference sways back and forth. The conference ended yesterday in Chicago, but here you are in Middle-Of-Nowhere, Ohio, to do research for a screenplay. One of the characters hails from these parts. You're trying to get into her head, but your own head is thick from last night's drinks with fellow film academics at the hotel bar.

This day trip has gone all kinds of wrong. You overslept and woke hungover. Since leaving Illinois, it's rained non-stop. Near a town called Sinking Spring, a tire blew. You pulled over and—rapping your knuckles several times—put on the spare in a gravel lot before sunset. The blown tire was nearly bald. The other three tires aren't much better. When you called the rental company, they offered to exchange the car if you'd drive it to their closest location—over thirty miles away in Hillsboro.

That's where you're going now, except your international data plan has gone wonky. Your map app is glitching, and the phone keeps slipping out of the dashboard mount. So you're clutching the phone while navigating through the dark on this twisted, narrow country road.

The rain intensifies, overwhelming the slothful wipers. You wish you were home with your wife, playing games or watching a movie or even reading a comic. Something bangs under the car—another blown tire.

The car pitches to the right.

You yell, "Fuck!" but it's drowned out by squealing tires. Spraying gravel. You try steering into the skid but the world pitches upside down. The car's momentum halts abruptly like a slap in the face.

One jarring impact later, you're hanging sideways in your seat. The car must've slid into a ditch. The only light comes from your phone which now rests beside your feet. You try reaching for it, but the wheel and dashboard have you pinned. Everything's crumpled up. Enclosing you. Raindrops rattle above you against the passenger side window. You reach forward in the darkness but sharp teeth bite into your fingers. Broken glass. You check your body, trying to ignore the rising flood of panic. Everything aches. You probably have a hundred bruises, but nothing seems broken despite the fact that the airbags didn't deploy. Fucking rental cars.

Enclosed spaces terrify you but you'll survive this. Your whole body trembles. It's nearly pitch black, you still close your eyes to push away the sense of being restricted. The inability to move. The car closing in on you.

You breathe away the bad, but that's when cold water seeps into your left side. It's oozing into the car from the ditch. The phone's light goes dark. You struggle against the twisted metal and stubborn seatbelt and bent steering wheel. The car becomes a cackling demon clutching you. Raindrops needle against glass and metal.

The water rises still higher. You flail until you're bloody and exhausted. Your heart has tripled in size, now filling your throat. Your pulse pounds so loud it almost eclipses the rain. Almost.

Darkness grips you. Controls you. Mocks you.

Water inches higher. Surrounds you. Smothers you.

Help could still come. Maybe someone in a distant farmhouse heard the crash. Maybe a car will drive by. Maybe the rain will stop.

Those possibilities keep you fighting—even after the water laps over your face and you're craning your neck and thrashing your body and a jagged piece of metal tears into your side and you take one last breath before the water covers you, yet you hold your breath still longer until your lungs burn like fire—an unlikely, unseen flame in this cold dark wet pit that your life has become. Your body betrays you then, and you inhale water that tastes like blood and motor oil before that burning somehow turns inside out.

Kaley sat on her bed, the sterile room swirling. An artful spray of lilies, roses, and carnations sat on the corner table. She imagined Graves and Wells had stolen it from a cemetery. While Wells cleared this morning's breakfast tray and fluffed the flowers, Graves listened to a stethoscope pressed to Kaley's chest. She wondered how many emails must be piling up in her inbox. How many new positions to process? How many requests for interviews? It didn't really matter now. All that mattered was getting out of here. Graves scribbled in his notebook.

"You barely touched your breakfast," he said.

"Your coffee sucks," she said.

He chuckled. "That's my fault. Ms. Wells makes much better coffee than me." He looked back at her. "Don't you?"

Wells nodded.

For a moment, she channeled Hugh. "I'm having trouble figuring out my motivation for this scene."

Graves raised an eyebrow. "Your motivation is to be a good test subject for your doctor so we can understand the Demiser's side effects."

"What exactly are you a doctor of?" Kaley said, the words thick and fuzzy like caterpillars shuffling over her tongue.

He sat back. "A doctor of life, I suppose."

She closed her eyes to escape the whirling room, but rain pounded in the encroaching darkness. Black water crawled over her. She jerked sideways, expecting to splash into cold water. Instead, Wells caught her. They looked into each other's eyes. The rain was gone—for the moment. Side effects, indeed.

Wells eased her onto the mattress. Their eyes locked. Kaley basked for a moment in the intimacy of the act—in the comfort of Wells' strong embrace. When was the last time Kaley had shared a bed with another?

It'd been the Saturday morning she woke next to Chris. The sun hadn't yet risen. She'd slept fitfully. The previous night they'd had a terrible argument. They'd gone to sleep angry, sheets simmering with resentment. How she'd dreaded the dawn. She knew the fresh day would usher in a terrible ending. And so it had.

Graves snapped his fingers in her face. "Still with us?"

"What're you drugging me with?"

"Drugs are primitive. Your suit has many functions. One of those is producing electric fields to stimulate key points in your body. It keeps you relaxed."

"Docile," she said.

He shrugged. "Receptive."

"Both dead men," she said, "came from elsewhere. Are all your bodies from out of state?"

"No. But it's remarkably easier to snatch a corpse if you don't have to dig it up. Better to grab it from the airport before it's loaded onto its plane. We have a client who works in domestic funeral shipping. He misplaces an occasional body in exchange for services rendered."

She tried focusing on his masked face. "Earlier, you said *for the most part* people pay for peaceful deaths. Who the hell would pay for otherwise?"

He frowned. "Most clients opt for the White Light Package—often with the Serenity Upgrade. However, we do offer a Reprisal Package."

In the distance, relentless rain. A steady knocking. Black water lapping against the walls of her cell.

She ignored those dreadful sounds. "Which is?"

His brow furrowed. "Some of us endure a life-long relationship, say a *paternal* one, with someone who consistently damages us." For a moment, his gaze seems to focus somewhere distant and terrible. His hands clenched. "Often, those villains slip this mortal coil before we can find retribution. In those cases, clients often find it...therapeutic to experience that person's death—even if, or sometimes especially if, it's brutal. Few experiences offer more robust closure than death."

"You should put that on your brochures," she said.

He laughed sharply at this. Perhaps even Wells chuckled. Kaley laughed, too, a dry snicker that sputtered out of her throat except it didn't stop. No, the laughter kept coming—a frantic drumbeat to drown the rain and to eclipse her desperation.

Later, they wheeled her again to Room Number Six.

This time, the body in the other casket was of woman with shoulder length brown hair and a sturdy frame. Half her face was caved in. One leg was misshapen and swollen. She had a ragged hole in her chest big enough to toss a softball through.

The casket lid lowered.

Darkness. Peace.

Graves called to her through the void, "Your name is Jennifer Petitti. You're a 41-year-old woman from Columbus, Ohio."

A fucking tornado. Seriously?

In the distance, warning sirens scream into the wailing wind. Above, a wall of menacing clouds crashes down upon the Circle P Sanctuary—a storm of biblical proportions. A gust flaps your brown hair across your face. You take a breath to focus yourself—to stay calm. After all, Wilson is counting on you.

Outside the horse barn, you toss back the dregs of your Starbucks coffee barely tasting its rich sweetness. You mouth a silent prayer before checking your phone. A new text from your son Griffon awaits. "Here w dad. We are ok. Be safe!" Heart emoji. Thumbs-up emoji.

Thank God. You give yourself a moment of relief. The wind hurls hay through the air. The forecast called for storms, but the bad stuff was supposed to hit south near Columbus, not up here in Marengo. The first chunks of hail plunk against the barn. A gentle tapping at first. Head low, you dash inside. The other horses are already outside, all except for Wilson.

Even over the roaring storm, you hear him neighing in his stall. He's over 20 years old—a beautiful chestnut-colored gelding. The thoroughbred raced in over 80 races in the early 2000s before being sold to a couple who only ever neglected and abused him. Eventually, Wilson ended up here. A pitiful sight. Frail as a skeleton. Missing most of his hair. Now he's a happy member of the sanctuary family.

You leave your Starbucks cup outside his stall. He bumps his head against you as you fumble with a brown halter with the sanctuary's phone number on it in case he gets loose during the storm. The sanctuary can't afford an expensive stormproof horse shelter. The resident horses' safest option in the storm is to roam the large pasture and dodge whatever's coming.

First, he needs his fly mask to protect him from debris. With trembling hands, you manage to fasten it into place, a white mesh mask that covers his eyes and ears. The hail intensifies—a hundred angry fists slamming against the barn's roof.

The lights flash three times before winking out.

"Fuck," you say.

Wilson neighs in response.

You wish you were napping on the couch or watching a Blue Jackets game or a cooking show. Alas, Wilson needs you. You open his stall door but he won't budge. He's spooked. The darkness. The cacophony above. You grab his halter and pull.

The sweet fella follows.

Now the wind rages with bestial ferocity—a monster thrashing against the barn. The beams groan and tremble. You pull Wilson toward the exit, but he resists.

The tumultuous clamor boils over. The roof buckles. Wilson rears back, eyes as wild as this storm. You fall. He thunders over you, hooves smashing your thigh, your chest, your face.

Each impact, a sledgehammer crunching into you. Breaking you.

In the ringing darkness, you dimly hear his hooves galloping to safety. When your vision clears, a section of the roof above has been torn free, revealing an ugly, twisted sky. Greenish clouds swirl. Fist-sized hail drops down.

The barn groans. You have to get outside. It isn't safe here.

Your leg must be broken. It screams and crackles when you roll over, blood raining from your face. Something rattles in your chest. One of your eyes isn't working. You drag yourself toward the exit while the sky falls.

Outside, bits of splintered wood soar through the air and stab through your clothes. Something crashes behind you. You chance a look back. The barn has collapsed. You're trying to decide the best place to shelter when the raging gale slows down. The air goes still. Peaceful. You've survived this terrible ordeal.

That's when you see it.

A mighty funnel of wind twists out of the sky. It roars like a gigantic beast. In the resulting chaos, your Starbucks cup flies past—close enough that you could pluck it out of the air. The world tilts sideways. Everything blurs. You can't breathe.

Wind as strong as the ocean hurls you sideways.

The next thing you know, you're miraculously upright again. A splintered fence post protrudes from your chest. You try to scream for help but all that comes out is blood. So much blood.

That night, Graves visited her alone for the first time. He stumbled into her room stinking of gin. Having no windows, she imagined it was nighttime based on his weary face.

He left the door open—the hallway's light penetrating the dark—and sat in his chair, only much closer to her bed. He sipped beneath his mask through a metal straw from a rainbow patterned Tervis cup. "Ohio has a long proud tradition of body snatching," he said.

"A fucking tornado," she answered. "Seriously?"

"The state had many medical schools yet no anatomy laws." Another sip, the straw clinking against his teeth. "Those schools needed corpses to teach their students about the body's mechanisms. Some professors or students dug up their own cadavers. Most schools hired resurrectionists."

She swallowed the taste of blood and high winds, sniffed the stench of manure. "I'd kill for some Starbucks. And I fucking hate Starbucks."

Graves fumbled the lid off his Tervis and stared down into it. "As my father never failed to remind me, I come from a long, proud line of resurrectionists. My ancestors' preferred method was to dig down to the approximate location of the head, saw a hole in the coffin lid, loop a rope around the corpse's neck, and drag the deceased up out of the hole."

While he spoke, she scratched at phantom splinters in her shoulder. Tons of rock pressed upon her. Chilled waters consumed her. She struggled to sit up. "That willful horse."

"There were no laws directly forbidding body theft, but stealing clothes would've been illegal," he said. "So first priority was to strip the corpse naked. Often the face was then mutilated to prevent identification." He raised his Tervis. "Cheers." He tilted it back, likely forgetting about his mask. Liquid sloshed down his chin.

She managed a hollow chuckle. "I wonder if they ever filled that assistant provost position at University of Miami."

"By the late 1800s, the mourners fought back." He tore off his wet mask. "They put stones or metal over coffin lids to block entry. A patent was filed for a goddamn coffin torpedo to blow up resurrectionists tampering with the deceased."

She reached for his Tervis, took a drink, and tasted gin and juice, olives, accents of salt. "The most alive I've felt since losing Chris is when sleeping in graveyards or experiencing other people's death. How fucked up am I?"

At last he made eye contact with her. "I've seen far worse, thanks to my father."

"Have you ever been in the Demiser?" she said.

He shook his head. "I haven't had the courage."

At that moment Wells stepped into the doorway, her bulk eclipsing the hallway light. She stood over them.

Graves looked up at Wells. A lone tear slid down his cheek. "What did he do to us?"

She wiped his cheek, patted his head, and lifted him into her arms with surprising tenderness. His metal straw dropped onto Kaley's bed. She covered it before Wells could see, and a plan formed.

Hours later they wheeled her to Room Number Six.

This time, the body lying in the casket was a tall man with short brown hair and a tidy salt-and-pepper beard. A few extra pounds. A crack in his forehead revealed grey bone beneath. His hands were torn. His bare chest was caved in—almost cartoonish in its broken concave shape.

The casket lid lowered.

Darkness. Peace.

Graves' gravelly voice punctured the darkness. "Your name is Victor Twynstra. You're a 47-year-old man from St. Thomas, Ontario."

Six hours into the drive south, your eyes tire. You've been driving since your shift ended last night—making the most of what time you have. Florida is more than a dozen hours away, but you're veering east toward the Unofficial Toy and Plastic Brick Museum in some little town called Bellaire, Ohio. The museum has three stories of LEGOs. You've been collecting a long time, and you're damned excited to see this.

It's not often you're able to do something entirely for yourself. As a nurse, you work long hours. As a member of the sandwich generation, you spend the rest of your time parenting your teenage daughter and caring for your own parents. Except this week, your daughter is on a field trip for school, and your older sister is visiting from Boston to see your parents. So here you are—driving the open road with a suitcase full of horror novels and swimming trunks.

You're mentally bracing yourself for the museum. Something about large, man-made objects like statues or cruise ships deeply unsettles you, but you've prepared yourself by studying pictures online, especially the Guinness Book of World Records Largest LEGO Image—a 13.6 by 5.9 meter image of a LEGO tractor trailer using no less than 1.2 million bricks. It sounds both exciting and terrifying. Hopefully it's worth the detour.

A few miles past Columbus, your navigation app alerts you to a major back-up on I-70 East. Dammit. Still two hours away. Up ahead, brake lights glow, so you take the next exit.

You head south but your navigation app keeps rerouting you back to I-70. After a series of confusing turns, you end up on State Route 33 South. You try heading east again on State Route 22, but winds have taken down some powerlines—so it's back on 33 until you hit a town called Logan.

Its Main Street is quiet and dark just before dawn. Debris from the high winds litters the streets. Now you seriously need to pee. You don't want to waste time at a gas station.

Right off Main, you spot a desolate factory—a three-story brick building called Columbus Washboard Company. You pull in the side lot with your headlights off and slip out of your car. The winds have calmed, though the trees still sway. Bladder groaning, you barely make it to the side of the building before unzipping and releasing your stream.

That's when you hear the rattling. You haven't even put yourself away and zipped up yet when you step back and look up. The impending dawn illuminates the monstrosity lurking overhead. Your mouth falls open.

Above you, a giant fucking washboard is mounted to the factory's side. The massive thing stretches the full height of the building's top two stories. The rattling noise is the oversized tool banging against the bricks. The wind must've knocked it loose.

You try stepping back except your feet won't cooperate. Your blood has frozen, although your heart rattles in your chest.

The washboard falls. It lands on its feet, but the bottom of its frame smacks you on the forehead. The impact knocks you onto your back, your vision streaked red. Stunned. You touch your face, and your fingers come back bright red, hot, wet.

There's a crack in your forehead, but somehow you're alive. You survived it. Your vision focuses overhead. The washboard looms over you, still standing on its frame but very nearly ready to fall. If it does, it'll slam right into you. Your legs twitch violently but otherwise seem useless. You must drag yourself out of the way.

Your palms scrape against the gravel and concrete. Frantic. Urgent. The last thing you see is the gigantic tool tilting forward. You open your mouth to scream, "Cun—"

The massive frame slams into your chest. A loud cracking noise sends you floating into a world of hurt. Your hands flop against the ground like fish out of water until finally, mercifully, your body shuts down.

Kaley woke in Ms. Wells' arms, curled up like a baby. This was her chance. She patted the metal straw hidden in her sleeve. It was flattened now, made so by pressing under the bed's legs.

Glimpses into four dead lives had prepared her for this moment. Now everything came together.

Daniel's work as a defense contractor provided basic knowledge about electric shielding. She guessed stuffing the straw into her sleeve might disrupt the suit's electric field—allowing her to wake sooner.

Hugh's knowledge of character motivations—vital to writing screenplays—gave her insight into how Wells cradled Graves last night with such gentleness. She resembled a brute but was no killer.

Jennifer's experience with horses provided skills for Kaley's next task. She sprang out of Wells' arms. Escape then would've been futile.

Rather, she swung onto the woman's muscular back and rode her bareback as Wells slammed her bulk into the hallway walls. Each impact rattled Kaley's bones, but she clung on. No matter how much Wells bucked and galloped, Kaley held fast to that wild mare.

Victor's nursing training was the final piece of the puzzle. His knowledge of the human body informed her exactly where to apply pressure to Wells' throat to cut off the oxygen to her brain. Once Kaley managed to get her arm wedged under Wells' chin, she squeezed with all her might at the sides of the woman's neck.

A hundred bruises later, Wells pitched over with a wet grunt. Kaley dug into Wells' pockets until she found a key card that opened a door at the end of the hall. That led to a flight of stairs to a garage where she discovered her trusty bike, backpack, and bivvy bag.

Kaley pedaled—still in her onesie—down a street she vaguely recognized. She was still in Dayton, only a short ride from home. On Main Street, she passed a parked police car. She could've stopped and explained everything, but something held her back—something she wasn't yet ready to face. She told herself she just needed to get home.

At home, she told herself she needed a shower.

After the shower, she told herself she needed a cup of strong coffee.

One French press later, she told herself she needed to check her email.

After scanning her messages, she realized that the world had been largely unconcerned with her absence. She sat back in her chair, sipped her coffee—so much better than Starbucks, and considered. Who really, aside from herself, had Graves and Wells hurt? The deceased didn't care. If dying so many times had taught her anything, it was that death was the ultimate act of forgiveness. Graves and Wells should've been punished for what they did to her, but what—ultimately—had they done? Hell, she'd probably received thousands of dollars' worth of White Light Packages.

They'd kept her prisoner for six nights. She'd never be able to forgive that violation, but nor could she forget the Demiser's power.

That evening, she called Mom to apologize for missing her birthday. Her parents had been worried about her, but she made up a lie about a spontaneous walkabout-style bike excursion. She almost called her older sister in Boston but then remembered that sister belonged to Victor. The next day, she caught up on messages at work. She was woefully behind, but explained away her absence with a story about her mother falling ill unexpectedly and a lost phone.

Days passed. She tried returning to normal life. Hell, she even planned another microadventure in a cemetery, except at the last minute she took her car instead of her bike. She went to a different cemetery, and she brought a shovel to a grave where she'd spilled many tears.

She brought her bivvy bag, too, but she didn't sleep in it. In fact, she didn't sleep at all that night. Instead, she dug and dug.

As she stabbed the shovel into the soil, she found herself once more lapsing into that final Saturday morning she'd woken next to Chris. Her eyes were raw from restless sleep. Dawn wasn't yet nudging at the window blinds. She ran last night's argument through her head, forming the perfect apology that she could only hope would heal this.

As the sun rose, she waited for Chris to stir. She lie on her side watching her sleeping lover. Waiting. Light stretched across the floor. Over the sheets. Chris never twitched. Never snored. Minutes turned to hours.

When at last Kaley dared to put a hand on Chris's bare shoulder, it was as cold and lifeless as rock. The doctors later said it was a brain aneurysm—a random pointless death.

Kailey dug all night, pausing only to sip water.

Six feet of dirt later, she stuffed the bivvy bag full of the putrid meat and lifeless bones that had once been the love of her life.

The next morning, she returned to Graves and Wells. Almost as soon as she pulled up, the garage door opened. She parked inside. Graves and Wells were waiting for her. Neither sported a mask this time. Kaley exited the car wearing her onesie. Wells lifted the bag filled with Chris's remains as easy as hoisting up a bag of laundry.

They walked down the hallway together to Room Number Six, where Kaley handed a slip of paper to Graves. He unfolded it and studied the words she'd written. She lay down in the casket and watched the ceiling mirror. There, Ms. Wells' reflection dumped what was left of Chris into the other casket.

The lid lowered.

Darkness. Peace.

Dr. Graves' familiar voice read to her, "Your name is Chris—"

Author's Note: Many of the details about Ohio's fascinating history of body-snatching come from Curt Dalton's book, *Body Snatching in Ohio*. If you dig (pun intended) macabre tales that take place in the Heart of It All, Dalton's book is well worth a read!

THE GARDEN OF LOVE IS GREEN

Tim Waggoner

B renton stands in moonlight, night air cool on his exposed skin, bare feet in grass. The blades gently stroke his flesh, and he smiles.

I love you too.

It's three a.m. in Ash Creek, Ohio, and he's standing in the middle of his backyard, wearing only a pair of gray satin shorts—they're all he ever sleeps in, regardless of the season. He's looking down, marveling at how the moon makes the separate blades seem like thousands of tiny silver sculptures. The six-foot tall white wood fence that encloses the yard glows in the moonlight, a frame, he imagines, for a work of art titled *Night and Silence.* Except the grass isn't silent, is it? It never has been, not for him.

He hears a multitude of small voices, speaking as one. To anyone else, it would sound like an almost inaudible breath of wind, if they heard it at all. Brenton has no trouble hearing it, of course. He closes his eyes and listens, opening himself to the meaning contained within those strange soft syllables. He has no idea how long he stands like this, waiting for some sense of meaning to make itself known to him, but at last it does, and his eyes open.

He knows what he needs to do.

He walks to the gate, unlatches it—the ground is slightly sloped here, and the door swings open by itself—and steps through. He heads for the wooden shed where the lawn equipment is stored. It's less than twenty feet from the gate, and he reaches it within seconds. There's a padlock on the door, although it isn't necessary. He lives in a safe neighborhood, and besides, who would want to steal weed trimmers, edgers, leaf blowers, and wheelbarrows? Still, better safe than sorry.

He has a pair of objects in the pockets of his shorts, one of which is the key to the shed. He uses it to unlock the padlock and then opens the door. It creaks, and as he always does, he tells himself to remember to oil the hinges next time he comes here. Not that there will be a next time. Moonlight spills into the shed, illuminating the reason for the padlock. Now *this* is worth stealing. The push mower—Brenton would never resort to something as gauche and impersonal as a riding mower, not on *his* grass—cost him in excess of five hundred dollars, and it was worth every penny. It has a powerful easy-to-start motor, optimized air flow for superior mulching, four cutting surfaces that create extra-fine clippings, and a smart drive system that matches the user's stride. Only the best for his lawn.

He tucks the key back into his pocket, wheels the mower outside, and checks to make sure it's gassed up. He keeps the tank topped off, but he always checks anyway. Satisfied, he replaces the gas cap and pushes the mower through the gate and into the backyard. He stops then, regards the grass, frowns. For the first time since he and Charlene moved into this house, well over forty years ago now, someone besides him has mowed the lawn—a service that Charlene hired—and while they didn't do a terrible job, they were, by Brenton's standards, sloppy. The blades are uneven, the cut pieces only partially mulched, and there are several spots that they missed mowing altogether. Disgraceful.

He hears the voice-that-is-many-voices speak once more, and this time he has no trouble understanding its meaning. *We do not blame you. Now begin.*

He primes the gas, pushes the power button, and the motor roars to life. The sound cuts through the night's quiet like a chorus of angry chainsaws, but he finds the noise sweet, soothing even. He then removes the second object from the pocket of his shorts: a roll of black electrical tape. He wraps the tape around the mower's safety shut-off lever to hold it down, so that the motor won't cut out while he does what he needs to do next. He carefully tilts the mower onto its side, exposing its whirling blades. He watches them for a moment, transfixed by their wavering blur of motion, then he kneels. The grass speaks once more.

Come to us.

Brenton leans his head forward.

"Stop moping."

Brenton responded to his wife without looking at her. "I'm not."

He stood on the wooden deck at the back of his house, arms crossed over his chest, scowling. The yard was only half-mown, and the sight of it filled him with a level of anger approaching rage. He didn't like to leave a job unfinished, and he'd *never* abandoned his yard like this before. He could feel his heart attempt to beat faster, but the new beta blocker he was on kept it restrained.

"You should be inside resting," Charlene said.

Three days ago, he'd been out there, pushing the mower, listening to the grass sigh in contentment as he trimmed it, when he suddenly felt short of breath and his pulse skyrocketed. Less than an hour later, he was in a hospital bed, hooked up to a heart monitor, and waiting to get an MRI.

Minor tachycardia, the doctor had pronounced once the test was over. She prescribed the beta blocker and told him to follow up with his family physician in a few days. *And no more mowing the yard,* she'd said. *Not with a push mower, anyway. You're too old for that shit.*

Old? He was only sixty-six, for Christ's sake.

As soon as he'd come home from the hospital, he'd wanted to go into the backyard and finish mowing.

If you're determined to make your heart explode, I won't stop you, Charlene had said. *Just don't expect me to call an ambulance this time.*

Had she meant it? Maybe. Probably.

Charlene went back inside, to call a lawn service to finish the task he could no longer perform. He continued standing on the deck until they arrived, and then he retreated into the house and didn't come back out until they were done.

When Brenton was a child, his family lived on a farm. Brenton, along with his five siblings, was expected to do chores, and a lot of them, but whenever he got a chance—which wasn't often—he liked to lie on the grass in the backyard, gaze up at the clouds, and relax.

He was eleven when he first heard the grass speak to him.

It was a hot August afternoon. He'd just finished helping his dad fix the tractor—mostly he handed tools to Dad whenever he asked for them —and he was drenched with sweat. Drops rolled off his skin, fell to the grass, were absorbed. He could feel the dampness being leeched from his shirt and jeans, pulled into the ground, greedily swallowed. It was an odd sensation, one which he supposed should've been disturbing but which he found strangely comforting, almost intimate.

He listened to the whispering's rising and falling cadence, found it so soothing he had to fight to keep from drifting off to sleep. There were no words, none that he could discern anyway, but there *were* emotions, and these created pictures in his mind. He saw the god-demon sun blasting down its unrelenting heat for days, weeks, without a single drop of rain falling from the sky. He saw the grass's green fade, become yellow, then almost entirely bleached of color. Lastly, he saw himself, lying on the ground, watering the grass with the moisture from his own body. When the images faded, he was left with a warm, almost loving sensation inside which his mind translated as *Thank you.*

The next time the family went into town, Brenton visited the library and checked out a book on plant life. He read the chapter on grass and ignored the rest of it. That night at dinner, he attempted to share what he'd learned.

Did you know that grass developed 60 million years ago, during the

Cretaceous period? It's one of the strongest, most versatile plants, and it can live in rain forests, deserts, and cold climates. It even lives in some parts of Antarctica!

His family was usually silent while they ate, and they barely looked at him as he spoke.

His mother gave him a quick glance and a half smile. *That's nice, dear.*

He wanted to tell them more about what he'd learned, but there was no point. They might hear him, but they wouldn't *listen* to him.

That night, he had a dream. He stood in the middle of a sea of grass, an endless field stretching outward in all directions, blades almost as tall as he was. The sun hung high above, huge and hot, and warm winds stirred the grass, made it ripple and sway like currents of green water. This time when the grass spoke, he understood every word.

We've been waiting a long time for someone to hear us, Brenton. Someone like you.

Then the grass closed in around him, wrapped him tight in its embrace, and squeezed until he could no longer breathe. The sensation was alarming at first, but he calmed as his mind began to shut down, and then he knew no more.

Brenton would have no memory of this dream once he woke, but it remained with him the rest of his life, always just below the level of conscious thought.

July Fourth, a couple years later.

Every Independence Day, Brenton's family had a big meal outside to celebrate. Afterward, they'd play games and, when the sun went down, shoot off illegal fireworks. Brenton liked holidays because they were the only times his family really interacted. The rest of the time they kept to themselves, and at thirteen, he was starting to do it too. What was the point of spending time with people who didn't want you around, who didn't want *anyone* around?

One of the games his family played after dinner was lawn darts.

These weren't the safe, soft-headed lawn darts of later years, oh no. These things were murderously dangerous, with thick metal spikes at one end and a plastic handle at the other, with a trio of flared-out flat plastic "feathers" to help control the flight. The object of the game was to hurl a dart into the air and attempt to land it in the middle of the other team's circle, which was defined by a thin, round plastic hoop placed on the ground. Brenton was more than a little intimidated by the darts—especially by how fast his older siblings threw them—so he tended to stay on the sidelines and watch. This year, when it was his older brother Martin's turn to throw, their sister Dora shoved him as a joke. Off-balance, he released the dart and it flew high up into the air...

...and it came down straight toward Brenton.

Panicked, he ran, hoping to outdistance the dart, but when he glanced back over his shoulder, he realized he was instead running directly into its path. He tried to veer to the left, but his foot caught in a small depression in the ground, his ankle twisted, and he fell face-forward onto the grass. He lay there an instant, expecting the feel the metal tip of the dart pierce the back of his skull any moment, but then he felt pressure beneath him, as if a large hand raised up from the ground and gave him a hard shove. He flipped over onto his back a split second before the dart *thunked* into the ground exactly where his head had been. He stared at the dart for a moment, heart pounding, breath caught in his chest. His parents and his siblings were looking at him, none of them speaking or moving. He had the feeling that it wouldn't have mattered much to them which way his race against the dart had turned out. Then their paralysis broke and they came running toward him, shouting *Are you Okay?* and *Goddamn, boy, you were lucky!* But Brenton knew luck had nothing to do with it.

He reached down and patted the grass, felt its blades brush his palm.

He met Charlene when he was twenty and she was eighteen. She graduated from high school the same year Dora did, and the two of them were friends. He didn't know that, of course. He barely knew his

siblings, let alone the people they hung out with at school, and Dora
had been two years behind him. After the ceremony—which had taken
place on the football field—Dora and Charlene were posing for pictures
together, and she caught Brenton's eye and he caught hers. He wanted
to ask her out, but he was too shy, but then he heard the grass urging
him to be brave, and when the picture-taking was completed, he walked
up to her, introduced himself, and asked if she would like to go with
him to see a movie in town sometime. She shocked him when she said
yes. He didn't know that her family's farm was failing, and that—in the
back of her mind, at least—she feared being poor and hoped to find a
spouse who would help her become financially secure. He had no
money of course, and eventually his brother Stan would inherit their
farm, not that Brenton wanted the damn thing. But Brenton had *potential*, or so Charlene hoped, and that movie date led to many more.

It was almost two months before they had sex for the first time. It
was a late June, and they were down by the lake, hidden in the woods,
blanket spread out on a small clearing that local kids called Lover's Lawn
instead of Lover's Lane. Was the pun purposeful or accidental? No one
knew, nor did they care, as long as they had a place to fuck. Brenton and
Charlene had fooled around before, of course, and had made each other
come in a variety of ways, but they hadn't gone all the way, hadn't done
it. Brenton was as nervous as he was excited, and when he entered Charlene for the first time, he expected to feel a closeness, a joining, a merging
as the two of them became one. It felt good—great even—but he didn't
feel anything inside. No, that wasn't quite right. He didn't feel anything
coming from inside *her*.

He leaned his head close to hers, kissed her, looked deep into her
eyes, searched for any sign that there was *something* in there, but all he
saw was another human being enjoying the sensations her body
produced. He could've been anyone, could've been a goddamn dildo for
that matter, and she would've reacted the same. He tried to pull out of
her then, but she grabbed hold of his shoulders, twisted her hips, and
flipped him over onto his back and straddled him. The maneuver moved
them off the blanket, and Brenton's bare back, ass, and legs were pressed
against the grass. Charlene rode him hard, shouting her enthusiasm so

loud it caused nearby birds to take to the air in alarm. Brenton remained quiet and listened to the grass whisper its love as it undulated beneath him.

Brenton married Charlene, more because it was expected than out of any real desire to do so. They moved to a new town in Ohio that wasn't significantly different than the one they'd grown up in, and Brenton found work as a machinist. The job was dull and repetitive, much like farming, but at least he didn't end up with shit-covered shoes at the end of the day. He and Charlene never had children. They never even discussed the matter.

One spring day, when he'd been working with the same company for thirteen years, he decided to take his lunch break outside. It was a beautiful sun, warm but not too hot, wind blowing but not too hard. He sat on the lawn in front of the building and took off his shoes and socks so he could feel the grass beneath his feet. As he was eating a ham sandwich, Glenn Siler exited the building. Glenn was his immediate supervisor, a hard, humorless man who had been with the company almost as long as Brenton had been alive.

Glenn's upper lip curled into a sneer when he saw Brenton sitting on the grass barefoot.

"What the hell is wrong with you, Dowling? You some kind of nature freak or something?"

Brenton felt the grass stir beneath his feet.

It's okay, he thought. The grass stilled, but he could feel its anger toward Glenn burning hot.

"I like the grass," Brenton said.

Glenn snorted. "You are a fucking weirdo, Dowling. I'm going to be watching your ass, so shape the fuck up."

Glenn walked off, the grass's furious whispers following him.

That weekend, Glenn was working in his front yard, edging the grass near the curb. Somehow he tripped, fell, and cracked his head on the curb's concrete surface. He died less than two hours later in the hospital. When Brenton heard about the man's death at work Monday morning, he smiled.

As Brenton leans closer to the mower's whirling blades, he digs his fingers into the cool grass.

Will this hurt? he thinks.

Yes. Very much so.

That's what I figured.

Brenton takes a deep breath, then shoves his face the rest of the way forward. The grass was right. It does hurt.

Very, *very* much.

"No, I don't know why he did it, and I don't care. I'm just glad he's gone. Yes, I know that sounds terrible, but we were married close to fifty years. That's more than enough time for a woman to put up with any man, don't you think? Especially one that's as...empty as Brenton was."

Charlene stands on the deck of their—*her*—house, phone to her ear. She's talking to Brenton's sister Dora. They've remained close ever since high school, and Dora's long been aware of how dissatisfied Charlene was with her marriage to Brenton.

"I mean, there just wasn't anything *there*, you know?"

Charlene looks at the spot where Brenton shoved his face into the spinning blades of his precious $500 mower. The lawn is still dark there, and she imagines his blood soaking the earth, feeding the grass. *Nurturing* it. A fitting end, really. He cared more about the goddamn grass than anything else in his life.

Charlene and Dora talk for a while longer, and when the sun begins to go down, Charlene ends the call and goes inside. A few moments later, Brenton—truly *in* the grass now—stretches forth new fingers. Blades of grass lengthen, slither up onto the deck like thin green snakes, move toward the patio door and find it unlocked. Brenton isn't surprised. Charlene never remembers to lock the damn thing. His new fingers reach into the kitchen and continue to grow as they feel their way through the house in search of Charlene. Maybe Brenton was empty during his life, or maybe no one ever bothered to take notice of what he did have inside him. Either way, he's full now, full to fucking *bursting*, and he's going to teach Charlene, and everyone else on the goddamn planet, an important lesson—*The future is green.*

THE INFERNAL GIFT

David L. Day

"Whose blood is that?" Reverend Flarido stands just inside the doorway of his quarters at the back of the church, his well-weathered features rigid with shock, eyes widened behind rimless glasses. "Where have you been, my son?"

I hoover in the hallway, my bloodied shirt in shreds. I swipe sweat from my dirt-smeared face and push by him, falling into the corner of his little living room. "Water," I croak, then close my eyes, stare into the void.

A brief silence, followed by footfalls as the good reverend shuffles off to the kitchenette. The clink of glasses. The brief rush of the faucet. "Oh, Nain," he says, using my name in a sigh of disappointment. "Don't worry, my child, we'll get you help again."

"I hate myself," I mutter, the words dry husks. I open my eyes, and he hands me the water. I sip, tentative at first, then take a few gulps until I feel my throat is sufficiently soothed. "I hate myself," I say again, and let the words sit there with us like unwelcomed guests.

He slips down the wall next to me, places a hand on my knee. The weight of his touch reminds me of my inhumanity, but I'm too weary to try to make him move it. I know this moment matters no more or no less than any other, that he may as well be long dead, that everyone may as well be long dead, too. Everyone except me, and the woman I met earlier, and the old man who waits for us. The three of us exist perpetually in the state of the undead, gifted an eternity of moments, a gift that reduces every moment we pass through to nothingness.

"I remember," I say, but I can't bring myself to look at him knowing I'll repay his kindness with blasphemy. "I remember it all, and I hate myself even more."

"Tell me," the reverend says in his soft, soothing voice. He moves closer, and I feel sick from his touch, from the smell of him, that furry human odor, and I want to kill him, but I won't do that, not today, and so I tell the story, the last story I'll tell him.

───────────

The diner I work in is a perfect square, red brick on the outside, that sits on the corner of Main and nothing. Inside is old linoleum flooring, cracked vinyl counter tops, everything painted a chipping off-white. Table and chairs sit scattered throughout, mismatched rescues from yard sales.

The young woman comes in, the crunchy type who likely has been hitching across the country in search of the best weed America has to offer. She wears leather sandals, a long white skirt, and a salmon strap tank top. She carries a black boho backpack loosely in one hand. Her expression hides behind oval sunglasses. She is maybe twenty years old on a good day, slender and trim, if not just a little bony. Her long, obsidian hair drapes over her shoulders. Like me, she is some shade of Mediterranean that doesn't quite fit in rural southwestern Ohio.

It is between lunch and dinner, and I sit behind the register, staring out the window at the empty park across the street by the banks of the lazy Ohio Brush River. I am dressed in my plain white tee, faded cargo shorts, and well-worn canvas sneakers. A greasy apron hangs loose and untied from my neck.

She finds a table, seats herself, examines the menu, each action an independent statement of confidence, her very presence an act of narcissism. Her lipstick is a touch too bright, her hands still damp from being cleaned. My intuition says she's done things, horrible things, and at least one of those very horrible things she's done recently. I have to chase off the worry that I've also done horrible things, things deep in the chasm of my missing memories. Memories scattered to the four winds by an overdose nearly a year ago.

In spite of these certainties, seeing her is like seeing an old friend, and for the first time in a long time, hope caresses me, hope of recovering the lost stretch of time from before the reverend found me. Hope of knowing myself again. I know her, the feeling of ice water on my spine, clear and undeniable.

She looks at me, smiles slightly.

She knows me.

She knows me in way that scares me. The chill deepens, nearly breaks my back, and though I want to unlock my memories from before the overdose, I'm too afraid of what I might find there to ask her who she is and who I am.

She's dropped a fifty on the table, essentially making it hers for the day. She is quiet, patient, sits sipping her coffee, not even on her phone or reading, just staring out the window, the world reflected in the oval mirrors of her sunglasses.

Our regulars come and go throughout the afternoon, the handful of locals who can afford to eat something other than canned meat and homegrown vegetables. Their faces are plump and comfortable and nearly indistinguishable from one another, their regular, plain Midwestern features a blend of happiness and hard work and an underlying fear of God, a fear I seem to have forgotten along with everything else. They pay in small bills and tip with even smaller smiles.

It's getting late by small town standards, and I want to go. I finish wiping down the counter, toss my apron and rag in the bin by the kitchen door then take her handwritten check to her, slip it onto the table by her cup. "We're closing up soon."

She looks at it, looks at me, those maddening oval mirrors masking her expression. "I'm almost done with my coffee. Why don't you grab a seat and join me for a few minutes." She presses the tines of her fork, flipping the handle up with a soft *twang*.

I glance around at the exhausting emptiness of the diner. "I'm not supposed to hang out with the customers." But the owner's in the back, an old man hard of hearing, probably having a smoke and a beer, so I slip into the chair across from her anyhow.

"What are you doing here?" She flips her fork again, smiles like a cat.

"I work here," I say, knowing full well that wasn't what she meant.

Her smile drops. "I mean here, in this town. Are you from around here?"

There's no reason for me to tell her, but there's also no reason not to. I have nothing to look forward to, nothing to look back upon, and in this moment sharing with her feels right.

"I don't know," I begin. "I've been here maybe a year, but beyond that is all darkness."

She frowns, which could be empathy or could be disgust, I simply can't tell because of those damned glasses. "You don't know," she echoes.

I turn and stare out the window, toward the living river, water that calls to me like a faint voice from a previous life. "The local reverend takes care of me, a mostly kind man with mostly kind words. Nursed me back to health after an overdose nearly a year ago. Hooked me up with this job. Kept me out of jail.

"The reverend found me naked and unconscious in the old hilltop cemetery behind his church. I was a stranger to the area, and he should have called in the sheriff, but I reminded him of someone, someone he loved very much and lost, I think, so instead he took me in, clothed me, got me this job. I'm a memory for him, and somehow that brings him some peace."

I look back, find her staring at me with what I hope is mild interest. She tilts her glasses down a tick, just enough for me to see her eyes are brown and deep and hint at the darkness of the abyss.

A heartbeat later she slips her sunglasses back in place. The fifty is still on the table, and she settles it on top of her meager bill, slides them both across the table to me. "Keep the change."

I linger in the longing for the void in her eyes, a longing that seems somehow familiar, a memory within a memory. Then I gather the bill and money and get up.

"Where are you going now?" She joins me, helps clear her table, and put the chairs up for the night.

"I don't sleep much, and I like to wait until the reverend is in bed before going home," I say quietly. "I'm going out to the Serpent Mound for a bit." Then, stuck between wanting to know what she knows and not wanting to know who I am, I add, "You can come with me if you like."

We walk the road at sunset, make our way out to the mound. I shuffle along. She tends to dance and twirl, back and forth across the road. There is no traffic out here, only stretches of cornfield cut by concrete and drainage ditches. I get the sense she's hiding something. She knows something.

From out of the nowhere, she asks, "Do you believe in a god?" She twirls her skirt, spins, skips forward.

"The reverend does. He tells me that God is everywhere."

"And do you feel His presence?"

I don't answer, don't dare give voice to my unshakable doubt.

We make a detour and stop down by the Ohio Brush River, itself curving like a snake just to the west of the mound. I sit on the bank, and I take off my shoes, set them aside. I spread mud up my legs to my knees. I feel like there's some ancient ritual involved here, but I don't remember anything of the sort. It's just a thing I do to chase memories.

She settles down next to me, proceeds to spread thick Ohio clay up her legs as well, up to the knees. "What do you think happens when we die?"

I smooth the mud on my legs. "The reverend tells me we go to Heaven and live in God's glory forever."

She pauses, hands on her knees, thick mud squished between her fingers. "Do you think living forever is a good thing?" The evening light sparkles on the water, in the lenses of her glasses.

"Isn't it?" I furrow my brow, uncertain.

She smirks, resumes spreading the mud evenly on her calves. "We don't regret or mourn the time before someone's born, why do so after they die? In fact, we spend most of our time not existing, and the dead don't complain or argue or fight or suffer. Existence is an exercise in futility. We're only truly at peace when we stop."

I finish, wipe my hands on the ground, stand up. "Stop what?"

"Everything," she says. "Breathing and eating and shitting and fucking. Stop infesting this reality with our insufferable presence."

She stands as well, skirt tied around her thighs. She rubs her hands, mud clumping and scattering back to the earth. "Eternal life is no blessing. It's the most heinous of curses."

Deep down, my gut tells me her words hold a truth, a truth too unbearable to face, a truth too undeniable to resist. I hurt, I always hurt, and the hurt would always be there.

And then this time, with her here, with her questions burrowing into my brain, I remember a little...me as a boy, my mother spreading mud up my legs to my knees by the banks of a similar river, mud to keep me cool during the heat of the day while I played. It's a fleeting memory, though, and as soon as it arrives it is gone, leaving an aftertaste of sorrow.

We make our way up to the mound itself. The sun sits on the horizon, casts its harsh hues across the empty park, and I can almost see the serpent slithering in place, its maw poised to devour the earthen sun disk. Then the earthen effigy emerges into view, some thousand plus feet of winding dirt starting with a spiraled tail and ending in an open triangular mouth. The park is carefully manicured, the grass kept short and clean, with a path leading along the side of the snake from the park entrance to the ring representing the sun the snake is about to swallow.

"Why do you like coming here?" She steps off the walkway, flexes her toes in the grass, causes the dried mud on her feet to crack and flake.

"I guess something about the idea of the sun being devoured by a great serpent is comforting. And the impact crater itself, it's an energy I can feel, an energy that might help me remember. Maybe it's magnetic, or maybe it's something else. Whatever I was doing before I lost my memory, this seems as good a place as any to hide."

She stops flexing her toes, stares at me, head tilted. "Hide? From whom?" That smile again. Cat-like. Predatory.

I turn away from that smile and the biting anxiety it brought, make my way to the snake's mouth. She follows, catches up to me, and together we crest the mound of the solar disk, then descend into the heart of the sun.

She draws a simple knife from her bag, doesn't even try to hide what she's doing. When she stabs me the first time, I feel the blade slice through my abdomen, and there is surprise and anger and fear and curiosity. I see her face, the clean expression of disinterest sliced in two by frustration.

The knife is quick, digs deep, severs my intestines, my stomach. The blade slips cleanly between two ribs and pierces my heart. Blood, blood, and more blood, all of it draining from my body, my consciousness seeping out after it.

"Don't ever—"

She breathes into my face. I stand there dull and dumb, let her yank the knife out.

"—pull—"

The knife digs into something vital, slips out again.

"—this crap—"

She brings the knife to bear a third time, and I can't breathe.

"—again."

The knife lands in my chest, stays there, pinning that word to my heart.

"Why do you keep making me hunt you down?" she whimpers, then withdraws the blade and steps back. "Won't you ever just remember on your own?"

And I do remember. I fall to my knees, life seeping from my body, the blockage of my memory finally relieved, and I can remember it all, the drugs I took, the wishing for the end to come, the perpetual hurt and hate in my heart. And finally the rage has a target. At first, it is her, for bringing it back again, for letting me bleed all over the place right out where anyone could see.

Tali, I remember. *Her name is Tali.*

And then there is him, the one who gathered us together, that old man Lazarus always pulling strings in the background, and I hate him, too.

But further back is another memory, one so ancient it almost looks like someone else's. My young-man's body is still fresh, and my widowed mother is still grieving at the loss of my father. They come for me, the men who took my father's life, and I can no longer remember the dispute, but they take my life the way Tali pretends to take my life now, by stabbing me until there is nothing left to stab.

And I remember the bliss of oblivion, the great chasm of nothingness stretching before me forever and ever and ever. Then the void is ripped from me, or I'm ripped from it, by that cursed Nazarene, Yeshua ben Yosef, who used me for his own glory.

Resurrection is no gift. It is unforgivable theft.

Tali kneels next to me, her glasses off, and stares at me with hope. I see it in her eyes, that slice of deep desolation, and I want to sit in it for eternity, become it, but I can't get behind her eyes, I can't hear it or touch it or feel it, I can only see that it is there, always just beyond reach. Beyond my reach. Beyond hers, isolated behind the trauma of eternity, a trauma that strikes deep and, like us, is enduring.

I don't know which is scarier, knowing or not knowing. Remembering is an act of excavation, unburying nuggets of truth under the cruft of our brains, especially one as old and corrupt as mine.

I lie in the center of the sun disk, forever on the verge of being devoured by the serpent, bleeding out and staring at the stars, and a thought occurs to me. Some gaze at those twinkling lights out of hope. Others out of hopelessness.

I am the latter.

I dream of a long ago ancient city, a place of sand and dust and life, of my mother the widow, of life in a simpler place, but no less dangerous. I can still hear my mother crying, not at the loss of my life, but at the return of it, the cursed prophet summoning me back from the soothing abyss leaving me forever poised at the doorstep.

I dream of the ensuing weeks, where I lived with my mother, but our connection severed. There was nothing to tether us. She was dead already, they were all dead, are all dead, will always be dead. Only the old man and Tali and I remain, the unholy trinity of the Father Lazarus, the Daughter of Jarius, and the Widow's Son.

"And then I came here," I say to the reverend, who has moved away from me. "I remember the desperation when pumping myself full of ketamine and opioids, washing them all down with a fifth of rum. Part of me knew I could never get all the way there, but forgetting for a while brought me comfort."

I look at the poor man, his glasses off, disbelief in his eyes. "It takes courage to admit to the world that you're a monster," I say, "and even more to admit it to yourself."

I get up from the floor, the bloodletting of my story leaving me both empty and fulfilled. Hot tears run down my cheeks, tears for me, tears for Flarido, tears for the dead.

"I'm so sorry," I say, my heart empty and cold and heavy. "I needed to tell someone, and I didn't know where else to turn."

The reverend comes to me, puts an arm over my shoulders. I cringe at the weight and burden of his human touch, shake him off, then shuffle to the door and pause. "He's waiting for us."

"He?" His voice is pure confusion. "Us?"

Back to him still, I open the door.

Tali stands there, expressionless, emotionless. "Ready? Lazarus is waiting, and I'm sure he's pissed."

I look down at my tattered shirt, at the dried blood, my blood, the shreds of fabric, feeling powerful and pitiful. "As ready as I'll ever be."

She touches my chin, raises my head, looks me in the eye, and I see that warm oblivion again, long for it. "Don't ever pull this crap again. We'll never figure out how to undo ourselves if you keep avoiding your memories."

And I know she's right, of course she is. "I'm sorry," is all I can think to say.

She smiles once more, steps aside. I don't turn back or offer anything more to the good reverend. What else is there to say? He's dead already, along with everyone else. I go with Tali because there's nowhere else to go, and no one else to go there with.

I am who I am because of what happened to me, what was done to me, both by those men and that prophet. I'm not a mindless zombie or a ravenous vampire. I don't eat brains or drink blood, although I have been known to kill, which I suspect is inevitable for anyone who lives long enough. I'm not any of the monsters, I'm just reanimated, a window into the oblivion that awaits all of us.

Well, almost all of us.

WISHING YOU THE BEST YEAR EVER

Patricia Lillie

People constantly tell me I think too much. How is that possible? I'm pretty sure most people don't think enough, especially about what comes out of their mouths. Or their fingers.

On New Year's and birthdays, social media is always full of people wishing each other the *best year ever*. Seriously? I'm seventeen. If the next year is my best ever, why would I want to hang around for any more? I'd rather they wished me the worst year ever, then any that follow would definitely be something to look forward to. After last year, this year should be a winner.

And God. People are always tossing God into the conversation without thinking about what they are saying. After the Yankees won the American League Pennant, some player was interviewed and went on and on about God smiling on them.

"So, does that mean God's a Yankees fan?" I asked. "Or does he just hate Boston?"

"Don't be an idiot," my father said. I knew he wasn't bothered by the idea of God hating the Red Sox. He was no Boston fan, but once Cleveland failed to make the post-season—again—he became a fan of whomever was playing the Yankees. He really hated the Yankees.

"Leave her alone," my mother said.

I wasn't sure whether it was my question or the idea of God rooting for the Yankees, but the next morning, the three of us ended up at church for the first time ever.

It was okay. We sat in back, and nobody sat near us. The pastor talked about forgiveness. He sounded like he was improvising. He also sounded unconvincing. A few people gave us stiff smiles and said they were glad to see us there, but I was sure we were pushing their Christian goodwill. Mrs. Vohlpahl hugged my mother. Her face and body language implied she'd made full-body contact with a slime-covered tree toad. Mom's expression was worse. They'd loathed each other since they were kids.

We went back a few more times before we gave up.

My question about God and the Yankees wasn't answered. Pastor Benedict didn't think it was a suitable subject for theological debate. I thought he was probably a secret Yankees fan.

Baseball is the real religion in Ferrisville, Ohio.

In movies, the football team always rules the high school. Not here. Our football team is, and has forever been, mediocre. Less than mediocre.

Not the baseball team. In baseball, we have a string of state championships stretching back to my great-grandfather's time. The January snow may be deep, but when the notice for Little League sign-up appears on the town square message board, people start thinking summer. From late March, even if there's still snow on the ground, through October, when the snow returns, most of Ferrisville's population (2,925 according to the last census) can be found at the ballfields. We have six of them, outnumbering the bars by one and the churches by two. Age, gender, race, clique, it makes no difference. Anybody who can get out of their house and out of work is at a ballfield either watching or playing. The men play. The women play. The girls play. The boys play. When official league play is over—Little League ends before the summer's barely begun—Ferrisville has its own leagues. We even have a Snow Ball League so the most devoted can play all winter. In Ferrisville, we do a better job cleaning snow off the infield than we do plowing the streets.

I'm a klutz. When I was ten, my parents gave up hope and handed me a scorebook. I'm the best scorekeeper in town and in demand in all leagues. Or, I used to be.

Ferrisville's never produced a major league star, although we've sent more than a few boys to the minors. Doesn't matter if they never go any further. When they come home, they're not failures. They're stars.

My brother was once Ferrisville's great hope for real major-league, all-star, Cooperstown-level stardom.

When he was ten and I was nine, we were home from school on Christmas break and playing King of the Hill on a mountain of plowed snow.

Just as he stood at the top shouting, "I'm King of the Hill," I nailed him from behind. He didn't go straight down. His foot caught in a hole, and his ankle was trashed.

In the emergency room, he repeated one line over and over. He asked the doctor, the nurses, the x-ray tech, the guy mopping the floors, anybody who would listen, "Will it be better before baseball season?" I suspect my parents were worried about the same thing, but the question sounded better coming from a kid.

The ankle wasn't broken. Peter played ball that summer. He never told Mom and Dad I pushed him, but my father told his bar buddies what he'd said at the hospital. The story made the rounds. Everybody laughed and called Peter a true son of Ferrisville.

I wanted that put on his headstone.

He was a True Son of Ferrisville.

My mother said it was inappropriate. They had him cremated.

We never told anyone where we scattered his ashes. It was safer that way.

The first of January may be the official calendar-based beginning of the new year, but there are variations. Orthodox New Year begins on January 14. Rosh Hashanah is in September. In Ferrisville, the year begins on the Monday of the last full week of February. In the world of professional baseball, pitchers and catchers have been at camp for at least a week, and it's time for the rest of the squad to join them. In Ferrisville, it's time for tryouts, and indoor practice begins for all leagues and teams. The most important is, of course, the high school team, the Hawks.

The upcoming season, Peter's junior year, was crucial. We'd already had some unofficial sniffing around from the pros, but Mom and Dad were insistent he attend college, preferably one with both strong academic and baseball programs, and one offering a full ride. My brother's grades were okay, but they weren't going to earn him any scholarships. Neither was his bat, but his left arm could be the key to riches, or at least to tuition. His senior season would be important, but this was the year for scouts and schools to sit up and take notice.

No pressure at all.

Had she arrived anytime between September and February, she would have been the subject of gossip. A couple of people asked if she planned to try out for the women's or coed softball leagues. The Websters campaigned for a new town zoning ordinance outlawing giant women living in backyard trees, but as usual, everyone ignored them. Other than that, few outside of our house paid her much attention. Ferrisville had its priorities. Scandal was an off-season hobby.

Before you ask, no. I didn't think it was strange everyone took the presence of a ten-foot-tall, barefoot woman dressed in bedsheets in an oak tree in a backyard in a small town in Middle America in stride. I did too. It felt right. Natural.

I saw her first. On Monday morning, Ferrisville New Year's Day, I was standing at the kitchen sink, staring out the window, daydreaming big dreams about the coming season, and there she was.

"Mom?" I said.

I got a grunt in return. She was still on her first cup of coffee.

"There's someone in our backyard. In the tree." When I was younger, I begged Dad to build a treehouse in the giant oak that shaded half our backyard. He never did, but the place where the thick trunk split and curved away into two halves had been my favorite place to hang out.

No answer from Mom.

"She's barefoot and wrapped in a sheet or something. She looks...large."

"That's nice."

The only sure ways to get Mom's full attention before her third cup of coffee involved fire or fresh blood. Hoping it wouldn't come to either, I pulled on my boots and coat and went out the back door.

A giant woman sat in my place in the crook of the oak. It was hard to tell from below, but I guessed her height to be ten feet, give or take an inch or two. She wasn't beautiful by movie star standards, but she was beautiful. She reminded me of statues I'd seen in the museum. Greek or Roman, I wasn't sure, but something old and classical. She had her nose buried in a book. I liked her immediately.

"Hi," I said.

She looked up from her book, gave me the once over, and went back to reading.

"Would you like some breakfast?" Ferrisville's main non-baseball related social rule was "always offer food."

"No, thank you." She turned a page, not bothering to look at me.

"We have Pop-Tarts."

That got her attention. "What kind?"

"Strawberry and brown sugar cinnamon."

"No chocolate fudge?"

"No, sorry." No need to tell her I'd just eaten the last one.

"I'll pass."

"Anything else I can get you? A blanket? Socks? Shoes? Pants?" I wanted to ask who she was, why she was in our tree, and what she was reading. For some reason, I couldn't get the words out.

"No, I'm good." Her tone was dismissive. She returned to her book.

I could have taken the hint, but I didn't. "Do you have a name?"

"More than one."

"Are you going to tell me?"

"Nope."

"Then I'll call you Sibyl." If she wasn't going to tell me her name, I'd give her one.

She closed her book and looked at me as if I just might be worthy of her attention.

"That's as good a name as any and better than most," she said.

My parents mostly ignored her. I enjoyed chatting with her, if you could call our terse conversations *chats*. Peter appeared obsessed with her. When he wasn't at school or practice, he spent more and more time in the backyard, sometimes climbing the tree to sit next to her.

His girlfriend, irritated at his lack of attention, broke up with him.

I couldn't figure out what they could be talking about, so I finally asked him.

"She says this year will be the Hawks' best year ever," he said.

"Knows a lot about baseball, does she?"

He gave me the sibling look, the one that said he'd prefer to be an only child.

Peter and Sibyl's backyard tête-à-têtes continued. He barely spent enough time on his schoolwork to keep his grades high enough to make him eligible to play ball. I may or may not have done some of his homework for him.

"What's he doing out there?" Dad said.

"Maybe he's thinking about asking her to prom," I said.

"I guess I could make her a dress," Mom said. "But shoes are going to be a problem."

"We'll have to hire a stretch limo to get them there," Dad said.

My parents. Ever the practical ones.

The Hawks won their first game. And their second. And their third. Nothing unusual there, but by their fourth game—which they also won —it was obvious something unusual was happening. Something special.

I kept score and had a ringside seat for all the fun.

The Hawks threw the ball fast, far, hard, and on target every time. They hit the ball on the ground, in the air, out of the park, whatever the situation called for. Even Peter was batting over three hundred. Catch the ball? The thing landed in their gloves like it had a homing device.

The pitchers had it all. Fastball, slider, curve, sinker, cutter, changeup, slurve, and few more that didn't have names. Peter's slider had always, when it worked, looked like it was falling off a table. Now, if he threw it, it worked.

And speed. These guys were fast. Outs on the bases were a rarity. Something that happened to the other team. Even Richie Oslawski, the short-legged shortstop, gained speed. He was still slow, but it didn't matter. He led the team in home runs and was on his way to a new state record.

When anybody questioned how such a little guy hit such long balls, he pushed up his glasses and said, "Launch angle." Since he was the team's token math and science geek, his answer was accepted.

Stevie Doyle, the regular third baseman, wanted to pitch.

"You ever pitched before?" Coach Bannerman said.

"Nope."

"Okay. Warm up."

Stevie turned out to be a natural knuckleballer.

Knuckleballers may be out of fashion in professional baseball, but they sure are fun to watch. The ball went up, down, sideways, and may have done a loop-di-loop or two before making it to the plate. Just when you thought it was going to end up in the stands, it floated through the strike zone, and just when you thought it was headed over the plate, it ended up in a dugout. The real miracle was that Marcus Baxter, the catcher, snagged every pitch that made it past—or anywhere near—the batter. Stevie pitched one inning, struck out the side, and made the side look bad doing it.

The starting nine, aka "the Nine," rotated positions. When Peter wasn't on the mound, he played first or centerfield, and the first baseman or centerfielder moved to another position. Wherever the Nine played, infield or out, they were as close to perfection as humanly possible. No one is perfect all the time. Someone needs to make outs or games would never end. I suspected the Hawks made outs on purpose, just so they could go home.

The bench players, the second-stringers, weren't too shabby either. That may have had something to do with the fact that by the time they entered the game—usually the sixth inning—the score was so far out of hand they would have had to work hard to lose.

"The object is to win, not humiliate," Coach said. I'm not sure even he believed it. Humiliation can be fun if you're on the side dishing it out.

The bleachers filled with not only birddogs, but with scouts and recruiters, both college and pro. The coaches carried copies of the entire team's birth certificates, ready to produce on demand when opposing teams demanded proof of age. The state High School Athletic Association demanded drug tests. Everyone passed, clean as a whistle, which surprised me knowing some of them as well as I did. I guess they were only looking for performance-enhancing drugs or growth hormones.

The Ferrisville Area High School Hawks varsity baseball team always swaggered, but by game six, their swaggers developed swaggers. The Nine were young princes. The golden sons of Ferrisville. Superstars. Gods.

And Peter was their supreme being, the center of their orbit. ESPN was there the day he pitched his perfect game. I was happy for him, but pissed when they aired the shot of me crying in the dugout.

The population of Ferrisville increased by two. Both new babies were named Oscar, after Coach Bannerman. Both were girls.

Everyone forgot the woman in our oak tree, or nearly forgot.

Midseason, one of the classic movie channels aired *Damn Yankees*. There was a ripple of speculation involving Sibyl and who might have sold their soul. My money was on Peter. Every morning before school or breakfast or anything, he spent a half hour outside with Sibyl. On game days, he spent an hour. When he came in, he wouldn't talk to anyone.

Mom questioned whether this was healthy.

"Don't mess with him," Dad said. "Game day. Rituals. You know the drill."

Mom dropped the subject. She knew about ballplayers and streaks and superstition. Morning visits with Sibyl were preferable to Peter refusing to have his jockstrap or socks laundered.

On one hand, I knew *Damn Yankees* was just a movie and deals with the devil didn't really exist. On the other, I had a ten-foot-tall mystery woman living in a tree in my backyard and, well, I think too much. I asked Sibyl.

She snorted and spat the word *soul* as if it was synonymous with *booger encrusted butt-nugget*.

In the end, if there was a deal with the devil, Ferrisville approved. As far as they were concerned, no matter whose soul was sacrificed, Satan got the short end of the stick. Like I said, priorities. Sibyl fell off their radar.

When we made the playoffs—not that there was ever any doubt— the rules required an official responsible adult as scorekeeper. No students. I was relegated to the stands and cheering fan status, but like the rest of Ferrisville, I didn't miss a game. Mr. Jeffers, the official responsible adult, texted me whenever he had questions.

The state championship was a given. The trip to Florida for the National High School Invitational was a coronation procession, not a tournament. No other team stood a chance.

Exactly one hundred people flew to Florida to watch the Invitational. Far more drove to the airport to meet the team and escort them home on their triumphant return.

We didn't see the accident. Mom, Dad, and I were miles ahead of the caravan, racing back to get the welcome home party set up before the team arrived. Half of Ferrisville travelled with the team bus, but not us. We were happy and clueless until our phones rang.

Leading the citizen's convoy, right behind the bus, were Mr. Otto, the mayor; Mr. O'Neill, the council president; and Mr. Oliveira, the school superintendent, all in Mr. Otto's Cadillac Escalade. They claimed to have seen everything.

A flash, they said, like an explosion. The inside of the bus filled with fire before it broke through the guardrail and went off the bridge into the gorge below. Mr. Otto said he nearly followed the bus over the side. Other witnesses backed them up.

When the emergency crews made their way to the bottom of the ravine, they found a tangled mess of metal and bodies, but no sign of fire.

The driver was still alive and conscious. Rumor has it he said something about Peter before he died. No one knew what exactly, but that didn't stop them from talking.

People need a scapegoat. It absolves them of all personal guilt, real or imagined.

Ferrisville had lost its young gods, its nine golden sons and their acolytes. Someone had to pay. Ferrisville chose Peter. In their minds, he grew into a legend, a monster. The rest of the family wasn't far behind.

People stopped speaking to us, if they could help it. Dad lost his bar buddies. He drank alone while painting over the obscene graffiti that appeared and reappeared on the front of our garage and the side of our house. Mom lost her job. The bakery said she was killing business. The good people of Ferrisville didn't want her anywhere near their doughnuts.

I worried they might come after Sibyl, deranged villagers with torches and pitchforks. They didn't. She was as dead to them as the rest of us.

For the rest of the summer, we were the only Ferrisvillians who couldn't be found at a ballpark. Life went on, but it went on without Mom, Dad, or me.

Being a pariah left me a lot of time to read.

And research. I did my searching online. I found basic information on my own, but the best stuff came from a library's electronic "Ask a Librarian" service. A library in another state. I could have gone to the Ferrisville Public Library. The librarians there would have helped me even if they hated me. It's their job. And they couldn't have told anyone—that's also part of their job. But I didn't want anyone I knew to know what I was looking for.

I got lucky with whomever was on the other end of my texts and emails. They sent pages and pages of info telling me everything I needed and more than I wanted to know.

She sat in the crook of the tree, one leg dangling and the other curled under her, her nose buried in her book, exactly as she was a year ago.

"Is your name Albunea?"

The woman formerly known as Sibyl closed her book and hopped down from her perch. "That's one of my names."

"Are you from Tibur or Cumae? Are you the Tiburtine or the Cumaean?" It didn't make any difference, but there'd been some disagreement in my research. I figured I might as well ask the question while I had a chance.

"So you finally figured it out," she said. "Took you long enough."

"How long do we have?"

She leaned over and whispered in my ear. Instead of answering my question, she rattled off three short sentences. All unrelated. All easy to interpret. All minor prophesies. She straightened up, patted me on the head, and disappeared, book and all.

I stood alone under the oak and thought about her last words. Two minor prophesies and a major one. She had answered my question.

Mom and Dad waited for me at the back door.

"Is she gone?" Mom said.

"I think she is."

"What did she say?" Dad sounded worn out. Since the accident, he always sounded tired.

Her first two prophesies were personal, for me alone. Certainly not things I could or would tell my father or anyone else. The third was different.

"The Guardians are going to take it all."

Dad's grin was no doubt reflex, the result of a lifetime of hope and conditioning. I decided not to tell him any more. Let him have his hope. Maybe I was wrong. I hope I am, but if Cleveland winning the World Series isn't the final sign of the apocalypse, I don't know what is.

In summary, the TL;DR version: Last year sucked big time. Next year is going to suck even worse. So, for this year—or what's left of it—I sincerely wish you your best year ever. Enjoy the season.

IT CAME FROM THE LAKE

J. Thorn

Danny didn't *really* want his parents to die. The stupid thought popped into his head when his mom interrupted his game of *Zombie Squad*.

"Did you hear me?"

"Yeah, Mom." Danny pushed a curly lock of blond hair off his forehead. His blue eyes darted across the screen while his tongue hung from the left corner of his mouth.

"Danny. Pause the game and acknowledge your mother," his father said.

He dropped the controller into his lap and flipped the microphone up on his headset. Danny didn't want his friends hearing him talking sweet to his parents.

"What?" Danny asked.

"Did you hear what I said about the laundry?" his mother asked.

Seven loads, all smelling like cold, wet socks. His mom stacked seven piles of dirty laundry on the back wall of the playroom floor. He couldn't believe four people could make so much dirty laundry. Then again, his sister changed her outfit three times a day.

Danny sighed and waited for her to continue, knowing exactly what she was going to say.

"We have to go through this every time. You don't listen to anything we say when you're playing that stupid video game."

Danny's dad stood behind his wife, arms folded across his chest with a furrowed brow.

"It's not stupid, Mom. It's a highly sophisticated, live, multi-player—"

"We have to go," Danny's father said, interrupting him.

"For the last time, you have to check the laundry," his mother said. "Sometimes the drain backs up and the water will spill out into the rest of the basement. Last time, we had to pull up the carpeting and—"

"Okay, Mom. I got it."

"I mean it," she said, determined to finish her explanation. "I scrubbed the mold and mildew for days and I'm not doing it again. Check the laundry and make sure it doesn't overflow. Keep your eye on the drain, Danny."

His father put on a sport coat before grabbing his wife's purse and handing it to her. He pointed at Danny.

"Keep your phone nearby. I don't want to have to call you seven times in a row before you answer."

Danny glared at his father before reaching for the game controller.

"Nobody makes phone calls anymore. Text me if you need something," Danny said. "I promise I'll text you right back."

"Yes. God forbid anyone *talks* to another person in this world." Danny's mom tossed the purse over her shoulder and smiled at her son. "Have fun shooting monsters."

"Zombies. They're zombies," Danny said.

Danny smiled at his parents and offered them the top of his head. He would not let his classmates at Central Junior High see this, but his social standing wasn't at risk if his parents kissed him goodbye in the privacy of their own home.

"Call us—I mean text us if you need something. I love you," his dad said.

"Geez. Go to dinner already. I'll be fine. I love you guys."

Danny's mom winked at her son before she followed her husband up the stairs and out the side door. Danny flipped his microphone back into place and rejoined the zombie slaughter on the screen.

Ajax89, also known as William, tossed a hypoblast grenade into a nest of zombies behind the prison's perimeter fence.

"Bull's eye," William said through Danny's headphones.

"So what? Easy kill. They were trapped behind the burnt out car."

"Shut up, Danny. You couldn't have hit them. Why don't you go kiss your mommy goodnight?"

Danny sighed and shook his head. He hoped William hurled a random insult and did not overhear Danny's conversation with his parents.

A massive explosion rolled through his headphones as another member of the team used a shoulder-strapped rocket launcher to blow out the guard tower at the north end of the prison yard. Danny watched as digital zombie guts splattered the ground in pixelated pinks and reds. When the dust settled, Danny heard the washing machine rumble. He spent enough time gaming in the playroom to recognize the washer's final cycle. He tried closing the door between the game room and the laundry room but the old clunker always seemed to make more noise than a high school pep rally.

"I gotta go," he said.

"Wuss."

"Pansy."

"Whatever," he said to the succession of taunts coming from the rest of Team Alpha Dog. "I'm totally grounded if I don't watch the drain."

"One more level. C'mon, dude. You can iron your mom's panties later."

Danny felt the blood rush to his face.

I'll show you who's a wuss, William.

"Fine. You all suck. You'd never make it to Zone 5 without me."

The other boys in the game laughed, the sound in Danny's headphones drowning out the moans of the washing machine.

Danny's neck stiffened and he rubbed at his eyes. They burned and began to water. He felt the muscles in his legs vibrate and the beginning of a cramp twitched in the bottom of his right foot.

"Seriously, I gotta go. What time is it?" Danny asked.

"Time for you to sack up," William said.

Danny tapped his phone and saw 11:45 p.m. glowing on the screen.

"Holy crap. We've been playing for four hours."

"Wasn't like we were going to stop after plowing through Zone 5," William said in Danny's headphones. "You're a zombie killing machine."

Danny smiled and shook his leg. The impending cramp softened into a prickly dance of pins and needles.

"So we saving the game here? I'm hungry."

The disembodied tween voices agreed as the avatars dropped out of the game.

"Cool," Danny said. "I'm out."

He set the controller on the floor and placed his headset next to it. Danny stood and the lights in the house flickered. He looked up at the fluorescent bulbs in the drop ceiling. They buzzed at him like angry flies. Danny took a step toward the laundry room, his mother's voice reverberating in his head amongst the sounds of zombie-fueled explosions.

When he got to the laundry room doorway, the lights flickered again and went out completely. Danny stood in the windowless playroom, staring at the afterglow of the LCD screen. He turned to climb the steps out of the basement, reached into his pocket, and felt the smooth plastic case of his phone.

Might have to call the old man after all, he thought.

———

Danny walked through the kitchen and looked out the back door. The night covered the patio and yard like a thick, dark paste. He turned his head around, scanning the backyards of the houses on the next street over backed up to his. On any given night, porch lights and streetlamps softened the night in a weak copper haze. But tonight, Danny saw only silhouetted shapes trapped beneath inky blackness. He lifted his head and gazed in the direction of downtown Cleveland where the city lights kept the horizon in a state of perpetual dawn. Again, he saw nothing but black swatches of darkness beneath wispy, slow moving clouds. Instead of the usual aroma of grass clippings, Danny caught a faint whiff of wet garbage and mold. He shook his head and thought he could almost taste the foul stench on his tongue.

He tapped his phone and the screen flared in the intense darkness. He squinted and turned it away for a few seconds. Once his eyes adjusted, Danny looked down. He saw his usual widgets and apps on the home screen and the battery indicator showed fifty percent. But a circle with a line through it replaced his network bars. He tapped a green icon to see his messages, checking the arrival time of the last one in order to determine when the network went down.

He saw a few texts—some came from his friends. Several kids didn't have a headset so they texted during game play instead. He scanned the other messages until he saw his dad's.

Dad texted me. I didn't answer. I'm in big trouble.

He tapped the conversation string and saw his dad sent five messages over the course of the previous hour. Danny gulped and a knot balled up in his stomach. He read the first message.

Lock yourself in.

Danny fell for his dad's pranks all the time. He chuckled and shook his head. He read the next message.

You're probably in game. Pls son. Lock doors.

"What the—?"

Danny saw two more messages in the conversation. He used his forearm to wipe a bead of sweat from his forehead. He looked out the back door again and let the silence wash over him. It was almost midnight on a comfortable September Saturday. He expected to hear traffic on Mayfield Road or the teenagers laughing and teasing each other on the sidewalk, ignoring the curfew and angering the old folks on the block. The smell of wet garbage grew stronger and Danny expected to see a raccoon climbing out of an overturned garbage can. When nothing moved, he looked at his phone, scrolled down, and read the next message.

Stay quiet. No lights.

He liked to tease his parents about their texts. Adults never used shortcuts or abbreviations because they thought their texts had to be grammatically perfect. Yet his dad's texts became shorter. And abbreviated.

Hide. Hide now.

Danny felt dizzy and shut the kitchen door before sitting in a chair. He looked first at the microwave and then at the stove. At night, the glow from the LCD clocks would cast a blue hue about the room, one familiar and soothing to Danny. But tonight, the kitchen sat beneath the same ocean of darkness as the rest of his world.

He saw one last text from his father sent fifteen minutes ago.

Covered rains.

Danny shook his head and read it again. He scrolled to the top of the conversation and back down, thinking his phone scrambled the characters in the text.

Covered rains.

Danny stood, thinking about the last two words his dad texted. His brain started to wrestle with the bizarre message when the house shook. A sound like a jackhammer on old concrete came from the living room. Danny walked from the kitchen and toward the front door, his eyes buzzing with confusion. He saw thin shadows moving back and forth beneath the window as the banging intensified. Danny stood in the middle of the room before his father's second text message popped back into his head like a movie subtitle.

Hide. Hide now.

Regardless of the other times in his life he didn't listen to his parents, Danny knew this time he had to obey his father. He had to hide.

———————

Danny thought about his sister as he ran up the steps to the second floor.

Where was she tonight?

He remembered his mom arguing with her about a curfew but

Danny paid little attention to any conversation in the house when he played *Zombie Squad*.

Danny glanced out of the high window on the landing, halfway between the first floor and the second. Downstairs, the pounding on the front door continued, falling into a rhythmic thumping like the beat of a war drum. He used the first two fingers on his right hand to split the venetian blinds so he could peer across the driveway at the neighbor's kitchen window. The Sandersons moved into the neighborhood almost nine months ago, yet nobody in Danny's family knew their first names. His mother commented on the family's comings and goings, often whispering under her breath to Danny's father about the hours the mother kept. Danny saw an upside down tricycle in the driveway. Movement in the neighbor's kitchen window caught his eye. A shape flickered in the darkness, and at first Danny wasn't sure if it was the night playing with his vision or if the neighbors were home.

Stay quiet. No lights.

He bit his lip, hoping to punish himself for making noise. The pounding on the front door sped up as if his question taunted whatever wanted inside.

Shut up, Danny. Don't be stupid.

Danny took a breath and tried to clear his head.

The grid went down. Whatever it is, it happened while we killed zombies on Level 5. Dad tried texting me and I didn't notice because I was too busy playing. I'm in the dark in more ways than one.

The thought sounded silly inside of his head. He knew every kid in every horror movie hid underneath the bed. And then the monster would come and yank the frightened dweeb out by his ankles. He'd seen it so many times, the scene would make him laugh instead of shake with terror. So when Danny stood in the threshold of his room, looking at the floor where dog-eared issues of *Gamer Mag* poked out from beneath the box spring, he laughed.

The chuckle seemed to agitate whatever was outside of the house because the banging on the front door intensified in both volume and frequency. The walls shook. Danny heard thumping coming from the back door now. It started with random thumps until it fell into syncopation with the banging on the front door.

Danny walked to the window and pushed the curtains to the side. His bedroom window overlooked River Lane and, in fact, the street appeared to be a deep, still river in the darkness. The concrete sidewalk glowed with a faint gray, accentuating the space between the street and the grassy lawns. His eyes darted from house to house. Still, Danny saw no movement and no lights. The absence of people, cars, or the police made him shudder.

Danny sat on the edge of his bed and tried to apply the same logic he used in *Zombie Squad* to this situation.

Strategy is strategy, he thought. *I can figure this out.*

Danny ticked the facts off on his fingers.

Something bad happened while I was gaming. We were so focused on killing zombies, we didn't hear about whatever was going down in the rest of the world. Dad texted me. He knew something, but didn't have the time to call or text me the details. The power is out. Something is pounding on my door.

He turned his head sideways like a dog hearing a high-pitched tone.

They haven't broken a window. They haven't knocked the doors down.

Danny jumped up and looked out of his window again. He stared at the front door of the house across the street. At first, he saw nothing out of the ordinary. But as his eyes lingered and adjusted to the meager light, he saw it.

There.

He waited, daring not to blink for fear of missing it.

Again.

At first, Danny thought the house caught fire and smoke oozed from beneath the door. But the haze flowed in deliberate movements, morphing into and out of shapes, like...

Tentacles. The arms of a giant, evil squid.

Danny remembered hearing about the algae bloom on Lake Erie that summer. Most people dismissed it as a fungal growth explosion caused by industrial fertilizer. But what if the government hid the real reason for the bloom? The conspiracy theorists online started talking about the Lake Erie Monster again. They believed an entire colony of fresh-water squid lived in the deepest part of the Great Lakes, waiting.

The shapes outside looked like long, thin whips—like tentacles. And they searched for a way to get inside, to get at Danny.

Why couldn't they break down the door or smash the window?

The questions raced through Danny's mind faster than he could contemplate an answer. He didn't know why. He might never know why.

The entire house shook and he heard dishes crashing to the ceramic tile floor in the kitchen. The walls vibrated, shaking dust and chunks of plaster from the ceiling. Flecks floated through the air, catching the scant light like miniature snowflakes. The floorboards rattled and the trophy Danny won in U8 soccer toppled forward and landed in a pile of dirty clothes.

The Lake Erie Monsters can't figure out how to get inside, so they're going to shake the place to rubble to flush me out.

He stood up and took a step toward the door when a force knocked him sideways and into the wall. Something smashed into the side of the house so hard, Danny thought the roof would cave in on top of him. He regained his balance and sprinted for the hallway. Something slammed into the house again, this time from the other side. Danny wondered if it was only his house under attack or if the creatures infested the rest of the city, the rest of the world.

Another noise caught his attention, this one softer than the others. He heard a soft thump, like a wet sponge dropped into a bucket of mud. A dark shape on his bedroom window smothered what little light came from the street. He saw a tiny mouth on the outside of the glass, pulsing. It sat within a mass of dark gray flesh and looked like the mindless jaw of a Venus flytrap. The mouth's dark lips pressed against the pane. Danny gazed at the sharp points of thin teeth and he shivered when they scratched the glass like frenzied rats.

The next impact knocked Danny to the other side of the room. He slipped on a T-shirt, fell, and smacked his elbow off of his dresser. The floor thrummed and vibrated as if the engine of a monster truck revved beneath it. He crawled on his stomach into the hallway and saw the tub in the bathroom.

Danny moved on instinct, pulling himself along the carpet. He hoped to survive the same way people survived tornadoes—hunkering down in a tub.

He looked at the bottles of shampoo and conditioner, the pink razors and luffa sponges. Danny would never admit it, but he loved his sister and hoped she found a safe place. He thought of his mom, and the jasmine rose scent of her shampoo made him smile. He used both hands to clutch the tub as tiles rained down off the walls. Toilet paper rolled back and forth across the floor into green puddles of mouthwash spilled from plastic bottles like alien blood. Danny wanted to cry out, and even though the house screamed in agony from the destruction, he did not make a sound. He turned on his side and felt an object digging into the top of his thigh. The phone.

One last look, he thought.

Danny flicked at the screen and the light nearly blinded him. He squinted, using his finger to flick down to view his messages. The screen showed the text conversation he had with his father. Danny's eye scrolled down to the last message.

Covered rains.

He shook his head and looked again.

Danny remembered his father complaining about his new phone. About the—

Autocorrect.

He stared at the screen and used his mind to reorder the characters.

Covered rains.

Cover ed rains.

Cover the drains.

Danny slid the phone into his pocket and used his feet to push until his back pressed against the wall opposite of the drain. He looked at the shiny chrome grate and saw the usual mound of moist soap shreds. And something else.

What appeared as thick strands of black hair came through the drain, lengthening and expanding out like tiny snakes. The house stopped shaking but the tub vibrated as the long, greasy black hairs crawled from the pipes. They snaked up the side of the tub and wrapped around the waterspout, the ends dangling in mid-air like a serpent's tongue. The stench of rotten eggs and sour milk made Danny's face twist. He wrinkled his nose and felt a nauseous rumbling in his stomach followed by a sharp pain in his abdomen. He held his breath, bit his lip, and let the tears fill his eyes.

The thing from the drain paused, and then, as if sensing his presence, sent more hairy tentacles in his direction, threatening to pull him down the drain. When the first one touched his leg, Danny wanted to vomit. He turned his head sideways and dry heaved, feeling as though the dirty hair crawled inside of his mouth and crept down his throat.

Cover the drains.

Danny used his foot to try and push the drain stop, but he missed. The hairs pulsed and intertwined, becoming thick like rope. The strands weaved and circled about the tub.

"I got this," he said.

He kicked again, and this time his foot hit the drain stop and triggered the plate. It slid across the opening. The drain closed and the levitating black fibers vibrated. They shook and whined like the cry of an injured puppy before dropping back into the tub. He took a deep breath, the air still holding the smell of wet garbage but the odor no longer as strong.

I did it. Oh my god. I did it.

Danny heard the banging on the door again as if the Lake Erie Monsters retreated through the plumbing and re-gathered at the front door. He was not sure how or why his dad knew, but Danny now knew how to protect himself.

Cover the drains.

He leapt from the tub and ran into his parents' room where his father left a roll of duct tape sitting on top of his dresser. Not the handiest, his father always seemed to have a roll of duct tape nearby. Danny grabbed it and ran back into the bathroom. A rumbling noise came from the first floor and he wondered how long it would be before the monsters would refocus their attack. He ripped a piece of tape from the roll and slapped it over the opening. He repeated the process three times until he covered the drain. Danny turned to the sink and pulled the plunger up. He used more duct tape to cover this drain as well.

Danny heard the pipes pinging behind the walls and cracks raced through the plaster. He looked at the tub and sink one last time before running out of the bathroom and jumping down the steps.

He stood in the hallway between the kitchen sink and the half-bath. The banging on the doors subsided as the walls groaned. The plaster covering them ballooned out and Danny saw the old, black pipe inside the walls. It throbbed.

Cover the drains.

He ripped strands of duct tape off the roll, peeling it like raw, dead skin. The first piece would not adhere to the wet sink basin so Danny applied several more until he felt certain the tentacles would not be able to break through. He ran from the bathroom sink to the kitchen sink, using tape to cover the drains.

Danny stood in the middle of the kitchen, shards of dishes and glasses littering the floor. Cabinet doors hung askew on hinges broken like a bird's wing. He listened, hearing nothing inside the house. The pipes stopped pulsing and the pounding on the doors ceased. He held his breath, fearful even one noise would start the fury again.

They can't get in so they've moved on to another house.

Danny tiptoed into the living room. He stared out of the window onto an empty street. The doors stood still and silent. He collapsed into the couch kicking up dust and plaster from the attack. Danny felt the adrenaline ooze from his body and he guessed it was two or three in the morning. He didn't know the fate of his family or if the sun would rise, but Danny took comfort in the fact he fought off the attack. He closed his eyes to rest, just for a moment.

The first black filament slithered up from the pipe with the smell of rotting carp and through the water on the floor—the puddle where the washing machine overflowed. Two more greasy hairs entwined with it and they snaked up through the floor drain in the laundry room. Past the forgotten clothes and up the steps toward the couch in the living room where Danny talked in his sleep.

"I won't forget, Mom," he said. "I'll watch the drain."

IS ANYONE THERE?

Rami Ungar

T he blond man holds up the two L-shaped copper dowsing rods in front of him, his arms tucked into his sides, so he can stand as still as possible. He holds the rods by the short ends, which are wrapped in plastic cylinders so he's not directly touching the metal, while the long ends swing freely back and forth. To me, they look like antennae searching for a signal. Which I guess, in a way, they are.

The blond man stands in front of the glass wall keeping people from getting too close to Old Sparky. He faces it, expectant. Off to the side, another man in an argyle kilt is filming the blond man with a mobile phone, while the rest of his tour group wait in anticipation. Except for their tour guide Catherine, all of them are vendors for the convention the prison is hosting tomorrow, and all of them are at least open to the idea of a world beyond this one.

A world which, if the rumors are true, is especially thick and active here at the Ohio State Reformatory. And I know from personal experience that it is.

The blond man clears his throat and says in a loud voice, "Cross the rods for yes, push them apart for no. Is anyone there?"

I don't know why I do this. Before I know what's happening, I step in front of him and force the rods together in a cross-shape. I'm not sure how I'm able to manipulate these things. It's something to do with willpower and how energetic I'm feeling, but the specifics elude me. Nevertheless, I'm able to make them move, and the blond man's face lights up. He and the others in the room can't see me, but they can see the results. In their minds, a spirit is answering him.

Which, in actuality, a spirit is answering them. *I* am answering them. But they don't know that. They only have what they see and believe to go on.

Whatever their beliefs, they're excited, none more so than the blond man. "Uncross the rods, please," he says. I uncross and straighten them. The blond man asks his next question, "Did you die in the electric chair?" I cross the rods again. Yes, I died in Old Sparky over there. I uncross the rods on cue and the man asks, "Did you die here, in the Ohio State Reformatory?"

Now that's a trick question. He knows no one was ever executed at this prison, let alone me. Catherine, the tour guide, just told them five minutes ago how Old Sparky was only used in executions in Columbus before being retired and thrown in a warehouse for storage. It was then brought to the Reformatory, the state's official prison museum, where it became part of the collection. And every time it was moved, it brought all the spirits still attached to it, including myself, along for the ride.

Ghost hunters, both amateurs and professionals, ask trick questions to establish they're actually speaking to an intelligent spirit. If the answers match up to the historical record, it's supposed to prove to skeptics that the hunters really are communicating with something, rather than mistaking random movements of the rods for communication.

I push the rods apart to indicate a no. The blond man turns to Catherine, who's standing by the door. "You said nobody was executed here at the prison?" he asks.

Catherine nods her head. "That's right, there were no scheduled executions at OSR." She then cocks her head, listening. "We have to wrap this up. One of the other tour groups is on its way."

"One more question?" He gets the okay, then says to me, "Were you innocent of whatever crime got you sent to the chair?"

I am not expecting this sort of question. From watching plenty of other spirits interact with the living, I've learned that most people seem to assume that prison ghosts deserve to be one. After all, if you were innocent, wouldn't you have gone straight to Heaven after you died? If you're still here, this is probably your eternal punishment.

He waits for my answer. I reach up and cross the rods again. Yes, I was innocent. But because I was of the wrong race, the wrong class, and I had relatives with criminal records, I was still convicted, sentenced to die, and eventually executed via electric shock. And as far as I know, nobody else has figured out an innocent man was sent to the chair that day.

The blond man nods, thanks me, and drops the rods back into his bag before retrieving his phone from the man in the argyle kilt. "Did you get everything?"

The kilted man nods. "Yep. You, the chair, and the rods moving. It might even go viral."

The blond man laughs. "That's the hope!"

They follow the tour group out of the electric chair room and up a flight of stairs to the Warden's Residence on the second floor.

I stay behind. I'm tired. I don't know how a ghost can be tired, but I am. It's one of many mysteries that, despite over sixty years attached to that damned chair, I still can't answer. Sixty years in a special kind of Hell.

Of course, I wouldn't be tired if I had stuck to my usual routine and not answered. After all, how does answering the blond man's questions help me? I've been in this prison for many years and witnessed many ghost hunters and paranormal TV shows, so I've picked up on a few things. He'll use the video on his phone to try make himself famous, and I'll have expended my energy for nothing. Trying to have a conversation with the living, with beings who can leave the Reformatory whenever they want and leave us behind, is a waste of time. Makes me wonder why I even bothered answering in the first place.

I sit outside Old Sparky's room and relax until my energy comes back. When I was alive, I mostly worked and slept. Relaxing meant bills would go unpaid, so I did very little of it. At the very least, being dead means I get to rest whenever I want to. It's a small consolation, but I take what I can get in this existence.

I'm still resting an hour later when the blond man comes back. There's something tucked under his arm and he looks determined. Catherine follows behind, exasperated and nervous at the same time. With a key, she opens the door to Old Sparky's room and lets the blond man in.

"We gotta make this quick, okay? If we get found here after the Ghost Tour is over, we'll both be banned from the prison."

I'm curious, so I get up and follow them inside. I walk through the door, of course. Very ghostlike. To my surprise, I find the blond man on the floor in front of the glass, the thing he had tucked under his arm placed flat on the floor. It's a Ouija board.

Oh hell.

Already other spirits, including ones who have never walked the Earth in human form, are gathering around. They materialize out of the floor and walls, or drift down through the ceiling, drawn by something that can't be heard or felt. Some wear prison garb or guard uniforms like they did in life and have glowing lights within the dark holes where their eyes used to be. Others are just shadows in the shape of people, unable to take a more definite form for reasons unknown. The ones who have never been human take all sorts of forms, and looking at them fills me with dread, so I don't look for too long.

All of them watch and salivate as they gaze at the blond man and the board. I quickly jump onto it, establishing myself as the only one who will be allowed to communicate with the man. Having lost a chance at whatever opportunities that board would give them, some spirits leave. Others, especially the diabolical ones, hover like vultures over a kill. They still hope to attach themselves to this guy and use his energy for their own nefarious purposes.

Off to the side, Catherine is filming on the man's phone. I ignore them both as the blond man starts messing with the Ouija board. He takes the plastic triangle with the hole in the center, the planchette, and makes a circle on the board with it three times. "Is anyone there?" he asks.

I bend down and put my hand on the planchette. A burst of energy goes into me, and I understand that it's coming from the blond man. He's using his own energy to give me a chance to talk. Boy, he doesn't know what the wrong spirit can do with that power, does he? I'm going to have to yell at him a bit before I let him go.

But first, I move the planchette to the YES. He says my answer aloud, then asks, "Are you the same spirit I spoke to earlier?"

Again, I force the planchette onto the YES spot. Inside, I'm boiling. I want to give this guy the biggest verbal smackdown possible, even if it's just through a stupid wooden board and a piece of plastic. I know what people say about these boards and what's portrayed in the movies. They don't come close to the terrifying reality. Ever seen someone's soul ripped out of their physical body and have something occupy it, making the victim essentially a ghost? It's not pretty.

Before I can chew him out, however, the blond man throws me for a loop again. "If I promise to help you, will you be honest with me?"

I slide the planchette off the YES, then slide it back on. Give me an opportunity to speak my mind already, dammit! I want to tell him how this stupid stunt of his is the exact reason blonds always die early in horror movies!

"Were you telling the truth when you said you were innocent of the crime that got you in Old Sparky?"

YES.

"Did anyone ever clear your name?"

I freeze and my mind blanks so that I can't move the planchette. Someone figuring out I'm innocent? Before I died, I prayed like crazy every day for someone to do just that. But then I got executed and found myself haunting Old Sparky, unable to get further than two hundred yards from its wooden frame. That was the day I stopped praying.

But what if someone did figure out I'm innocent? It's not outside the realm of possibility, that's for sure.

The blond man is expecting an answer. I spell out, *I don't know*, and the blond man thinks for a minute. Then he says, "Would you like me to look into your case?"

Who is this guy? Why is he willing to help me? And what good would it do me?

As if reading my mind, the blond man fills the silence. "I know you have no reason to trust me. And I have no reason to trust you. But maybe...maybe it's what I'm supposed to do? Does that make sense? Forget that, do you want me to look you up and see if anyone ever figured out you were innocent?"

He feels like he's supposed to help me? This living guy, who just saw me as something cool to get on camera earlier? He wants to help me because he feels like he's supposed to? For the first time in my life and death, I know what "gobsmacked" means.

And yet...and yet I felt like reaching out to him. I've never felt like reaching out to the living when they're trying to find proof of the para-normal. I'm one of the many ghosts here who just don't give a damn. And yet this evening, with this guy, as he shows up in front of Old Sparky with his stupid dowsing rods, I felt like interacting with him. Why? Was I compelled by a higher power I don't believe in or something?

I think for a moment, and then I move the planchette to YES. It can't hurt to find out. And maybe knowing will make my personal Hell a bit easier to live with, so to speak.

The blond man smiles. "What is your name?"

I move the planchette around the board. The blond man says every letter out loud so his phone can record it. When I finish, he says it aloud. Then he repeats it, but with his brow furrowed. Like he's trying to remember something.

He takes a deep breath. "I'll see what I can dig up. Goodbye."

He moves the planchette to the big GOODBYE at the bottom of the board. Like that, the connection is broken and I'm no longer drawing energy from him. The other spirits in the room—God, I forgot they were there!—leave with annoyed grumbles. They won't be using the connection the blond man made through the board for their own purposes.

I watch, almost shellshocked, as the blond man picks up the board and planchette, stands, and heads for the door. Catherine hands him back his phone.

"Come on," she says. "If we're caught—!"

"I know, I know! Did you catch all that, though? Can you believe what we got? And I know I've heard that name before. Recently, too. I think if I Google it, I can find out who this guy is and why he was executed. And maybe...well, we'll see what I pull up."

Catherine and the blond man fall silent as they walk quietly through the prison to the west cell block. As I'm not drained from speaking to him, I follow behind. I pass many spirits, some of whom call out to me, but I ignore them. I want to hear what the two flesh-bodies ahead of me have to say, if they say anything else.

But they don't. Instead, they place the board on one of the tables for the convention tomorrow, sprint up a flight of stairs, and sneak out a side door to the parking lot.

I'm left to wonder if the blond man will keep his promise, or if he, like everyone living who visits this prison, will forget me as soon as he's gone.

***

In life, I was nobody remarkable. I graduated from an Ohio high school and started working at a country club as a gardener. I hoped eventually to save up enough to go to college, get a degree, and get a better job than anyone in my family. When I wasn't working, sleeping, or keeping my brain sharp by reading one book a week—mandatory while living with my parents, though I never complained—I drove around in my secondhand Volkswagen, attended church on Sundays, played games or hung out with my brother and sister, and hoped that someday I would live a better life than my parents did. You know, just the usual stuff for someone my age.

But then The Incident happened.

I still remember it as clear as day, which is ironic because it happened in the middle of a summer evening. I was doing some last-minute work on the shrubs around the building. I should've been done long ago, but one of my coworkers had been fired that day. Why? Among other things, he goofed off, and his neglect had led to the flowers and bushes wilting in the summer heat. Because of that idiot, it was up to me to pick up his slack and try to coax some life back into them.

Anyway, the shrubs were my last task for the day. I was hot, thirsty, and looking forward to going home and getting some sleep. At that moment, a figure walked past me with a raised hand and a "Hey."

I looked up and spotted a blonde-haired teenager in a two-piece swimsuit, a towel hanging from her shoulders and her purse on her arm. From the direction she was heading, I could tell she planned to swim at the club's pool. Which presented a problem that I had to let her know.

"The pool's closed. There's no lifeguard on duty. You can't go swimming tonight."

The girl turned around. I expected her to yell at me for telling her what to do. Most members of the club, including their underage kids, treated the staff as servants.

Instead, the girl walked over to me, smiled and held her fingers up to her lips. "I'm meeting my boyfriend by the flower garden. My dad doesn't like me dating, so I told him I was swimming with friends. He can never remember when the pool closes."

I chuckled. The girl reminded me of what I was like when I was her age, about ten years ago or so. Back then, I used to come up with all sorts of plans to meet up with girls. It would appear things never changed.

"I'll be done here in a few minutes," I informed her. "If I stop by the pool after I'm done and find you swimming in there—"

"Then I give you permission to drag me in front of my father and tell him I was breaking rules."

Having reached an understanding, I smiled at her and said, "Don't do anything I wouldn't do."

She gave me a mock-offended gasp. "Why sir! I don't know what you mean!"

We both laughed, and she left for her rendezvous. I finished up my work on the plants, put my supplies back in the gardening shed, and headed to the pool. When I got there, the lights were off, and nobody was around. True to her word, the girl was not going for a late-night swim.

Satisfied, I signed out in the staff lounge, crossed the front lobby, nearly had a collision with a state senator's son who was rushing in, and then walked through the parking lot to my car. I headed home listening to the radio and looking forward to a shower before bed.

I had no idea that my life was about to be turned upside down.

In the morning, the girl would be found dead in the flower garden. Someone had raped her before strangling her with her own towel.

I was the last person to see her before she died.

That is, besides her murderer.

***

I don't like to think of what happened after the police showed up at my parents' house because it still upsets me.

To put it simply, I was their only suspect. I had admitted, before I knew I was a suspect, that I had seen the girl. I was on camera talking with her, and then I was on camera walking after her a little while later. As to the part of the story where I visited the pool and saw no one, there was no way to verify that. I apparently had been in the cameras' blind spots, and no cameras are mounted in the flower garden. After all, what's the worst that can happen in a flower garden?

Not only that, but the coroner said the girl likely died before I signed off for the night. And the state senator's son, the one I'd nearly bumped into on my way out, said I looked hurried, like I couldn't wait to get out of that country club. Which was true, but not for the reasons the police thought.

But the thing that really cinched it for the police was that, because of my background and the color of my skin, I seemed like the perfect suspect. To the cops, and to the judge and jury and prosecutor at my trial, and even to the defense attorney who did a half-assed job defending me, that was enough to turn circumstantial evidence into proof positive.

My trial took two weeks. The jury deliberated barely an hour before finding me guilty. I was put on death row, and none of my appeals went anywhere. After three years, I finally took that long walk to the last chair I would ever sit in.

And thus, my Hell on Earth began.

The Ohio State Reformatory used to be a facility to try to put wayward boys back on the right path. It later became a regular prison for nonviolent first offenders, though at one point it did house some of the roughest and most dangerous criminals in the state when a fire burned the prison in Columbus.

These days, it's a tourist attraction and a film set. People visit to learn the history, make movies and TV shows, and, of course, try to interact with the spirits that supposedly haunt the place.

And there are numerous spirits in the prison. Former prisoners and guards who died here or found themselves here even though they left the prison as living, breathing beings; one of the former wardens and his wife, who still occupy the residential section of the prison, as they did in life; spirits that were never human to begin with, drawn by the many lost souls and the living that they can maybe possess; and there are those who were brought in with Old Sparky, like me.

We're all packed into this old building like sardines, and the living who pass through only get a tiny fraction of what's happening behind the veil. Except for the nonhuman ones or the ones here because of Old Sparky, I have no idea why so many ghosts haunt the Reformatory. Perhaps it's something keeping the ghosts here, or because God wants us too. Who can say? Sometimes the afterlife is as mysterious to the dead as it is to the living.

Anyway, this weekend the spirits of this prison are only part of the attraction. That's because the Reformatory is hosting a paranormal convention. The vendors here sell electronic equipment that's supposed to pick up on spirits, crystals that allegedly make you feel better, and things I have no idea what they're for or why anyone would buy them. They're spread across three rooms along two floors, with a makeshift auditorium in one of the shower rooms for so-called experts on the paranormal to give lectures.

Today, Saturday, is the first day of the convention. To say the least, it is the both the strangest, as well as the most fascinating, thing you can witness as a Reformatory spirit. And that's saying something!

I wander through the packed convention, unnoticed by even my fellow spirits. They're too busy taking in all the weird booths and the many people who have come to buy from them. I'm trying to find the blond man. I want to see what he came here to sell. And I want to know if he has done anything to help me like he promised me the night before.

I don't find him in the Western Cell Block, which mostly holds big tables selling Eastern statuary, jewelry based around birth signs, and so-called magical equipment, or with the celebrities from ghost hunting shows and the like as they greet their fans and sign books. Nor do I find him in the Central Guard Room, which has an array of alternative medicine types, big-name authors, ghost hunters, and horror-themed memorabilia. Finally, I step into the East Diagonal Room, where most of the small retailers, lesser-known authors, ghost hunters, and one or two psychics hang out, and spot him four or five tables away.

I wade through the sea of humans towards his table, which is covered by a Halloween tablecloth and several books. He's a novelist. And according to the sign next to him, he sells both books and does Tarot readings. I guess it pays to be multitalented.

I watch him work for a little while. Several times he tells people about his various books, all of them horror stories and all of which sound weird as hell. Women turning into plant creatures, mafia-hunting serial killers, and maids working for mad scientists, among others. It's not my thing, but it is for a lot of patrons, because he sells four books in just the first ten minutes I stand beside his table. Not bad.

He also does his Tarot readings, telling people's fortunes with colorful playing cards for ten bucks per question. That's not the definition he uses, but I'm pretty sure that's what he's doing anyway. And he appears to be good at it, because what he tells people seems to jive with whatever's going on in their lives. I want to ask if he's making up the meanings as he goes, but, of course, that's not possible.

And in-between being friendly with the guests and the other vendors, cracking jokes, and trying to get people interested in his weird little books, he sometimes looks in my direction. Like he knows I'm watching him.

But that's stupid. None of these so-called mediums and psychics notice most of the spirits hanging around their tables. How can the blond man know I'm there?

I leave after a while and retreat to a quiet corner of the prison where no one is walking around. Finally, evening falls and the prison empties. There was supposed to be a special celebrity ghost hunt after the convention, but for some reason it's been canceled. I'm glad. Even if I have the energy to talk to the living, I'm in no mood for it. Instead, I just wander around aimlessly, chatting for short periods with this or that ghost.

And eventually, my wanderings lead me back to Old Sparky's room.

The blond man and Catherine are there. This time the blond man only has his dowsing rods. He looks like he's just arrived.

What's going on? I thought the stupid celebrity ghost hunt was canceled.

The blond man says my name and asks, "Are you there?"

I don't want to answer him, so I don't. He asks for me again, but I still don't answer. As the dowsing rods wave aimlessly back and forth, again looking like antennas searching for a signal, he sighs in frustration. "Is anyone there?"

I'm scared. That's the problem. If I were alive, I'd be shaking in my shoes and looking for the nearest exit to run through. I'm afraid of what he might reveal. I'm afraid of what he might have found out about me. About what went on after I died, convicted when I didn't even commit the crime.

Well, screw that! I'm dead, what do I have to be scared of?

I stride over to him and cross the rods. Yes, I am here!

The blond man's face lights up and he says my name again. I cross the rods again. Yes, it's me.

He sighs again, but this time it's a happy one. "I was able to find some stuff out about you," he says. "Turns out, there's a reason I thought I'd heard your name before. You were in the news recently."

I was in the news? I lean in, waiting for him to go on.

"Late last year, somebody confessed to the murder you were accused of," the blond man continues. "It was a big story, given who the real killer was." He says a name I recognize, and if I could gasp, I would.

That's the state senator's son, the one who said he saw me leaving the country club in a rush.

"And that's not all. After that, he went to college, majored in business and politics, and went to law school. Last year, he left his law firm to run his first campaign for state office. Follow in his dad's footsteps, I guess." He pauses and continues, "Of course, those plans went out the window the moment he was arrested. He had murdered another girl, a student interning for his campaign, and had left some DNA behind. That was how they caught him. And after his arrest, he revealed he'd raped and killed eight women and girls between the girl at the country club and the intern. Ten in total. From what I hear, he confessed it all to the police with a smile on his face. A creepy sort of smile."

I'm floored. My legs are shaking and I want to sit down. However, the only chair in the room is Old Sparky, so I don't sit. Instead, I wait for the blond man to say more.

"So, you're exonerated. The real killer is likely going to plea out. Life sentences for every victim. That way, he avoids the death penalty." He scoffs. "Not like he'd face that, anyway. The governor's suspended all executions until a more humane method can be found, whatever that means."

He's going to be punished for what he did to me as well as to those girls. For the first time in forever, I'm happy.

But then the blond man's face falls. "I do have some bad news." He pauses and takes a deep breath. "Your family never stopped believing in your innocence and trying to get you a new trial. Unfortunately...your younger siblings went to New York back in 2001 to talk to a law firm that wanted to take your case. The firm there wanted to see if they could at least prove you never did anything and get your family some closure."

His face is heavy with emotion. "Your brother and sister were meeting with the firm when the building was hit by an airplane. None of them survived. They left behind no wives, husbands, or children. I'm so sorry."

All my happiness evaporates. The blond man is still apologizing, but I can't hear any more. I run from the room and keep running until I reach the bullpen on the lower floor and to the back door. I don't slow, but instead speed up. I need to get out. I need to leave. Surely, I can leave now, can't I? My business here on this plane is resolved. I should be allowed to leave—!

An invisible wall keeps me from running through the doors and pushes me back like a kid on a trampoline.

I fall back onto my ass, but then I get up and try again. Once more, I fall.

No, I can't let this stop me. I get up again and run at the wall. This time, the barrier sends me through the bullpen, out the main prison, and back into the residential section.

I'm still bound to Old Sparky. I can't leave the prison.

I let out a loud wail that only the dead can hear.

The dead. My family are among the dead. They were the last people I saw before the hood was drawn over my face and I was executed. And they died trying to clear my name. And if the theory that ghosts become stuck to a place if they have unfinished business is true, they might still be stuck in New York. Stuck and unaware of what's happened since they died.

They never got to hear my name cleared, or that the real killer had been caught.

The real killer. If I had blood, it would boil. It's all his fault! He's not just responsible for the deaths of those women and girls. He's responsible for the death of me and my family! They never would have been in harm's way if not for him. But that monster, protected by power and money and his white skin, was never even looked at. He went on to have a gilded life, probably with a pretty trophy wife and perfect kids and a giant house that cost twenty times the one I grew up in, along with fancy cars and a host of servants. And he probably would still be killing and living his fancy life if he hadn't gotten sloppy with the campaign intern.

I bet he's sitting comfortable in a cell right now. I bet he's congratulating himself for getting away with it for so long. Not only that, but he's looking forward to a long, comfortable stay in a nice prison, one with air conditioning and decent meals and opportunities for him to earn a little spending money for the commissary. Hell, he may get money from fans who think he's sexy because he's killed people. He thinks he'll be set for the rest of his life.

At least I know that, when he's old and gray, his body will become as much a prison as wherever he's locked up. His limbs will grow weak, his organs will fail, and maybe his memory will go. He'll look forward to when he's free from his body.

And then, when he's finally on the other side, he'll find it's not the release he was hoping for. He may find that he's trapped in his prison or his hospital or his graveyard with thousands of other spirits. Some of them may be worse than him and want to play with him. Believe me, just because you're dead, doesn't mean you're invincible. You can be harmed. I can see plenty of spirits wanting to make an example out of the senator's son when he's on our side.

I just wish that I could be there to see him die. I wish that the governor who put executions on hold had been in charge when I was on death row, so my own execution could've been forestalled. Then, when the senator's son was caught, I could be freed. I could have a life with my family, who would still be alive. And I could tell that senator that he may have thrown me into prison, but he didn't break me.

Now I can hope he'll eventually make his way here. Old Sparky and all the ghosts attached to it did, after all, so who's to say the senator's son and whatever's he's attached to won't? Perhaps someday I'll find him in the Reformatory, and I can give him the torment he truly deserves.

Him and me, together forever, in Hell on Earth.

ALL GHOSTS ARE LIARS

Matt Betts

1 Tom Hart tossed his fork onto the plate, knocking pie crust crumbs onto the table. "What am I supposed to do then, Mary? Should I just go back to guest starring on *The Love Boat*?"

"*The Love Boat* was canceled decades ago." Mary rolled her eyes at her father. "I think there was even a reboot of it, and that got canceled." She gathered up the dishes and headed for the kitchen.

"What the hell? When did that happen?" Surely it was just a couple of years ago that he'd sailed to Puerto Vallarta as Connie Sellecca's husband. He took another sip of Mary's overly sweet lemonade and winced at both the taste and the thought that *The Love Boat* had sailed without him.

"What's Grandpa cussing about now?" Tom's grandson, Spencer, thudded down the stairs like a bowling ball. "And is there any pie left?"

"The network passed on your grandpa's new series, so he's a little unhappy," Mary shouted from the other room. "Sit down and I'll bring you a slice of apple crumble."

Spencer sat down and took up space at the table. Twenty-one, no job, no desire to go to college. Taking up space *and* a leech on Mary.

"Sorry, Grandpa. Was this another shot at reviving *Jack Bracken and the Saturn Spacestation* thing?"

"What? Jack Bracken was never even near Saturn. The Rusatians ruled Saturn with an iron fist, Jack would've been disintegrated if he even approached Saturn. *That* show was *Savage Galaxy*. Jack Bracken was my best character." Had his family even watched his shows? Tom sighed. "This was a paranormal investigation show."

"Another one?"

"Yes, *another one*." Tom was beginning to feel like the visit was a bad idea. His family had absolutely no idea how the entertainment business worked. Admittedly, the fresh Ohio air was a nice change of pace from Los Angeles, but it was one of the only perks. If he'd stayed home, he could have leaned on some of his contacts, maybe worked the phone. Here, Mary frowned at how much he used his cell.

"They had nice things to say, I'm sure. Didn't your agent talk to you about a role coming up?" Mary returned to the table with an oversized slice of pie with a mound of whipped cream on top. "That sounds nice."

She meant well, Tom knew, but he wasn't really interested in playing the principal in a high-school comedy series with that tattooed comedian and his cronies. "My agent suggested I go off and make my own show. *On the interwire*. What kind of advice is that?"

Spencer nearly choked on his pie. "You? On the net?"

"What's that supposed to mean?"

"Does she know you're, like, seventy? Did you tell her you still haven't figured out your voicemail yet? "

It was true, but Tom wasn't willing to concede it to the parasite. "Oh, ha ha. That's funny. I'm sure I can figure this YouTube thing out."

Mary sat between the two with an uneasy smile. "Guys..." She shot a look that Tom remembered as her barely holding on by her fingernails expression. "Spencer, you keep talking about film school. Maybe it would make a good demo tape if you help your grandpa out." It was tough for Tom not to spew a stream of very explicit language at the ceiling. He wanted to ease into asking Spencer for help, maybe even talk the kid into offering to help before being asked. He could feel his chest ache at the idea of working with his grandson on something so frustrating as modern technology. Conversations already felt like talking to an alien from Venus, if he threw in some technobabble, it would be maddening.

"And Dad, you'd be getting cheap labor and an expert in the field.

Win-win." Tom heard her, but bit his tongue at the suggestion he had
an ego. Plus, it wouldn't be *all* wins, and Tom felt several excuses
bubbling up in his throat, but he was pretty broke. Cheap help would
be nice, but he wasn't sure if the scales balanced between saving money
and spending time with Spencer. Across the table, his grandson was
quiet too. No doubt weighing his own threshold for bullshit.

"Can my friend Moira help? She's great at lighting things."

"Ehhh..."

2

"Can we listen to something else?" Tom asked from the back seat of
his own car.

"This is Nirvana," Moira said. She sat with her feet up on the dash
in the passenger seat next to Spencer, staring at her cell phone and
swiping constantly.

"We seem to have different definitions of paradise, so I'll take your
word for it." He loosened the collar on his dress shirt, unbuttoning a
couple of buttons for air. It was the first time he'd been on location since
his short-lived FBI series *Special Agent Leo Steel* was canceled at the
network. His work for both of his paranormal series, *Holy Ghost* and
Our Strange, Strange World, was all done in various studios somewhere
in Burbank. Even his cameo appearances on various sitcoms were done
on soundstages. Wardrobe provided everything he wore, did his makeup
and hair, and pampered him with snacks and ice cold water.

"What did you bring to eat?" Tom asked.

"What?" Spencer looked in the rearview mirror.

"Food? What did you pack for us to eat?"

"I didn't pack anything. You didn't tell me to pack anything."

Tom leaned forward and looked at Moira.

"I've got some Funyuns in my bag." She started digging through her
bag and pulling things out.

"Funyuns? Are you shitting me?"

"What? It's not even lunchtime. Why would we pack food?"

"It's a fucking shoot, isn't it? I can't perform on an empty stomach,
with parched lips. Shit."

Spencer sighed a little too overdramatically for Tom's taste. "Look, Grandpa. We're almost there, I'm sure there's a gas station or a burger joint there at the Wapak exit. We'll get whatever you need there."

A gas station? Eat at a goddamn gas station? Tom thought. *Jesus. How the mighty have fallen. Is this what happens when stars lose their shine? They eat gas station food on location?*

They drove in silence for another half hour with the two in the front seat mumbling and laughing until Spencer said, "Hey, Grandpa? When you planned this, you checked the forecast, right? Those shots of you outside with the jets and stuff need some natural light, but I'm seeing a few drops of rain hit the windshield."

"We'll just film inside. It's not a big deal." On the old show they never let something like rain ruin the schedule. They improvised. He focused on the script, researching the area around their shoot, googling facts about the Neil Armstrong and the Space Museum in Wapakoneta.

"So, this museum is haunted?" Moira asked. "That's pretty cool."

Now he was getting creative notes from the lighting girl? Great. "No, the place isn't haunted as far as I know."

"Then why are we shooting there? You said this web series was paranormal, right? Don't you want a place with a potential for a ghost sighting?" Spencer asked.

"This is just proof of concept stuff; we'll shoot the episode intros here for the effect and feel of things. Trust me." The rain drops started hitting the windows and Tom watched the cornfields that lined miles and miles of Interstate 75. Occasionally the scenery was disrupted by a field of cows, but not much else.

It was a strain to remember the last time he'd seen an actual cow up close. After he got a few high-profile jobs in the sixties, Tom bought a house near Burbank and moved there permanently. He was close to Studio City, far enough from the wildfires, and could drive to every audition his agent could get him. He didn't go home for holidays, his family came to him, it was California for God's sake. Once he landed the part on *Savage Galaxy*, he couldn't have gone home if he wanted to. He was way too busy. Sci-fi conventions with lines of geeks out the door kept him traveling around the country when he wasn't shooting, and, of course, he had his books to write. The memoir sold well, the sci-fi novels were at the top of the charts and optioned for a series on Fox. But that was years ago.

"I'm guessing that's it?" Spencer said.

On the right side of the highway, a huge white half sphere sat nestled in a white frame.

Moira laughed. "Looks like a giant boob."

"That's the moon, you dolts." Tom shook his head to clear his mind. A studio in Burbank to this.

"It does look like a boob, Grandpa," Spencer said.

"Can you stop with the 'Grandpa' crap? Maybe just call me Tom?"

They did stop at a filling station where Spencer gassed up while Moira searched for food and drinks inside. Nearby, the breakfast crowds were still filtering through the drive-throughs at the fast food restaurants, traffic disappeared down the nearby exit ramps. While he waited, Tom juggled titles for the web series and tried to come up with a catch-phrase for the endeavor.

The Midnight Hour was taken, which was too bad, because he liked that idea a lot. Would *Twilight Stories* be too derivative of *The Twilight Zone*? *Mysteries from Beyond Space and Time* was a mouthful, but maybe just *From Beyond Space*? Or only *From Beyond*? As he thought of that as a title he could feel his legs tingle like they'd fallen asleep. Sitting in the car, probably. He opened the door and stood up next to the pumps. Spencer was gone and Moira hadn't returned. Gas fumes assaulted Tom's nostrils as he stretched his legs. "Ugh." He covered his nose and moved back toward his door, not willing to stand in the stench. The flapping of the receipt at the pump caught his attention, as it was nearly the only sound on the chilly morning.

The lights on the pump flickered and the numbers faded until they were dark. Tom scanned the other pumps and the convenience store, looking for an outage, but everything else seemed fine. With a mechanical grinding sound, lights came on around the gas receipt. After some whirring and clicking, the receipt started printing again, inching out bit by bit. It seemed to speed up as it went, printing and spewing out paper until the end hit the ground and began to form a pile on the concrete step below.

Tom grabbed the paper mid-stream and tore it off. Repeated over and over for half of the ream of flimsy paper was the gas station's standard signature "Thank you for using PetrolUnited. Make sure to come back soon." But as the printing continued, the ink began to run low and printed fewer and fewer of the words until toward the middle it only repeated "you. come back" for a dozen lines or so. After that, it was only some sort of error code all the way to the end.

"What do you have there?" Spencer asked as he and Moira came from around the pump.

With a shrug, Tom held up the long strip of paper. "The computer crashed, I guess. Spit out a bunch of nonsense."

"We got you a chicken sandwich," Moira didn't even look at the paper Tom held out. "Hope that works for your dietary needs."

At least Spencer glanced at it before moving to the driver's side door. "Entrance to the museum parking lot is right over there. Let's get going so we can get this over with, *Tom*."

The lot was nearly empty. The group sat in the car, forced to eat there by the pissy rain that refused to end. Tom realized he'd tossed the rope of a receipt on the seat next to him. He glanced at it, not interested in forcing a conversation with the other two. From that angle, something about the gibberish error code caught his eye and he slowly picked it up. Turned on its side, the numbers and letters formed a pattern that repeated half a dozen times. Tom pulled out his reading glasses and looked closer.

"Shit," Tom said. "This looks like the logo for the Coalition of Galaxies." He waved it at the two in the front seats.

"The what?" Spencer's mouth was full and dripped catsup.

"The Coalition. You know, from my show?" Tom traced the swoop as it formed from the paper. "It's on all of the merchandise, the movie posters."

Spencer shrugged as he looked at it.

Moira said, "Gibberish."

3

The rain slowed to a sprinkle outside, so Tom tossed the last of his food back into the bag with a resignation he hadn't felt in years. "Let's just get this over with." He hoped Spencer could get some good footage and was half as good at it as he claimed. At least it would be something.

They walked in the morning gloom past the jet fighter and space capsules on display by the parking lot with a little more than a glance. Moira stopped and giggled as she took a picture of the enormous façade of the moon that made up the museum's exterior, but otherwise, everyone seemed happy to get out of the rain.

The ticket taker recognized Tom. "Holy shit. You're Admiral Jack Bracken. What are you doing here? I wasn't told you would be coming." His lanyard of identifications and keys sported a button with the Coalition logo on it.

"I just dropped in to take a tour and maybe get some pictures and a little video." Tom affixed the smile, the one that he used at all of the sci-fi cons, the photo ops, the press conferences when the old show grew another year older. It was his toothpaste smile, from a commercial he'd done in the sixties, and he could hear the *ding* they added when the light caught his teeth, he could smell the mint. It was Pavlovian by now.

"It was over thirty years ago, but I'm still pissed they canceled your show. It was so tragic."

"Thanks."

"And the cliffhanger at the end of the last episode where everyone had been mind-controlled except for your character? Ugh. That was sad. I wish you could have shot the next episode to resolve it."

Tom nodded. "But then, what would we be speculating about at cons today, right? All those panels, all those theories." Tom knew, of course, that he'd prevail and save everyone, somehow. No matter how bleak it got, no matter how improbable, Jack Bracken came through.

The ticket taker, Jerry or Jeremy, led them through the hall to the main exhibits, and in a room with the moon rock, something clicked and Tom nodded. "This is it. Let's just film here. The rock will be a good background." He pulled some masking tape out of his suit jacket so he could tag the floor for his mark and the best spot for the camera.

As he knelt, a glare suddenly hit his face. "Jesus, girl." Tom shielded his eyes from the harsh light that suddenly flashed on. "Maybe point that thing away from my face?"

The light faded, and when Tom looked up again, the others looked confused.

"She hasn't even turned it on yet," Spencer said. "And it's pretty weak, anyway. It's just a selfie ring that runs on a couple of double A batteries."

The light was still there, but weaker when he found it again. "There. Something is glaring off that display case over there. The one with the moon rock in it."

His sorry excuse for a crew turned and looked at the rock and the area beyond. "There's no light over there, either."

Tom pointed and walked toward the case. "Here, right here. You don't see that? None of you see that?" Tom looked at the museum employees that had begun to follow him around. He got close enough that he put his finger on the plexiglass case, directly where the yellow-blue illumination was brighter. "Right fucking here."

"Please, Mr. Hart. Could you keep your voice down?" One of the museum's employees said. "And please don't touch the display cases."

"Grandpa?" Spencer was looking around at the few other patrons who'd stopped to stare. "Maybe we need a break?"

"A break? We haven't even started." The light on the moon rock seemed to pulse, with the colors growing bolder and then fading. He stared at it and then looked around the room to see if he could find the light that caused a reflection.

"Yeah, but the drive was a little long, you've barely eaten."

"Maybe you would be more comfortable in another area of the museum with fewer people in it?" Jerry or Jeremy said. He looked sad to ask Tom for the favor.

"This is ridiculous. I'm a professional entertainer. I can do this without anyone treating me like a child." He pointed to Spencer and Moira, then their equipment. "Just get that stuff ready and we'll do it with my back to the rock display. That way the damn glare won't screw me up." He stomped around the display until he found an angle that didn't present a problem and planted his feet. "Here. This will work." He straightened his jacket and smoothed his lapels.

"Okay." Spencer shifted his position and reset the tripod, directing Moira to the best position for lighting and the microphone. Tom saw her make a goofy face at Spencer, which elicited a smile from both of them. "I'll give you a countdown from three and then point when you can start, all right?"

"I've done this before, thank you." He'd mulled over some script ideas on the way down, but decided to just wing it rather than write it down. Tom had done so many of these intros that they just came out on auto-pilot at this point.

"This is just the intro, right? We're just doing the short intro?" Spencer asked.

The answer was an exaggerated nod and a wave of Tom's hand.

"Okay." Moira's lights came on, dim, subdued. "Let's do it," she said.

With a deep breath, Tom said, "Here we go. First take, introduction. In three...two...one." He pointed dramatically at Tom.

Tom's mind went blank.

"Grandpa?"

"I got it. I got it. Give me the countdown again."

"Okay? "Here we go. Introduction, take two. In three...two...one."

"Welcome again, my fellow...world...travelers. I'm glad we could get together again for more...adventures through life. This is *Haunted Space*, and I'm your host..." Tom paused, distracted by something moving nearby. It was a mother and her child staring at the rock nearby. "Cut. Stop." He waved for Spencer and Moira to stop and walked over to the family.

"We're trying to work over here."

The woman seemed surprised, and put her hand on her boy's shoulder to pull him back a little. "We just wanted to see the moon rock."

Tom leaned down closer to the boy. "Oh, you want to see the rock? Well, I'd like to finish this so I can go see a glass of scotch. Which sounds more important to you?"

Spencer's hand was on Tom's shoulder, pulling him back.

"There's no need for this, Grandpa. It's a public space, okay?" Spencer turned away and half-shouted to the boy and his mother, "I'm sorry ma'am."

"Don't treat me like a child, Spencer."

When they were farther away from the mother and son, Spencer said, "*Shit*, Grandpa. You're a step away from being the creepy old man yelling at kids to get off his lawn."

"Less than a step." Moira flipped the light off and on a nearby handrail, giving Tom the stink-eye.

"And for the love of Christ, stop calling me 'Grandpa.' I've told you that."

"You have to chill out," Spencer said. "Are you sure you don't want to take a moment to write down or practice this?"

Amateurs. Giving him advice? Tom's hands felt heavy suddenly, thick. His muscles always got tight when his blood pressure shot up too quickly.

"Let's do it again, okay?" He looked around to make sure the distracting family had wandered away and the rest of the area was clear. He looked at the moon rock as he composed himself. It was a large sandy-looking chunk of the Earth's satellite, with pockmarks and ridges all the way around. It wasn't circular or oval, more of a free-form shape that defied Tom's ability to place in a category.

Deep within one of the small craters, something moved slightly. Tom leaned closer. His face was nearly up against the barrier around the exhibit. This time it wasn't a trick of the light, or an errant reflection; something moved. But what? How could anything be in there? Surely the air was thin in the sealed exhibit.

Moira arrived by Tom first. "What's wrong. What's so interesting over here"

"Something moved inside this hole in the rock." He pointed uselessly, as there was no way to get close enough to really show where it had appeared.

"Yeah." Moira turned and headed back to where Spencer was waiting by the camera.

"Wait, just look. Grab your light and shine it in there."

"Grandpa..."

His patience was low, but Tom pulled himself together. "Just let me see this and we'll do the intro. Just..."

Light in tow, Moira stepped over to the moon rock and flipped it on.

As the light hit the rock, Tom could feel the case shake, hear the grind of metal and concrete as the ground beneath him shifted. He looked deep into the depths of the unearthly rock and, for a fading second, something stared back. The eyes, all he saw were eyes, blue and black with flecks of the cosmos twinkling around the iris. The didn't blink and none of them closed.

Tom lost his balance and fell to his knees as the floor shifted. Tears welled in his eyes at what he had seen. All the eyes upon him, staring, curious. It was what he'd chased his whole career, an audience that watched his every move. They weren't fickle, like fans, or judgmental like critics, they stared in acceptance.

Moira was at his side immediately, and Spencer joined after. "Are you okay? Let me help you up."

His breathing was labored, but he found the air to speak, "Are you two okay? Don't worry about me. I'm fine."

"Why wouldn't we be? You're the one who fell."

He allowed himself to be helped up, and looked around. Nothing was disturbed, no cracks in the floor, no busted glass or broken exhibits. "But...the shaking. The floor rumbled. I thought it was an earthquake or something."

The museum guide took Spencer aside, but Tom could hear what he was saying. He was concerned that they could be blamed for Tom's falling, and worried for their liability.

Spencer assured him that they were leaving very soon.

He turned from the employee and looked at Tom. "Look. "Let's grab a drink, go outside, get a little fresh air, and maybe regroup on this whole thing. I mean, I'm worried about you. You're acting a little...I don't know...off?"

"Look, I swear I'm fine. I swear." Tom could feel sweat rolling down both sides of his face. "This stuff is just reminding me of the old show. I don't know why, it just is." He pointed at the rock nearby. "The eyes I just saw, they were like something out of season two, episode four, 'Eyes of Refalon.' There were these monsters in the forest...same eyes. Right? So it's just something triggering my memories. I haven't thought about them in years. It's fine." He gazed back at the moon rock, feeling cold without the gaze coming from inside that had warmed him, made him feel complete. The rock was only a few feet above him, yet it felt like it was in another galaxy.

"I loved that episode," Jerry the ticket taker said quietly.

"That's not normal," Moira said. "Telling us that your memories are sneaking up on you is not making us think this is normal."

The rock glimmered in the light and Tom traced his finger down the display as he watched.

"Sir, you really shouldn't touch the display," Jerry said.

Tom waved him off and leaned closer to the thick case. The new position brought new details into focus. The simple rock was dotted with pinprick holes and hidden craters that vanished into the bumpy surface. The pocked surface twinkled with silvery dust that blew across the surface of the dark object. Where the winds came from that moved the dust, Tom didn't know, but he could hear the sounds clearly.

"Sir..." the employee began again.

Tom heard him like he was far away, like the man was standing in another room. Hard to hear over the winds that swept the surface of the tiny piece of outer space inside the glass. Gusts that gathered until he heard it as one long shout for him. One long gasp that seemed to form his very own name.

"Grandpa?" Spencer was suddenly at his side. "Maybe you should sit down somewhere?"

"How many people look at this rock?" There was a pain in Tom's chest, and his breathing felt funny.

"What?" Spencer asked. His voice seemed just as distant as the museum employee.

"The damn rock. How many people come to see it?"

Spencer looked at Moira and she shrugged.

When they looked at the curator, he squinted in thought. "I mean, somewhere around forty thousand people come here a year. I'm assuming they all look at the rock at some point."

Tom braced himself against the case as his chest felt like a vise was closing around it. His last series on television hadn't even attracted forty thousand viewers.

"Someone call nine-one-one," Moira shouted. "I think he's having a heart attack." She stepped back and scanned the room, looking worried that no one was actually listening to her, or maybe not even taking her seriously.

It took a few seconds for Tom to realize he was on the floor looking up at the lights in the museum's ceiling. Out of the corner of his eye, he could see the museum staff scurrying to get people away. The curator, Tom's fan among the staff, stood frozen in place, with only his head turning back and forth to see who was helping. The visitors moved away, with only a couple curious enough to look back.

"Help's on the way, Grandpa." The ceiling lights were blocked suddenly by Spencer's terrified face looking down. Is there anything I can do? Is this a heart attack? What do I say to the medics?"

The pain in his chest began to restrict his breathing and it felt like someone was sitting on him. "You should film this," Tom said. "Maybe the tabloids would pay you something for it."

"What?" Spencer leaned away. "That's nuts."

With a clear line of sight again, Tom could see the case and barely make out the edge of the tiny moon rock. It glittered in the dense lighting, winking at him like the stars themselves.

As the pain became too much to fight off, Tom closed his eyes with sparkling lights blinding him.

After what seemed like a second, or an eternity, Tom opened his eyes in time to see the paramedics working on a body that looked so much like his own. He tried to stand up, but found he had no legs. He tried to look at his hands, but had none.

Tom turned around and looked at the museum displays on the wall, and the signs on all sides of him. He could make out Spencer's camera in the distance, and Moira standing off to the side with her hands over her mouth.

Somehow he was right where the rock had been enclosed in the tall case. When he turned again, he discovered he could see from multiple pinholes at once. And the more he concentrated, he realized he could see from all of the holes at once. His vision wasn't limited to two eyes in the sense he'd grown accustomed, he could see everything, he could see everywhere. And at times, he could close all of the eyes and just listen to the hum of the cosmos. The winds that had drawn him closer, now whispered his name as they slowly swept across the surface. When he opened his eyes again, he could see each particle of dust as it made its way around him, and he never moved.

"Hello?" His shout seemed to bounce around in the small space. Tom felt both cramped and free at the same time. There was infinite room to move, but as he tried, he couldn't reach the side of the case. He was as small as the moon rock, and yet there was nothing containing him.

"Help me," he bellowed.

A few feet away, his body was hoisted onto a stretcher and ushered out of the room. He tried to shout at Spencer and Moira but his voice was muffled, low, maybe even in his own head. His grandson and Moira followed close behind the paramedics, shoving their way past displays and the few onlookers who were stuck in the building waiting. Tom worried that the two of them looked afraid for what was happening, and wished he could figure a way to shout to them and show them where he was. He was feeling no pain at that point, and wanted them to know.

The small boy from earlier broke from the crowd and ran over to the moon rock display and stared. Tom was sure the kid could see him. He was just a few feet away. The closer the boy got, the more the sparkles of the rock reacted with the light, making copies of the boy's face until it seemed like a hundred clones of the boy were staring. It made Tom dizzy to look at, to try to process all the images of the boy coming at his at once.

"Sean?" The boy's mom, a hundred of her, got closer and grabbed the boy's arm to pull him away.

Tom watched them go, and felt a twinge of loneliness as they vanished into the hall. The room around him grew dark and his tried to focus on the exhibits to keep from panicking at the encroaching noth-ingness around him. He desperately hoped tomorrow would bring fresh eyes and new fans. There would be festivals every year. News stories about the space program would all surely come here to film. He would go on season after season. No one could ever give Tom notes again. And he would never be cancelled.

Never.

NAVIGATION BY STARLIGHT

Steven Saus

I f there's one nice thing about rural Ohio, it's that you can get sorta lost pretty easily, driving around back there on the state routes. Because sometimes you want to get sorta lost and pull up a streaming emo station on your phone and not worry too much about your eyes getting blurry from the tears, 'cause not much happens out on these straight bits of two-lane, edged by farmland and dotted with tiny towns.

Sure, there's the normal son of a bitch with those blue LED high beams every so often. The occasional deer here or possum there to avoid. But for the most part, you can just drive long stretches without having to think.

You remember, on an earlier, happier drive, telling them these towns look like they could have been airlifted off an old movie set. You remember them laughing at the idea. You remember and almost forget for a second that they're not there with you, until the second is over, and it hits you again in the center of your chest. The single stoplight in these small little towns—it seems like they all have a single pointless stoplight —gives you a chance to skip that song that's *their* song and shove the swelling choking feeling back down your throat without worrying about going off the road and hitting a power pole. Least, not yet. Not yet. Not on accident, anyway.

Nobody's judging. We've all had those thoughts. Those impulses. Those of us who know the answer to "How will I know if it's really love?". Those of us who found out knowing the answer doesn't always matter. We know.

Enough of that, put that thought back away, the light's green, and the guy outside the bar, the smoke from his cigarette pooling under the brim of his faded red MAGA hat, is staring at you and that's the last thing you need. You manage to hold it together, to not cry until you're back outside of town, back in the fifty mile per hour areas where signs along winter-fallowed fields proclaim what brand of soybean was grown there last summer.

It is the grey season: blue-shifted evening light fights its way through gossamer sheers of cloud; desiccated, desaturated leaves still hang lifeless and black on the trees, night racing up from the west in the rearview mirror. Your headlights, when you flick them on, inject a warm yellow light into the grayscale outside, flickering slightly as your heater cycles, just a little too high.

Its air does not warm your arm the way they used to, their body snuggled up against you. *They* would have made up something funny about red-hat guy, some story about why he was waiting outside a bar in early December, or maybe told you about something that happened last week, or maybe just leaned against you in silence, watching the night sky as you drove.

You realize now how you set yourself up for this. How you didn't stop and think that after all that time together, your comforts, your patterns, are all tied up with memories of *them* now. It's okay. It's okay. We've all done it. Found ourselves doing things that remind us of being together, driving down the same streets, going to the same stores. You've found yourself driving—by habit, of course it's just habit—to their place after work instead of your own.

Maybe you're torturing yourself. Or maybe you—we—just want to be close to *them* again. To that feeling again. That feeling of being "home," of being in the right place no matter where you were, from the fucking moment you met them, and yes, you're aware of how corny that sounds, and...

Like I said. We've all done it. Had to pull over because you can't even see the dash through your tears. Wait for the choking sobs to come, then pass, then come back again when another one of *their* songs comes up on the station and you scream out the desperation and frustration and pain and throw your phone across the car; shocked out of it by the sudden quiet and fear that you actually broke your phone this time.

After a brief scramble through the clutter that's accumulated, you retrieve your mobile, hit the power button. You let your breath out at the phone's annoyingly cheerful branded startup tone.

That's when you hear it, now that the music isn't anything you're streaming. It's just barely audible over the car's idle, just barely penetrating the fogging windows. A drum beat from outside the car. From out in the cold dark. Quiet, but clear.

For a second, you teeter on decision's edge; the soft near-numbness of driving back or the desperate need for distraction, of something, fucking anything else to think about.

The air is just the wrong side of cold, damp enough to carry a hint of decay. It floods into your car when you open the door and get out.

You're between tiny towns. Most of the land is flattish fields with a few small rises that barely qualify as hills. There is a farmhouse behind you, but the drumming, that's ahead. You're pretty sure it's coming from up on the small hill in front of you, a dark raised mole in the midst of farmland, covered with uncleared brush and bramble and trees. The drumbeat is deep and low, a vibrating bass *thumpthudthumpthud*, a rhythm the speed of a heartbeat. You raise your hand to your eyes, shielding them from your own headlights, and try to peer through the dark tree trunks in the hilltop grove.

You're pretty sure you see people moving up there.

The cheap binoculars in the glovebox are practically a kid's toy. You hadn't cared when you bought them. The "weekend camping birding expedition" they were for had less to do with looking for birds than an excuse for the two of you to get away from everything else, to focus on exploring each other. But the binoculars work. Even in the failing light they're enough to see the motion between the trees. To see the people. To see them dancing in a circle in that small patch of woods.

It takes a moment to be certain of what you're seeing. To try to focus the crappy binoculars.

It takes just long enough for a fire to snap into existence on top of that hill.

Long enough for you to make out the leather breeches and decorated ponchos against the chill air as the figures dance with the drumbeat on top of that hill.

And then you get it in focus, and see *their* face, see *them* dancing on top of that hill.

You're yelling *their* name in a reflex of longing before your mind starts to catch up. Even though you don't have the binoculars up, you swear *they* lock eyes with you before the fire goes out.

And then there is no light, no motion on the hill at all.

It takes a cold half hour to ascend, fighting your way through bramble and brush.

There is no fire pit. No sign of anything burning. No sign of people, no sign of *them*. Just a large worn circle at the top of the hill. Your thorn-scratched and scraped arms swear there is no path up to the circle, no way the dancers could have taken off so quickly without you seeing them. Without leaving some kind of evidence.

But *they* were here. You can smell *them*. It sounds strange to think it, but we know what you mean. Their scent. Not a bad thing, not a gross thing, it's just *their* scent, the one you could smell in *their* room, the one on you after you made love, the scent that told your hindbrain you were home. We understand.

You feel as empty as the sky on the long drive back to the interstate.

You feel as empty as the new apartment you refuse to think of as home.

You don't really want to, but your friends encourage you to go out again with the latest match on the Tinder account they made for you. You have to work to remember the name; you've saved it under "PeerPressure" on your phone. You are slightly surprised PeerPressure agreed to a second one after you spent most of the first date talking—indirectly, at least—about *them*, about how much you missed *them*, instead of, well, anything else.

It is fine, again. Dinner is okay, though your mind is out in the dark, on the highway. There's nothing wrong with PeerPressure—your matchmaking friends did a decent job of screening out the weirdos and crazies from the online dating scene. Your date knows you're rebounding, and swears they're okay with it.

You still don't share with PeerPressure that you're going to scroll your ex's (the term squirms hatefully in your mind) social media when you excuse yourself to the bathroom.

They haven't blocked you, just unfriended you, which is somehow worse. Your friends have tried to tell you that you're just seeing the curated happy face *they* present to the public world. Your friends try to tell you that's just how social media is. You know better. You know *them* better than that. That's how *they* really are. Happy. Just fine. Without you.

PeerPressure does not mention the red in your eyes when you come back to the table. Your date is that type of nice and kind, checking all the boxes you thought you wanted, so you let the date go longer than you originally anticipated. You actually laugh a few times, and then it's getting late, and the thought of that empty apartment is more than you can really deal with, so you take them back with you, and they check all the boxes you thought you wanted there, too.

And yet you fall asleep in your date's arms and dream of your ex dancing in the cold starlight on that small hill.

———

The online video explains, step by step, how to find location history on your phone. How to find out where you've been at any point recently. How to diagnose location data corruption from a sudden power loss due to, say, hurling your phone across a car.

———

If there's one awful thing about rural Ohio, it's that you can get sorta lost driving around back there on the state routes, where half-remembered soybean signs all blur together and all small hills look pretty much the same.

Your date from the other night texts again, you swipe the notification away unread. The emptiness inside you is hard; neither the cold wind from the half-open window or the billowing warmth from the heater penetrates inside, to the real you. In that cavern it is quiet, dark, always sixty-eight degrees, and empty. So empty.

You try to keep it that way, try to ignore the little bit of hope with each hill so you don't have to feel it drain away as you go past.

You almost miss it on the seventh night, distracted by the unusual aurora this far south. Then there's a sudden spark in the rearview and you skid to a stop on the dirt shoulder. It's a week closer to Christmas; the distant farmhouse has disguised itself by vomited gaudy electric decorations across its large lawn. But there, you're sure you see it. Just the spark of a small fire, the distant deep drumbeat, and—you're sure— your ex. Of *them*.

Pin dropped in the maps app, car off, toy binoculars on their strap thumping your chest with each footstep across fallow fields, all falling in time to the rhythm of the drumming. You only stop to look when you reach the edge of thicket and brush at the bottom of the hill.

Makeup distorts the dozen dancer's faces; draws cheekbones into sharp glacial valleys, sinks eyes into caves, but you know *them*. Not like easily confused facial recognition with a photograph, but *them*. The reality behind the appearance. The way it feels when it's close enough to yours that the hair on your skin touches *theirs*. The way *their* pupils used to dilate when *they* looked at you, the connection between your eyes and minds and bodies that you used to think was just another stupid toxic rom-com trope until you felt it yourself. Until you met *them*.

That look is not the look *they* have now, when your lips break your quiet vigil with the whisper of *their* name—a whisper no one should have been able to hear.

But they did.

Startled, spooked like deer, the drumbeat and dancers stop statue-still.

Fast—too fast, too damn fast as you push through the brush, rush up the hill, feel your coat tear—the fire is out, the dancers gone, no drum to accompany your wailing cursing at the empty clearing and darkened night sky.

Your ex does not answer the phone or texts, but PeerPressure does, and does not ask anything when they arrive, putting the questions aside at the sight of your tears and just holding you like you ask until the next morning.

PeerPressure asks all the questions over breakfast.

They are not happy with your answers.

You think it happened while you were in the shower.

It's supposed to be just a quick check of *their* socials after cleaning off and getting dressed. But it's gone. All of *their* social media has just...disappeared.

Part of you knows. Part of you has been expecting, dreading this moment. But that can't be right. The accounts must have been hacked, compromised in some way. It happens all the time. Ransomware, virtual blackmail, that sort of thing, right? Figures the first thing an attacker like that would do is cut you off from your contacts. From the people important to you. *They* might not even know the accounts are hacked yet, passwords compromised. You need to make sure that's not what happened. It's not about what you want—you have an obligation.

It's only a few minutes on your laptop to make some fake accounts, to check.

To find out it's just you that's blocked.

You text *them*—you don't call, see, you're showing restraint, being calm and rational. Surely it was a mistake. A misunderstanding of something, misreading why you keep liking all of *their* posts or something, there's no need to do anything drastic, just reply whenever you get a chance.

You check again with your fake accounts, looking over the posts that aren't friend-locked. The friend requests from your fake accounts go unanswered.

Friends and family you normally don't hear from start "checking in." It reminds you of the deluge of auto-prompted birthday wishes social media pulls out of the woodwork every year, more phone calls and texts and messages than you've gotten in months, and you start to worry that you'll miss *their* reply among the noise.

Your fingers learn the pattern quickly: I'm fine, I have plans tonight, thanks for checking in.

From their sudden questioning concern you realize that PeerPressure—you probably don't have to worry about changing the contact name any longer—must have told someone your answers to the questions asked over runny eggs and slightly-burnt toast. But they're getting the story wrong, twisted your reasons, making them sound unreasonable. They're misunderstanding.

Of course. Of course, it's a miscommunication. How can you communicate that feeling, that longing, that **pull** of real love? You would not have understood either, not before *them*. You **didn't** understand, back then. You were one of the "reasonable" ones too, texting platitudes about fish in the sea and bullets dodged.

But that was before.

Before you experienced it. Before you felt the swell of love every time you even saw *their* picture. Before you knew where home was. Before you knew where you belonged.

Before the hard empty aching gulf in your chest.

We know. We understand.

You read the latest notification as you swipe it away: "Feel your feelings, but you don't have to act on them." Their advice is interchangeable, rote. You know it all already. You know that it doesn't apply. This is **different**. They don't understand what's at stake. How colorless, how bland, how *cold* their advice is, blissfully ignorant of how passionless their own relationships are.

You sit on your bed, covers warm around your shoulders. You scroll through your gallery, through the pictures of the two of you together, waiting for *them* to reply.

Waiting for evening to come.

Clear up the misunderstanding. That's what has to happen.

It's all just misunderstandings. The breakup, the blocking, it's nothing more than a miscommunication, obviously. *They* kept telling you that text messages are breeding grounds for misunderstandings. There's no substitute for face to face communication, *they* said. You aren't going to just show up at work or the house like a creeper. You just want to talk. Face to face, so there's no miscommunication. We get it. You're doing the right thing. The thing *they* would want you to do.

The trees and brush on the hilltop do nothing to stop the cold air from wicking up the back of your coat and licking your spine as the sun sets in a brief flush of reds and orange. You are far enough back that you're hidden in the brush, barely able to make out the circle of trampled grasses worn down before by the dancer's feet.

With no clouds overhead, stars slowly appear in the darkening sky, the air going from chilly to cold under their hard light. You think you wiggle your toes and fingers; they're cold enough that you are not entirely certain. There is no moon tonight, but the aurora has returned. The slight light of the distant tacky farmhouse decorations blinking— red, green, red, green—echoes the shimmering glow overhead until even those small electric lights go out, leaving only the spectral glow of the aurora overhead.

And twelve stars detach themselves from the aurora and the vault of the sky.

You forget the cold as the twelve descend in gentle spirals to the ground. They dim as they descend, allowing you to make out limbs and heads. To see the intricate beadwork on headbands and belts, faces decorated with traditional paints and dyes, the way the Shawnee did before your ancestors ever set foot on this land.

Their luminescence fades further as they come closer to the ground, until you are able to see not just the paints, but the faces beneath.

You hold your hand tight over your mouth as you see *them*, as your lips form *their* name.

One of the twelve—you do not see which one, you're just looking at *them*, at *their* face—gestures, and in an instant the fire swells from the ground.

As moccasin-clad feet touch the ground, the twelve move together.

They dance.

The hill is the drum, footfalls echoing resonating through layers of mud and clay and stone.

They dance.

The trees are their arms, swaying, unburdened by the leaves of summer, energy focused inward.

They dance.

Their dance is the silent swirl of the planet through space, the shifting experience of the inexorable passage of time.

They dance, and *they* dance, and *they* dance past you, past you, past you again.

They are so close, so close, so clear in the firelight. You can almost touch *them*. Then—if you did—then it would be like one of the movies *they* love, where the music swells at the climatic reconciliation, so you know it's the right thing to do and you're doing it before you even really realize that you'd already decided and this is the time this is when the music swells—

There is no music when your gaze meets *theirs*, as all the dancers stop.

The sudden silence shatters the expectation in your mind.

Which is why you see that recognition does not lead to relaxation.

Why you see the sudden stiffness in their shoulders.

Why, instead of the deep connection you expected, you only see the quiet fear in *their* eyes.

Fearful of what *they* see.

Fearful of you.

The ground is hard on your knees as realizations crumble the emotionally load-bearing empty space inside you.

As quick and silent as it was lit, the others extinguish the fire. Without a word, the dancers begin to climb the long silent stairs of air. *They* ascend, growing brighter and brighter as they rise. As *they* get further away from you.

You watch until they are just dots of light, twinkling through atmosphere and tears.

You knew *they* would not look back. But you had to watch anyway.

We know.

But it is a long way home, and you are no longer sure you can find your way.

Author's Note: This story has at its base the Shawnee legend of Waupee (or "White Hawk") and the Star Maiden. That legend tells of Waupee abducting the youngest of twelve dancing star maidens and making her his wife. She later escapes after bearing Waupee a son, but then feels bad for Waupee and misses him, so she returns to her abductor. It is portrayed as a "happily ever after" kind of story.

http://www.bigorrin.org/archive124.htm

https://www.indigenouspeople.net/starmaid.htm

AMONG THE WOLVES

Ray Pantle

My best buddy Joel isn't bothered by the violence. He stands next to our van, feet from the bodies littering the campgrounds. His hands rest casually inside his shorts. There's a detached, clinical look on his face, the same one he had during our night shifts in the ER, before the government fell six months ago and the rebels seized most of the food.

Stepping over the dead, Joel nears a life-sized statue of some fertility goddess. I could almost see the dead hippies, alive and dancing joyfully around the stone figure. Now, dried blood covers her swollen, earth-shaped womb. Her head has been severed clean above the neck.

Joel peers at the stone head at its feet. "Welcome to Starwood," he says, the name of the renowned New Age festival that was held on these campgrounds, according to the highway signs we'd seen while driving along I-70 earlier in the day. "So much for peace and love, huh Seth?"

I can't speak. The stench wafting up sends nausea roiling through my gut, and all I can do is stare at the dozens of slain women and men in hemp bracelets and flowing shirts, bloated and rotting in the heat. Those who would have peacefully handed over their food, butchered by rebel scum.

Joel swats at a fly buzzing by his ear. His gaze shifts beyond the bodies and van to the thicket of woods. A crow shrieks from somewhere in the distance. "Well, no sense wasting time. Let's set up camp, bathe in the lake, get a fire going."

"Seriously?" I ask. "You want to stay?"

"Yeah," he says. "What's the problem?"

"There's no point now. Everyone's dead."

"Meaning any food left here is up for grabs, and we'd be idiots to pass it up. And I'm sure some of these folks have insulin on them."

I reach into my pocket to feel my glass vial. Last I checked, there was only enough insulin to last me a week, meaning we need to find a replacement soon.

"You said it yourself," Joel continues. "There are no pharmacies and stores left to raid, not with rebels guarding them, and we can't keep busting into homes hoping no one's there. So far, we've been lucky. Eventually, we'll get a bullet in the head."

"But the rebels would have taken the food. Or they haven't yet, meaning they're still here."

"Hold up," Joel says. He squats at the base of the goddess shrine, where the corpse of a portly old greybeard lies on his back, his neck blown up like a microwaved sausage. Joel studies the large gash in the man's skull, lifts his shirt, and turns him sideways, examining the blackened flesh.

"No bullet holes," he notes under his breath. Then he circles around to repeat the process with other corpses. Finally, Joel straightens his legs and wipes grass from his knees.

"The rebels aren't here. They never were."

"What are you talking about?" I gesture to the bodies. "Look at them."

"I have. Rebels use guns, not rocks and fists. This was an inside job. These hippies, they did each other in."

I roll my eyes. "Here we go again."

"It makes total sense. They come here for the festival six months ago, the shit hits the fan, they catch news of it on their phones and decide it best to stay put, hide from the rebels, ride it out. But with a bunch of people, all living here for months, knowing their rations will eventually run out, they get paranoid. Time goes on, they steal from each other, form rival groups. One thing leads to another, and violence breaks out."

Joel bends to lift the goddess head. He grips it in both hands and extends his arms to show me. A smug, self-satisfied grin oils over his lips.

"There, Seth. There's your proof. Everyone for themselves, like I always told you."

We fling back the flap and enter the first of the tents. Piles of clothes are strewn on the floor. A makeshift altar fills one corner, topped with two stones with the words "hope" and "peace" painted on them. The skunky fragrance of weed clings to the air, along with patchouli and sandals ripe with feet.

"Check under the mattress," Joel says. Grabbing a knapsack, he dumps out its contents and sifts through the clattering mess. Finding nothing in the way of food, we move on to the next tent.

A dead woman's inside this one. She's young, dreadlocked, with a dove tattoo and a deep gash across her neck. My insides twist, and I recoil back, gagging from the fetid odor trapped in the space.

Joel squats down and roots through her pockets. "Bingo," he says, brandishing a cigarette pack and a protein bar.

We check each tent along the dirt path, every mile we walk into the campground taking us farther away from the entrance where we parked the van. At first, I'm too shaken up to do anything but watch. After ten years as a nurse, you'd think I'd be used to death, but that was different. Cancer, heart attacks, even car accidents, they're somewhat expected, part of the natural order that existed before the world as we knew it collapsed. Not rampant, avoidable, and caused by human greed.

Finally, I'm able to lend a hand, and we manage to scrape up some trail mix, one Snickers bar, and two Fruit Roll-Ups. The two of us settle under a tree, Joel tosses me the trail mix and tears into the gooey red candy. Hunger gnaws at my gut, and I'm slightly lightheaded, two warning sights that I should eat. I know the risk of going without food, any lifelong diabetic would, and especially a nurse, yet I can't bring myself to eat. Too many thoughts whirl through my head.

"Something wrong?" Joel asks, pausing to wipe sweat from his brow.

I pull my knees up to my chest. "Remember those cardboard signs awhile back? Directing survivors to that town out west?"

"Town?"

"Yeah," I say. "Near New Mexico."

"Oh, right." Smirking, he air-quotes the name for it. "Eden."

"Yeah, Eden. There are cars out there, where we first parked the van. Tanks full of gas. If we head back and fill up now, we'd be on the road before dusk. I-70 west to I-44, that puts us at Eden in about two days."

"But I like it here," Joel says. "Just the woods and the lake."

"They've got livestock and crops. And *people*, Joel." A touch of wooziness ripples through me, and I'm sweating so much I can taste salt in my mouth, yet I brush it off. "A real community, just like before."

"Nature provides," Joel says, gesturing to the woods. "We rig up branches and vines, catch some fish. No trouble for miles. Not like out there, driving around with rebels patrolling the roads."

I don't doubt Joel's survival skills. I'd seen the pictures of his stepfather Ron when he was young, his *Rambo* mullet, the orange vest loaded with tactical gear, all meanness and grit. The Ron in my memory is from decades later, when he was my patient in The Ohio State University Hospital's critical care ward, reduced to a frail husk with dementia, but I imagine that for Joel, he would always be the tough prepper who taught him that weakness wasn't an option.

A sudden, intense dizziness slams into me. My muscles weaken, and I slump forward.

Joel yells my name. Confused and panicked, pure impulse seizes me, and I reach into my pocket for my insulin. I fumble to plunge the needle into the vial, to inject myself with it, but Joel grabs my arm, emphatically shakes his head, and forces the Snickers bar into my hand.

I devour it. Then I lay back on the ground and take deep, steadying breaths. Finally, my blood sugar rises enough for my mind to function again, and I'm able to process what just occurred and the awful fate I almost met. Somehow, in my disoriented state, I forget everything I'd learned and went for the one thing that would have dropped my glucose levels fatally low and killed me.

"Thank you," I say. "Wow, that was close."

"Don't thank me," Joel says with a smirk. "It's my job, watching out for your ass. Just quit arguing, okay? No more Eden nonsense. Right here, at Starwood, is where we stay."

I hit the emergency call button. "Get a team in here, now!"

The girl in the ICU had stopped breathing. The heart monitor's green line was flattening out, delivering an earsplitting beep. Her lips turned an icy blue. I was just a student, fresh into clinicals, not ready for this. I threw panicked glances into the hall, searching for an intern or resident to rush in and take over, but moments ticked by and no one came. It was just me and the dying girl and my heart pounding in my ears.

Someone touched my arm from behind. A stable voice whispered to me, one belonging to someone else in my class.

"A game," Joel said. "Pretend it's just a game."

Something changed inside me. My beating heart slowed, and I stepped out of myself and watched the scene from above. There was no girl anymore, no daughter someone would miss, no such thing as death. Just textbooks with terms and numbers on charts and an illustration of a nurse performing CPR.

I pressed my hands against the chest. One pump. Two. Three. Four.

"That's it, Seth," Joel said. "You're doing great."

I wake in the early dawn to birds trilling outside our tent. After splitting the protein bar and some trail mix, Joel and I part ways to comb the grounds for more rations. The morning is dewy and cool, and the wind stays at rest, keeping the stench of death at bay.

For hours, I poke around sleeping bags and heave over barrels of trash that hit the ground with a boom, then sift through garbage for edible scraps, yet the search comes up empty. After laboring all day over miles of campground, my calf muscles throb, and fatigue's a mountain on my back. Finally, as dusk sweeps in, I succeed at locating a box of granola cereal and some almonds.

Night falls, and the temperature plunges. Joel and I sit outside our tent, warming ourselves by a fire while he separates our rations into two piles. It isn't much at all, just what I found and two cans of beans.

"Good work," Joel says, lighting a cigarette over the flame and taking a quick drag.

"Seriously?" I say, staring at the piles. "That's not enough to get by."

"Sure it is. We'll split the nuts now, have the rest for breakfast. Then we hit the woods for berries and shrooms and fill up on water."

"We've been running around this place for almost two days. Don't you think it's time to consider Plan B?"

"Plan B?" he says. "What, this Eden thing again?"

"I don't know." I shrug. "Maybe Eden, maybe somewhere else. Either way, somewhere with people."

He takes a long drag of his smoke and blows it out in one dramatic huff. I brace myself for an angry rant, but he grinds his cigarette into the ground and scrapes one hand through his hair, and in an instant, all irritation has been wiped away. Then he settles his gaze on the fire, his features an unsettling mask of calm.

The two of us sit before the crackling tongues of flame, hanging in the ambiguous margin dividing us. Finally, Joel's silence breaks.

"Remember going out after our board exam? That shitty bar in Clintonville? The one with the moose head on the wall?"

"Harry's Hole."

"That's the one," he says. "Boy, were we shitfaced. All the stress from studying had me wound up like hell, but boy, when I left that bar, I felt calmer than I'd been in weeks. There I was, all ready to hit the bed and crash. But it didn't happen like that, did it?"

"No," I say, the long-ago events still clear in my mind. "We went and found that dog."

"No, Seth, *you* found the dog. That mangy thing could have been rabid. It could have bitten your damn face off, but you just had to bring it with us and find where it lived."

In the shifting orange light of the flame, Joel's features take on the contours of something else, some freakish beast. The long cigarette dangling from his lips looks like a single white fang. "Because that's how you are, Seth. Always sticking your hand out to a hungry mouth."

"What's your point, Joel? That I'm a fool for what, being nice?"

"I'm saying there are other dogs out there. Out on the road. In their homes. At Eden."

He stares at me hard, his coal eyes unblinking. "See, the thing about trust is, sometimes, you get lucky. People turn out okay. But sooner or later, your luck runs out. Sooner or later, the hungry hound bites."

The woods we trek through are monstrous. Twisted branches claw at our limbs, and tree trunks loom in the shadows like crouching beasts ready to strike. Only the thinnest slivers of light filter through the strangled treetops.

When Joel stops for a piss, I use my Accu-Chek to prick my finger and test my blood. My levels register within normal range for now, but unless we locate a source of food, I'll be in real trouble by nightfall.

I stumble along the rocky slope to catch up with Joel. We forge deeper into the woods, moving farther away from the goddess shrine. Earlier we passed a used condom and a half-smoked joint discarded near a bush, but we haven't seen the slightest sign of the berries or mushrooms Joel swore would be around here.

"Where are you going?" I call out.

"Toward water. Keep heading downhill, like I already explained."

He makes a determined little sniff and presses on through the trees, whistling a tune as he trucks down a decline in the earth. We squelch through grass. Brambles scratch my bare calves. My head throbs from the relentless heat. I fire mean little kicks at stones in my way. We could have been at Eden by now. We could be gorging ourselves until we're full and sleeping on pillows under actual roofs. We could be waking up to an almost normal life, surrounded by others committed to building a stable world. But instead, we're exhausted, most likely lost, cut off from anyone who could lend us a hand, all because Joel has to act like the misanthrope his douchebag stepdad taught him to be.

"Aha!" Joel yells, pointing to the ground. A stream of water flows through underbrush and dribbles over rocks. Unscrewing our bottles, Joel stoops to fill up.

We both see the footprints at the same time. A pair of them embedded in the mud, leading up the hill. Joel's features tense, he rights himself, warily sweeps his gaze through the trees, and creeps up the incline in the direction of the tracks.

When we reach the top, I catch sight of something on the ground and gasp, my heart fluttering like a moth.

A man lies with his back slumped against a tree. Dried blood crusts his tie-dye shirt, and his chest rises and falls from quick, labored breaths. Kneeling, I examine the wound. A deep gash runs parallel with his ribs, pus-yellow, angry with infection. He paws at my arm, wearing a dazed, doubtful look, like he's having trouble believing I'm real.

"It's all right," I say. "Stay still. I'm a nurse."

Straining to speak, his mouth opens and shuts like a fish stuck on land, but manages no more than a rasp.

Joel grabs my arm as I reach for the water. "He's septic. There's no point."

"Then we treat him," I say. "Rehydrate him first, then find antibiotics."

"What antibiotics, where?"

"The hell if I know," I say. "But we try and look, or do something, okay? Not just walk away and let him die out here."

"This guy *is* dying, Seth. Fussing over him, giving him false hope, it's cruel. He needs a quick end."

My vision seesaws. I shake my head.

"There's no other choice," Joel says.

"No way, Joel. No way." I search his face, needing to find some hesitation there, some sign he might change his mind, but his jaw remains stiff, and his eyes stare right into mine.

"We're nurses," I say, but my voice comes out hollow and weak. "We save lives."

"Not anymore." He stoops for a massive rock wedged against a tree. With a grunt, he lifts it with both hands and turns toward the injured man. "Now go back to the tent."

I recite the word *no* like it's some incantation or prayer that could heal the man, but my voice sounds far away, seeming to come from deep within a well. A pair of feet below me shift, take one step, then two, feet that must belong to me, though I can't feel them move.

"To be totally honest, Joel gives me the creeps," my date said from the passenger seat. "Seems kind of messed up."

"Forget what he says," I said, keeping my eyes on the road. "All that cynical crap he spews, it's just an act. I've seen him at work, how he treats patients."

"When you're around."

"What are you saying, that he's some kind of psychopath?" I frown at her. "He's had a rough life, but he wouldn't hurt someone."

"Yeah, because he's smart," she said. "And there are laws."

We fish on the lake. I sit on the shore, back hunched, my branch-and-vine pole inert. The water hasn't rippled once in the hours we've been here. Its ice-blue surface is as straight and limp as a heart monitor's flatline.

Joel smokes next to me, watching a dragonfly skimming low on the lake. His own line dangles motionless in one hand.

"Bass bite at dusk," he says. "Give it time."

But the sun remains at its fullest peak in the sky. It looms high above me, garish and strong, its wicked orange face mocking my growing frailty. I am eternal, it taunts. I'll survive eons from now, long after your name has been forgotten and your bones are dust.

"It was quick," Joel says. "That guy, he didn't suffer."

Oh yeah, the dead man. I should be riddled with guilt, questioning whether we did the right thing, but the initial shock has already been replaced by concern over my blood sugar. It last clocked in at the low end of normal, meaning the first waves of lightheadedness will soon begin.

I drop my fishing pole. "This isn't working. Joel, I need food."

"Then fight it."

"Fight? You want me to what, fight hypoglycemia? Fight death?"

"Yes," he says. "You fight like my stepfather did."

"Like your stepfather? Like Ron?" My voice grows frantic. "What the hell do you mean?"

"I mean, I was with him at the end. Mom brought pictures from home, thinking he'd come to and know she was there, but he'd just writhe in that bed, calling her someone else's name. I thought, *you sad sack of meat.* Here's the only person you ever loved, and you haven't a clue who she is. That instant, he woke up, like he could read my damned mind. Shot right off the pillow, grabbed me by the neck, and said, 'Bet you're enjoying this, you little prick.' Then he laughed so hard he choked on his spit."

I lowered my gaze, shook my head. "That's seriously messed up. I'm sorry, Joel, he shouldn't have—"

"I don't want your pity. What I'm saying is, that's how it is. When everything else goes, hate's the last thing to fade." He places the fishing pole in my hand. "So, figure out what you hate most, and use it to live."

Throughout the rest of the day, my blood sugar takes a steady dip south. A nasty fatigue soon claims me, sending a thick fog rolling through my head. Leaving Starwood is now out of the question. The van is miles away, back by the goddess shrine where we first entered the campgrounds, and my legs are far too weak to carry me back.

By nightfall, the sickness storms through me. I shiver inside our tent, my shirt drenched in sweat, delirium clouding even the simplest of thoughts. Joel's cigarette cherry floats like a firefly in the dark. I instinctively call out his name, but he tells me to shut up, get some rest, and I sink into black, bottomless depths.

I fade back to consciousness to discover Joel is gone. It must be hours later. The moon's glow casting light in the tent illuminates his empty sleeping bag. The mad gibbering of crickets sounds outside, but no footsteps. I try lifting myself up, but the dizziness slams into me like a terrible wave, and I fall back into bed.

Is he taking a leak? Fishing at night? Or peeling off with our van? *"Everyone for themselves, like I always told you."*

Again, I slip into blackness, the undertow dragging me down, down, down, toward an onslaught of dreams.

The faceless hunter wears camouflage. Two dogs circle around his boots. Barking, growling, jaws snapping wildly. His rifle aims at a dove in flight. The bullet rips through its underside and it falls from the sky, a mangled blotch of white and red.

"I couldn't let it live," Ron says and lowers the rifle. "Too damn soft."

One dog rears up on hind legs and shifts into humanoid form. The creature has Joel's piercing eyes; its canine snout towers over me. My perspective shifts, and now I'm the other dog, seeing through its eyes as I straighten into a stance and double in size. The Joel-Beast snarls. It lunges at me, and we twist and thrash, locked together in a violent dance, snapping our teeth, tearing through flesh.

I wake in the morning to Joel hovering over me, all wide eyes and guile and smirking like he's been up to something. He hands me a bottle of cranberry juice. "Hurry and drink."

Its nectar flows easy and sweet as I gulp it down, the most delicious and thirst-quenching thing I've ever tasted. Next, he produces a Fig Newton bar that I also wolf down.

"Where've you been?" I ask when the dizziness fades. "And where did you find this?"

"Come on. I'll show you."

After walking along the dirt road, we arrive back at the goddess shrine. Our van rests there undisturbed, and the countless bodies remain heaped on the ground, the flesh now blackened with more decay. I step over the dead, following Joel as he powers past the stone statue and its weird headless form, and crouches in front of some underbrush.

"I found it last night," he says. "Damned thing nearly broke my toe."

He pulls back the foliage to reveal a metal grate. Grunting as he lifts it, the grate creeks open to reveal a round hatch. A rickety ladder leads to blackness below. Downward we plunge, one rung at a time, Joel aiming the flashlight to brighten our path.

We set foot in a bunker carved under the earth. The flashlight's beam cuts through the dark, illuminating stone walls and long rows of wooden shelves. It takes a minute before my eyes adjust and the items stockpiled there come into view.

Food. Cans of vegetables and fruit and soup. Dried meat. Peanut butter. Boxed rice. Protein bars. Military-style, ready-made meals. Other supplies, too: blankets, coats, hats, and gloves, toilet paper, flashlights, and a handyman's set of tools.

"Tornado shelter," Joel says. "Those who knew about it probably died first, and no one else had a clue."

I must still be dreaming, or else we're already dead and in some weird afterlife, because this couldn't have existed here, right next to the van this entire time. I touch the shelf, expecting my hand to pass through it like steam, only to touch solid wood. I run my finger down its length, the slivers pricking my skin, then pick up the cans, their film of dust sticking to my palm. Real, yes, all of it's real.

The tight knots running through my shoulders unwind. A light, buoyant feeling swells inside me, and I burst out laughing. "It's over."

We both settle down for a hearty meal. Leisurely, joking, like old times again. After my close brush with death, I assume Joel and I are finally on the same page about leaving the campground.

Two hours later, once we've rested and I've gained back my strength, I mention Eden and stand to begin loading the supplies into our van, but he shoots a glance at me, the lightheartedness from seconds ago totally stamped out.

"Hold up," Joel says. "We're not going anywhere."

I laugh, thinking he's messing with me. "Sure we're not, Boss," I say with a smirk and proceed over to the nearest shelf.

Joel slowly stands. "I'm serious."

I turn to face him and stare, the words not registering. "What?"

"Look around you," he says, gesturing to the food. "We're totally set."

"For now. It'll eventually run out, and my insulin, it's almost gone.

We need more than just months of food. We need a normal life. We need *people*," I say and turn to grab a box of canned goods.

One blue vein in his head bulges. Anger flashes in his eyes, and he stomps over and pulls the box out of my hands. "This food is mine. *Mine*. Not theirs to take."

"Theirs?"

"Those people from Eden. The ones that'll screw us over first chance they get."

I stare at him, too stunned to speak. After a few moments, I collect myself, and the knowledge of where this comes from, and what needs to be said, hits.

"Your stepdad." I carefully hedge my words, parcel them out. "He was wrong, Joel. He was wrong, okay? So you can drop the front. You're not him. You never were."

"Front?" He laughs, slowly shaking his head. "No, Seth, there's no front. Everyone for themselves. That's what I've said, yesterday, today, every time. I'm not your wounded lamb." He spreads a hand on his chest. "I'm the wolf."

Realization sinks its teeth into me. I try to tear it off, to break free, but it's latched on too deep. There stands Joel, his cold eyes trained on me. The real Joel, uncaged.

"Fine." My voice sounds weary, but unwavering. "You stay," I say and turn to the shelves. "Half the food is yours. I'm taking the rest."

I climb up the hatch with a box. Danger caws a shrill note in my head, but I ignore it and bring the box the rest of the way, setting foot aboveground and carrying it to the van.

I'm opening the rear cargo door when I hear Joel's boots *thunking* up the ladder rungs. Leaves rustling behind me announce his approach.

I turn.

Joel raises the hammer over his head.

Before I can react, he drives it down onto my skull.

I'm splayed on my back. Blue sky spins above me. I feel warm blood trickling down the back of my head. The goddess statue looms nearby, her headless form blurry and vague, resembling a specter taking flight.

Joel sits propped against the statue's base. He idly rolls a thin tube-like object between forefinger and thumb, but my vision is too fuzzy to identify it.

"This is mercy," he says. His voice sounds monotone, stripped of emotion. "Driving off with the food and leaving you here to starve, that wouldn't be right. And the hammer, I could have finished you with that, but I wasn't certain you were out cold, and it would hurt. This way is best."

My vision clears enough to focus on the thing in Joel's hand. My insulin syringe. A single drop glistens at the needle's tip, but the liquid once filling it has already been emptied, has already been injected under my skin.

My blood sugar. I need to eat, to counteract its rapid dropping. I surge upright, but it's already too late. Wooziness hits. My legs go numb, and I tumble forward onto all fours.

Leaves rustle behind me as Joel rises to his feet. "I hoped you'd wise up and start thinking about us. But it's always them, them, them. Strangers who would just as soon slit our throats. You're a liability. A necrotic limb. So, I've got to amputate."

Black dots swarm before my eyes. Joel's voice drifts in and out. Trees, the grass, everything warps. I will myself forward on hands and knees, instinct carrying me away from him, toward the safety of the woods. My body is impossibly heavy, moving like I'm underwater.

"You knew what I was," Joel says. "Deep down, under your idealistic bullshit."

My hand swipes against brush. Thorns pierce my palms as I reach into the tangle of twigs, blindly groping for something to strike him with. Joel's voice sounds from behind, garbled and drowned out by the ringing in my ears.

My hand contacts something large. Something stone.

Darkness zips over me like a body bag. My consciousness failing, I scramble for good memories to keep me hooked onto life—my parents' smiles, summer camp, driving with my buddies in high school—but they crumble into dust and slip through my hands.

Joel's face rears up in my mind. Joel reclining by our hotel pool. Joel grinning in the hospital lounge. Joel sharing a beer after work, raising his glass and calling me brother.

I roar. My hands clasp the stone object. I swing it with all my strength.

I hit Joel with the goddess head. It nails him right between the eyes. His flesh cracks down the middle like an egg. He staggers backward and covers the wound with his hand, blood spurting through his fingers in rivulets. Again, I wield the head at him, clocking his jaw and knocking him flat on his back.

I raise the stone like an ax and slam it down on his skull.

Again.

And again.

And again.

I lose an hour chugging juice until the sickness clears and I feel steady on my feet. First, I work on the easy part, draining gas from the parked cars into an empty jug and using it to fill up the van. Then begins the long process of hefting boxes up through the hatch and trying to fit them into the back. I'm still quite weak, and the film of dust covering them burns my lungs and itches my eyes, but I'm grateful I won't have to raid any homes, at least for a while.

It's nearly dark by the time I squeeze in the last box and shut the rear cargo doors. The blood-trimmed sun is barely visible behind the thicket of trees, but I resist the urge to curl up in a tent for some sleep. The sooner I get on the road, the sooner I'll track down an abandoned pharmacy with insulin, and I want to be rid of this place.

Yet, there's one more thing I must do.

The stone goddess head is the perfect size for my dashboard. I mount it into the space, snug enough so it won't tumble off if I abruptly slam on the brakes. I flip over the engine, wait for its sputter and grind, and give one last look at the head.

Joel's blood covers the front. Blood on the outcrop of her nose; blood zigzagged across her left cheek. A disgusting sight, but one I cannot afford to forget. I need a reminder of how foolish I'd been. I need to make sure it doesn't happen again.

The van bumps over the terrain. Rocky campground gives way to paved country road, then to lonely sprawls of vast interstate. I drive for days, leave Ohio and all I've ever known. I cross homes with busted windows that resemble black vacant eyes, the low crackling of an old CD my only companion. I cross deserted truck stops with their mammoth big rigs, stopping only long enough to hand pump gas from the underground tanks. Always vigilant, surveying the parking lot for enemies lying in wait. At first, I have nothing but my two ready fists. Then, during one stop, I lift a shotgun from a corpse sprawled on the restroom floor and from that point carry the firearm, fully loaded, whenever I step from the van.

A cardboard sign for Eden surfaces on the side of the highway. Its white arrow directs me off at the next right-hand exit. I peer at the blood on the statue's head. And I feel the blood pumping in my heart, blood that was almost stopped cold by my best friend.

And I stay in the left lane.

And I press my foot on the gas.

And I pass up the turn.

And the road stretches on.

WHEN DADDY WAS ALL FIXED-UP AND EVERYBODY WAS HAPPY

Gary A. Braunbeck

Once, when Amanda's mom was working an extra shift at the nursing home and she was alone with her dad, she heard him scream a loud, long, scary, ragged, victim-in-a-monster-movie scream, and without thinking ran upstairs to see if he was all right (something she was *never* supposed to do when Mommy wasn't home). She found him sitting bent over on the edge of the bed, shuddering, face buried in his hands, crying so hard she was afraid he might break into a thousand pieces like one of her bigger puzzles. His hair was all tangled like a drippy used mop and his T-shirt was soaked with sweat; she knew the nightmare had been a bad one; he had so many nightmares. She bolted into the bathroom, grabbed a washcloth, wetted it with cold water, and then it was back into the bedroom, up on the bed, wiping his face and neck and giving him a kiss on the cheek, repeatedly saying "It's okay, Daddy, it's okay, I love you," but he just kept on sobbing, "I'm sorry... I'm...I'm so...*so sorry*..."

After he calmed down a bit, he tried to smile at her but didn't quite make it, then reached up and gave her left hand a gentle squeeze. "Thanks, sweetie. That cool washcloth sure helped."

"Who were you saying 'I'm sorry' to?"

For a moment he looked as if he were going to tell her, but then shook his head slowly and failed to smile a second time. "It's not important."

Amanda smacked his arm. "Yes it is! You *scared* me *real bad!*"

He put his arm around her. "It isn't a very nice story."

"Was it the person you were having the nightmare about?"

He looked stunned. "Wh-wha—how did you get so smart?"

"My daddy's a famous writer."

"*Semi*-popular, anyway. For the moment."

Amanda knew most of his real-life stories weren't very nice; he'd had —as her mother said to one of her friends—"One of the worst goddamn lives I've ever heard about...no wonder he's on a hundred different meds and writes horror stories!"—so she took a deep breath and looked him directly in the eyes: "I'm all ready, Daddy."

He reached over to the nightstand and picked up his wallet. "One afternoon, when I was about your age, my mother and I were sitting in the kitchen and she was reading the paper. I figured she was reading about Apollo 11—it was July 18, 1969, and we were going to land on the moon in two days. I was so excited I couldn't stand it. See, I was going to be an astronaut. I would be the first person to set foot on Jupiter." He grew silent, staring off at something depressing and faraway that only he could see; then he blinked, took a breath, and went on: "Dad came into the kitchen—*sober* and in a good mood, for a change, so nothing was gonna get broken and nobody was going to end up in the ER—anyway, as soon as he came in Mom gasped and he asked her what it was she said, 'My gosh, some woman here in Cedar Hill, just a few blocks away...she cut off her little boy's hand because he stole a cookie from the cookie jar,' and Dad said, 'What the hell?' and took the paper out of her hands and read the story, all the time shaking his head, and when he handed the paper back to her he said, 'Some people are just... goddamn just *evil*. Thank God they took her kids away from her. And at least it was his *left* hand. Story says he's *right-handed*. That's something to be grateful for, at least.' 'I suppose,' Mom said, 'but that poor little boy, he was only *three*...' And you know what she did next? *She showed me the picture of that kid!* Standing there, more alone than I've ever seen another human being in my life, with the stump where his left hand used to be all wrapped up in bandages and him looking at the camera with this expression...this broken-hearted, pained, shell-shocked expression because his *mother*, someone he depended on and *loved*, did this... this...grisly, abhorrent, *irredeemable* thing to him, this thing that could never be fixed, never be undone.

"The newspaper said his name was Anthony. Didn't give his last name. His mother used a hatchet. Doctors said the blade was dull so she had to hit his wrist twice to sever his hand. So, yeah, hon...I was dreaming about him." He pulled his arm from around Amanda's shoulder and slipped a folded piece of paper from his wallet. "And I was apologizing to him." He unfolded the paper and handed it to her. "I was apologizing to him because it seems to me that *somebody* should."

Amanda looked down at the yellowed but still visible newspaper photo of Anthony No-Last-Name with his bandaged stump and sad, confused face. Trying not to cry for the little boy, she said, "Wh-why... why do you have this, Daddy? Why do you *still* have this?"

"To look at when I think *I'm* having a bad day."

From the time she was old enough to hold one of six wooden pieces in her pink chubby hand, Amanda loved puzzles. She would sit on the orange rug in the living room, and she would lock the pieces into place, watching the picture unfold with satisfaction, then dump them back out of the wooden frame and begin again.

Oh, and she was good at them too, completing five-hundred-piece puzzles quickly when she was five and even seven-hundred-and-fifty-piece puzzles when she was six. She would roll a piece around in her hand, cheeks puffed out, blowing air, sometimes humming, sometimes making little clicks and clacks with her teeth before eagerly slapping it down in an empty space. She felt like one of those TV doctors, performing some life-saving surgery before the commercials came on.

When she was six, Amanda started a secret collection of single puzzle pieces she'd found lying around; on the floor in the waiting room at the dentist's office, on the playground during recess, on the school bus, or even just in the grass or mud around the neighborhood. There was one treasured piece that had been left out in the rain for so long that whatever had been on it—a color, some stars, maybe part of a face or animal or even a weird-looking movie monster—was long gone; the whole thing was just a dull faded white. In her mind, it could now be anything. She *loved* that, she loved thinking that one day she might be able to take all these missing pieces from other puzzles and put them together somehow to make a private, enchanted puzzle that could transport her to a secret world like in that *The Lion, The Witch, and The Wardrobe* book Daddy had read to her once.

Amanda liked her hair short and her sleeves short so nothing would get in the way of her "surgeries." Every Sunday her mother would bring her a new puzzle, and then take the old ones (as well as clothes that Amanda had outgrown, and a hundred dollar donation Daddy always gave her) to the Open Shelter downtown. The puzzles were a good distraction for the kids whose fathers sometimes turned into monsters.

Her mother explained it like this: some men were like the old black-and-white monsters in Daddy's favorite movies. They would turn into terrifying creatures that would hurt anyone who got close. Anything could make a man turn into a monster—like too much beer or too many drugs or too much noise from being in wars or other things that happened that scared them so bad they forgot where or who they were.

Amanda turned into a monster once when she was five. Her cousin Kristy was staying over one night and kept saying she saw a ghost outside their room; Amanda told her it was only Daddy checking on them but Kristy kept calling him a ghost, and she wouldn't stop, and even when Amanda said Daddy only wanted to make sure she didn't disappear like Suzy, his baby girl from his first marriage who'd died when she was six weeks old. Kristy kept saying "Ghost Dad, Ghost Dad!" Finally, Amanda slapped her twice, real hard, and Kristy's mouth bled, and after that she didn't sleep over anymore.

Amanda was afraid of turning into a monster again, and she made sure never to growl or bite or hit, and she checked her teeth in the mirror very diligently—that meant extra especially careful—every day and double before she went to bed to make sure she wasn't growing fangs.

Daddy wasn't a monster but sometimes he reminded her of one.

Mommy called him Frank-in-Stine or just Frankie and sometimes she called him Round-O Hat-On.

Mostly she called him Frankie when he got real bad.

Doctor Frankenstein was a man who wanted to see what would happen if you took a whole bunch of broke-down parts from dead people and stitched 'em back together and hit 'em with a lot of electricity and screamed "It's alive! It's alive!" It didn't end none too well; Amanda knew that from watching the movie with Daddy (watching the double feature of old scary movies on *Chiller Theatre* Friday nights— hosted by the one and only Fritz the Night Owl—was their Special Thing), and on those days when things were bad Daddy would shuffle stiffly around the house not talking clearly or right, and Amanda understood why Mommy called him that.

Daddy was like Frankie, or really like Frankie's monster, but since the poor monster didn't have a name, Frankie seemed as good as any. Her father was big and had a lot of scars that made it look like his parts were stitched together. Sometimes his hands would shake and break things, sometimes he'd set something down too hard, and sometimes he would crash into the wall or forget how to say some words or who she or her mother was but at least he wasn't scary like the Wolf Man or the Creeper (who was *played* by *Rondo Hatton*, who Fritz said had actually been a very nice man in real life). Daddy wasn't scary like them.

As long as he took his medicines on time: for his being so sad most of the time; for the awful pain because of his bad leg (caused by something called Complex Regional Pain Syndrome); for his insomnia; for his nightmares and the ones he sometimes had when he was awake (Mommy called them "flashbacks")...all of those were because of something called c-PTSD (Complex Post-Traumatic Stress Disorder), and it meant her father had experienced so many terrible things in his life that they had affected his mind and body in awful ways, which is why he sometimes turned into the Frank-in-Stein monster; her mother explained that c-PTSD was one of the worst kind, because in her father's case it was combined with something called *psychomotor retardation*, and Amanda didn't understand any of that at all, she only knew that he'd been sick and sad for a long time, even before she was born.

One evening, when he was in his office working on something called a "novella" that was giving him lots of trouble, Amanda asked: "Is Daddy ever going to be well? I mean, all that medicine and seeing the doctors and stuff? Is it going to make him well?"

Her mother looked at her, put down her embroidery, and said, matter-of-factly, "No, sweetie, he'll never be what the world calls 'well.'"

Amanda nodded. "But he'll get better, right?"

Her mother knelt down and took hold of Amanda's hands. "I need you to listen to me, sweetie, because I'm going to tell you maybe the two most important things I've ever told you—and you can *never, ever* repeat these to Daddy, do you understand? *Never.*"

Amanda, suddenly afraid but determined not to show it, gave a firm nod of her head.

Her mother smiled a nervous smile, took a deep breath, and began: "When you were born, I'd hoped having another girl would help maybe *fix* your daddy somehow, but it didn't. Now, I don't want you to think that you were a mistake or unwanted or anything like that, okay? We were overjoyed to have you, and we loved you—we *love* you, sweetie, with all our hearts, I swear it, but it was...it was stupid and maybe... maybe naive and selfish of me to think that another baby girl would make the grief over losing Suzy go away."

"How did she die?"

"It was a thing called SIDS—Sudden Infant Death Syndrome. Nobody really knows what causes it...maybe low birth weight, underdeveloped lungs, undiagnosed heart problems, maybe the mother smoked or drank during pregnancy. Daddy's first wife *didn't* smoke or drink, but Daddy used to smoke. Marcelina—that's her name, Daddy's first wife, *Doctor* Marcelina Hernandez—she's a child mental health counselor..." Her mother looked at Amanda, shook her head, and grinned. "...boy, she'd probably be able to write a damn *trilogy* about how living with your father and me's gonna make you turn out—anyway, Marcelina, she'd make your dad go outside, though, but he once admitted to me that when she'd fall asleep in front of the television he'd sneak a smoke or two in the house.

"The thing is, Suzy died while he was rocking her to sleep." She wiped at her eyes. "Right in his arms. He'd nodded off for a couple of minutes, and when he woke up, it took him a few seconds to realize that she'd...she'd stopped breathing. He tried giving her mouth-to-mouth and CPR but he couldn't press too hard on her chest, you know, her being so small and fragile, and by the time the EMTs got there Suzy was gone. He still wonders if sneaking those cigarettes might have been part of the cause, or if he hadn't fallen asleep he might've been able to call the ambulance sooner and she'd still be alive.

"He and Marcelina didn't stay married much longer after that." She reached over and gently touched her daughter's face. "And my having you didn't fix him.

"Not at first, anyway."

Amanda tilted her head to one side. *"Huh?"*

"Do you remember your first puzzle, that wooden one that had only six pieces?"

Amanda's face lit up. "I sure do! I loved it! I still have it in my closet."

"Well, one night when you were sitting on the floor putting it together for the umpteenth time, you suddenly stopped humming— you *always* hummed when you were really little and doing one of your puzzles—and you started putting the pieces into the frame really slowly. You had this terribly serious look on your face, and I asked you what you were thinking, and you said, 'It would be nice if Daddy was all better,' and I told you that was very sweet, and that you should tell him when he woke up, and then you finished the puzzle, got up to get yourself a drink, and said, 'Please don't put it away, Mommy. Please leave it alone for a little bit.' So I did.

"And then...and then there was your father, standing next to me, laughing and smiling and patting my behind like he does and asking if we wanted to go out for burgers. I thought he'd gone 'round the bend. I made him sit down. I checked his blood pressure, his heart rate, his sugar, I ran the penlight across both his eyes, checked his reflexes...he was *fine*. He didn't have any trouble walking, or speaking, driving —*nothing!* He was fixed, he was *well!*

"He was that way for about two hours, until we got home, and then everything started again. But for those two hours, sweetie, we had him back! And it was because of you and that six-piece wooden puzzle."

"Because of me and my puzzle?"

Her mother nodded. "You've done it a few more times since then. The last time was about a year-and-a-half ago. Remember that big Buster Keaton puzzle?"

Amanda sighed dramatically. "Boy, do I! His movies are *fun-ny* but I hated doing that puzzle. I wanted the front of that house to fall down and conk him on the head."

"Remember afterward?"

She stared at her mother for a moment, and then something in the back of her memory sat up, threw back the covers, and turned on the lights. "Yeah! You wouldn't let me put it back in the box right away, and Daddy was all better for, like...wasn't it almost...a couple of weeks?"

Her mother held up three fingers.

Amanda's eyes grew wide. "*No kidding*?"

"Cross my heart."

"So you mean that I...I can..."

"You can fix your father, after all. All you had to do, like I asked you, was think about your father being better every time you put the 'Daddy Puzzle' together."

"That's right! It's always in the same box." Amanda was all set to let out a *yippee* and hug her mother, but there was a look in her eyes that warned there was something else, something...not good. "What is it, Mommy?"

She reached up and removed the colorful scarf from around her head, revealing the mass of what she called "peach fuzz" that had covered her head for as long as Amanda could remember. "I told you I lost all my hair because I contracted alopecia. That's not what happened. I—don't interrupt, please? Let me get this out while I still have the nerve. The second time you fixed your father with the puzzle— you were almost five, and it was Godzilla—your father was fixed for ten days. Right off the bat, I lost all my hair. I had to tell everyone at work *something*, so alopecia it was. But only you and your father acted like I'd always been like this, so it was no big deal.

"The third time—this time it was Marvin the Martian—Daddy was good for two whole weeks, but...do you remember C.C.?"

"Huh-uh. Was he a friend of yours and Daddy's?"

"Sweetie, he was our cat."

Amanda was getting scared. "We had a *kitty*?"

"Right up until you finished that puzzle and your father was better. Then C.C. was gone, vanished, and I was the only one who remembered that he ever existed."

"Did anything happen that first time? With the wooden puzzle?"

Her mother shrugged. "I lost all my credit cards and had to replace them, but your father never knew about those in the first place."

"What about with Buster Keaton?"

"You said he started talking to you at one point."

"Uh-huh. He had a real froggy voice, but he was nice. He said to remember that..."

"Remember what, sweetie?"

"Remember that it wasn't my fault, and it wasn't Daddy's, either."

"Do you know what he was talking about?"

"*No!* Mommy, what happened after Buster?"

"I think it has to do with something called 'alchemical or theurgic' magic, sweetie. It requires an exchange of something of equal or near-equal value. My guess is I so *wanted* you to have the power to fix your father that you were somehow born with this ability and—"

"*—what happened after Buster?*"

Her mother stared at her, unblinking, her face an expressionless, granite mask. "All of our family photos and home movies."

"That's *it*?"

"I have no pictures of my mother or father, none of my sisters, my nieces or nephews, their birthday parties, weddings, picnics, none of it —I only have the vaguest *memories* of the events, and those fade more and more each day. Your father and I, we don't have our wedding pictures or the movies of the ceremony and reception, nothing from our honeymoon, we don't have the video tapes of your birth that were transferred to Blu-ray, we don't have any of your birthdays, we don't have film of that wonderful night in New York when your father won his very first writing award...I barely remember those things and he..."

remembers none of them. Oh, we remember the people, sure, but the events...gone."

Amanda put her arms around her mother. "I'm sorry...I'm...I'm so...*so sorry*..."

"Don't apologize, sweetie. To have him be his old self like that for a while...it was worth it. It was worth *anything*."

Amanda jumped when she heard the yell from upstairs but she knew better than to go running. That wasn't a Daddy scream but a Frankie yell. Sometimes if he was writing or if he was reading something or sometimes just because he'd see a ghost or hear a voice he'd yell and cuss and there'd be a bang or a thud and he never came down when he was Frankie. That's when he was scary and threw things. Sometimes things would be broken in his office and Mommy would be sweeping up a broken picture frame and biting her lip hard and pursing her lips tight and trying not cry...or maybe lose her temper.

Amanda knew what was coming, and for the first time, it terrified her.

Daddy didn't come downstairs for dinner and Mommy didn't go upstairs to sleep. Her mother got the puzzle box from the basement. It was largest Amanda had ever seen, with more pieces than ever before.

"Too goddamn big, I know," said her mother. "It's a lot, sweetie, and I know it's been a while since you did this, but you're only one who can fix him. How 'bout I buy a pizza and you can get a good start on it?"

Amanda gave a dutiful nod.

"Your friend Laura's not coming over tomorrow, is she?"

Amanda shook her head. Laura got tired of her canceling the last few times they were supposed to go to the movies. Laura said her mom thought Amanda was "flaky."

"We're not friends, anymore," Amanda said.

Her mother shrugged. "Yeah, well, she's a snotty little See-You-Next-

Tuesday, anyway. And now we can stay up late and you can get Daddy all fixed. Make it a Girl's-Only Friday Night." They both started pushing aside the table and chairs. Amanda might need the whole floor for this one. Mommy said she would put on movies in the living room since the two rooms were connected. The couch was in the way but she could move that.

The pizza was warm and gooey with cheese and breadsticks, and she could hear his staggered footsteps when Daddy smelled it and came downstairs. The Creeper—the nice man Rondo—had just strangled a woman to a lot of screaming and even though Amanda had seen this one before, she still stopped with the pizza halfway to her mouth. Mommy's head went up quickly with the snuffle and snort and the heavy step, and Amanda thought she would throw herself under him if Daddy looked like he was going to fall. They only had a short staircase, but when her father started turning into Frankie, his bad leg would lock up and sometimes he fell and cracked his head on stuff and bled and bled and the carpet was soft and it was really hard to get blood stains out.

"You girls order a pizza?" He took a careful step. Amanda held her breath. His leg was stiff and his hand half-swiped the railing. He picked it up, looked at his palm like he wasn't sure what it was or where it went, then grabbed the railing again and continued to shamble down. Amanda thought she saw his left leg wobble as he blinked a few more times in that half-Frankie daze. His voice was clear when he was Daddy, clear and strong, but it was rough and raspy tonight. He cleared his throat and Mommy asked if he wanted any pizza. Amanda set hers down before she dropped it.

"That's too much salt for me, babe," he said, staring at his feet as he took another step and lurched forward. He seemed so old and broken.

Sometimes kids in her class called Daddy her grandpa because he was older than their daddies, but as far as Amanda knew he had read every book, seen every movie, and had probably listened to every song ever sung—*and* he could answer trivia questions about almost everything. ("I don't know *everything*," he would say to her. "I probably know *most* of it, though.") He could pick her up over his head easily.

When he was Daddy, he was amazing, he was funny, he was smart, he was *unstoppable*.

Tonight he lumbered along like the Creeper and she knew his stomach was bothering him and probably his head and probably he'd have nightmares and start screaming and Mommy would tell her not to rush in because he would punch and kick, but Amanda knew just how to curl up behind him and hug his tummy and wake him up even if it scared her to see his puffy tear-streaked face glinting in the dark.

"No, I'm...I'm just gonna have a protein bar or a shake or a..." He stopped on that last step, staring at things far away, maybe seeing ghosts like Anthony No-Last-Name or dead little Suzy; he looked so lost and sad and Amanda wished every night that this time when they fixed him that he would never break again.

"There's some leftover chicken and broccoli from last night," Mommy said.

"*Veg-et-a-bles!*" Amanda exclaimed dramatically, throwing her right arm up against her forehead and rolling her eyes. "Oh, my G-uhd Lawd, *suh*, what ev-ah shall you do? The *hor-ah!* The *hor-ah!*"

He shook his head and offered soft applause. "Bravo, Miss Scarlett. Rhett was a Neolithic dipshit to leave you." He made the last step, shambling over to them. They stood and he kissed them both, ruffling Amanda's hair and giving Mommy's butt a pat that Amanda pretended not to see.

"I'm sorry about earlier, I just hurt and the novella is...well, I'll finish it or it'll finish me." His mantra about everything he wrote.

"It's only fifteen-hundred dollars," said Mommy. "The agency called to say Todd just deposited the money from the movie sale of *Please Look Down*. Christ, you said yourself that you'd never seen so many zeroes before the decimal point. We're in *great* shape, hon."

"Ah, yes, blessings from the Magnificent Mr. Skaggs. They don't call him 'Film Dude' at the agency for nothing. Man could get an illiterate walrus a seven-figure movie deal. As far as the novella goes—I've never let down an editor. *Never*. And I'll be damned if I'll start now because it's 'only fifteen-hundred dollars.' *Capiche?*" He leaned forward slightly. "Hey, sweetie, working on another puzzle?"

"No," said Amanda. "We're planning to rob a bank in case the story finishes you and we don't get that fifteen-hundred dollars."

"Very funny," he replied, half-absently, already shuffling toward the kitchen. "I'm gonna use that in a story sometime."

"It's Friday night," she called after him. "*Chiller Theatre*?"

"Not up for it, sweetie. Maybe next week."

Amanda realized he was still wearing Wednesday's clothes.

Amanda fell asleep sometime after *The Crawling Eye* ended and she woke up to see her mother laid across the floor over top of the start of the frame. Amanda always started with the frame. Six hours and even the frame was only half finished. She thought she could hear Daddy's nightmare screams but on the hard floor it felt as if something was preventing her from running to him. She listened closely, her heart racing. The clock on the wall showed it was four-thirty in the morning. Her eyes burned and she thought she heard another scream but sometimes Daddy's screams played in her head even when he wasn't there.

She thought about waking Mommy, or going up to her room to her own bed, but as she looked back at the half-finished border, the cries echoing in her head, she decided to get a can of Coke from the refrigerator and put in more pieces instead. She gave a quick look to the stairs in case Daddy had gotten up to check on them and fallen. The floor creaked as she walked. When Amanda was little she was terrified of the dark, of the shadows on the walls making monsters until she learned that the monsters had names, and they were so very different and fascinating and had history and stories and now she would see the blur of darkness and imagine the crawling eye with a soft giggle.

"The cloud has moved," she whispered to herself and could almost picture the giant eyeball with its slimy tentacles outside the windows.

Saturday, the screams were worse. Daddy had a pain in his leg that sometimes moved up into his back and sometimes also into his head and sometimes none of the medicines helped it. Mommy made him tea and rubbed his back and rubbed his leg and warned him if he took too many "Perkies" he'd run out before the next refill. Amanda worked on the puzzle as the border came together, the leftover pizza cold but still good. Her mother mixed up more of her "medicated goo" for Daddy's leg (it was heavy menthol cream) and some balm for Daddy's face because it was red and angry and burned like a vampire when the sun hit it.

———

After her mother went back to work, Amanda ducked into her parents' bedroom for just a moment to give Daddy a hug.

"I love you so much, sweetie," he whispered into her hair, and Amanda smiled as she struggled to breathe and fell asleep on the bed with him until he woke her up and asked her what time it was. She had a hard time convincing him it was still Saturday night. He sat up, his breathing labored, and unsteady, just as Mommy brought in pills and another protein shake. He took them from her and pushed past them both muttering about the fucking deadline. Amanda hurried back to the puzzle and had cereal for dinner. Her mother collapsed on the bed and was immediately asleep.

———

She heard her father throwing up loudly and violently all that night and well into the next morning. She saw Mommy wince before heading up, and Amanda touched her own throat, knowing how much it hurt from the one time she had gotten food poisoning from the gas station hot dog her mother had bought her in a hurry. She heard the shower run, and several minutes later saw her mother come down wet, tired, but smiling. Daddy was clean again. They had waffles and bacon. They saved a third plate. It got cold, so Amanda covered it in plastic wrap, put it in the refrigerator, and went back to the puzzle.

———

The puzzle was gigantic, at least five feet on each side. Amanda listened to the music the shrunken people were dancing to onscreen. She imagined she was one of the Puppet People shrunk by the ray, carrying one piece after another, trying to lay them quickly before the crazy scientist returned. Like them, she needed to work quickly. Tomorrow she'd have to go back to school and Daddy's hands were shaky and he was talking to the ghosts again. Her mother had to wash their clothes and make her lunch and get ready to go back to work because she didn't just take care of Daddy but cleaned and cooked and sometimes played cards with other sick people at the nursing home. But they couldn't be fixed like Daddy and sometimes Mommy came home just as sad as when she left.

Amanda wanted to stay home from school because Daddy's nightmares woke her up four times. Mommy got knocked off the bed and Amanda helped tape up a nasty gash on her back from where she'd hit the nightstand. Daddy hit her face too and Amanda was always scared people would start thinking he was a monster if Mommy didn't get better at dodging his Frankie fists. Frankie could be violent like the Creeper. He hugged too hard and forgot her name and fell into things and threw things at ghosts. Mommy said sometimes he didn't know his own strength.

When Amanda saw him Tuesday morning his hair was wild and more wispier white on top than she remembered. After school when Daddy was Frankie, Amanda would rush upstairs to her parent's bedroom and watch him from the doorway when he was asleep. She could see a little baby on the bed crawling over to him. It was Suzy. She was looking after him because Amanda hadn't been here.

Amanda sat on the edge of the bed where Daddy was curled up and stroked his hair softly, rubbing his forehead which was red and angry with a deep line between his eyebrows that she traced her fingernail between. He groaned and buried his face in his hands, low and deep like the monster, the sheets a mess, in disarray (which was messy times two) and Suzy sleeping near his head. He tried to talk to her but she imagined his mouth sticky stuck inside, his eyes swollen and gummed up with dark circles underneath and there were empty glasses all over the room. She tickled Suzy's arms and the baby giggled. Amanda couldn't resist; she pulled up the baby's gown, leaned over, and made belly-farts. Suzy laughed and laughed. It was such a joyful sound. It had been so long since the house had heard anything like it.

"I'll get you some water, Daddy," she said as he gave another grumble growl.

Suzy was gone. Again. She was glad her father hadn't been awake for the baby's visit.

She had to fix Daddy and fix him fast or it would be too late.

That evening the upstairs floor creaked like trees in a storm, there was yelling and something slammed into the wall and Mommy winced as she served up spaghetti and muttered that finishing the story was no good and fifteen-hundred dollars wasn't worth dying for and she put the spaghetti in the part of the fridge that contained everything Daddy wasn't eating.

That night came grunts and groans from the bathroom like an angry ghoul. Mommy slept downstairs on the pull-out sofa. Amanda stayed up, desperately working on the puzzle.

She couldn't figure out what the heck it was supposed to be. It was all fuzzy; black-and-white in some places, the sallow color of an old lemon peel in others. She worked faster than she ever had before, the pieces seeming to tell *her* where they went.

It was as if even the puzzle knew time was running out.

It was at three-forty-seven Tuesday morning, right after she heard her mother scream Daddy's name in terror from upstairs and fall twice rushing for the telephone, that Amanda realized not only was the puzzle missing several pieces right smack in the middle, but the picture—whatever it was *supposed* to be—kept blinking in and out like a TV show being messed up by static from a storm.

The puzzle was bigger than she was; if it had been a trap door she could have opened it and dropped down into—

—a secret world like in that *The Lion, The Witch, and The Wardrobe* book.

She bolted onto and over the couch, through the dining room, and up the stairs. She saw her mother on the floor of the bedroom, screaming into the phone for an ambulance, and Daddy on the bed, his body all twisted up, his face pale, blood coming out of his mouth, his eyes staring and unfocused, little Suzy sitting beside him, patting his face with her tiny hands and crying and looking at Amanda for help (Amanda knew only she could see the baby) but she kept on moving, slamming open the door to her room and barreling across to her closet, wrenching open the door and yanking out the box of her secret single pieces, then whirling around and zooming back toward the stairs, taking them three at a time until she hit the floor with a skid, almost losing her balance but regaining her footing at the last second to vault the couch in a single leap that would have made Buster Keaton proud, landing on her knees before the flickering puzzle picture and shouting, "Stop *fucking* with me!" and not caring that she'd just used the Big Bad Word that she'd heard both Mommy and Daddy use at least a dozen times, but she was scared, and she was mad, and Daddy was maybe dying, and she was having none of it, nosiree, not after all this, so she dumped out all of the lost, single, unmatched pieces, glaring at them, grabbing them one by one, slamming them down into the middle of the flickering puzzle and whattayaknow they fit just like she *told* them to, fit perfectly, every last one of them, and then she held the last one, the washed-out, nothing-on-it, all-white one, and she gave it a kiss, and she pressed it into place, and the puzzle was finished, and it stopped flickering, and there was the picture—

—and she found herself staring at the yellowed black-and-white newspaper photo of lost, confused, hurt face of three-year-old Anthony No-Last-Name, the stump of his left hand sloppily wrapped in bandages and the despair in his eyes so overwhelming Amanda could feel herself breaking in half.

"Please don't," said Anthony.

She couldn't believe he was talking to him.

He tilted his head at her. "Why not? Joseph talked to you."

"Who's Joseph?"

"Keaton. Joseph Francis Keaton. *Buster*."

"Oh. I didn't know that was his name. Listen, I, uh...I'm so sorry about what happened to you. It must have been—"

"You don't have to apologize. It wasn't your fault. And would do me a favor? *Please* tell your father to throw that newspaper photo away and stop it with the apologizing, already. Tell him I really appreciate his heartfelt sympathy and concern over the years—I kinda love him for it— but it started getting on my nerves a long time ago."

Amanda snorted a small laugh. "'Kay. I will."

"But now we have to make an exchange, you and I."

"I know."

"You want to fix your father forever, don't you?"

"Yes."

Anthony held up his bandaged stump. "Your left hand, please. No take-backs. No undoings."

Amanda nodded, holding up her left arm. "Deal. I'm right-handed anyway."

AVOCATION

Lucy A. Snyder

Τ he worst thing I ever did? Oh, my. That's quite the question for a
first date!

But I get it: we're both too old for trivia like our favorite movies or
cocktails. You want to see me prick myself on the needle of my moral
compass. See what colors I bleed.

Oh, honey, no...I wasn't calling *you* old. You're, what, fifty? Prime
of your life! Want some wine?

There you go. As for me...I guess it's not ladylike, but I don't mind
thinking of myself as older. Not like I'm a hag or something, but...I've
been around. Wisdom. Experience. Skills. Ought to count more than
how perky my tits are, right?

Right?

C'mon, don't make that face.

Oh, it's the merlot? Too bitter? Okay, how about a martini?
One sec.

So, your question. Stop me if you've heard about this: Allfine Insurance, 2015.

Not ringing a bell? Really? It made the national news for at least five
seconds, and they *are* a competitor to your firm...

Right. You're very busy. Who has time to watch the news?

So, let me give you my personal prospectus. I got my BS in nursing right after high school because I wanted to help people. I maintained a 4.0 grade point average, got a great job right after graduation with Cary Hospital here in Columbus. Things were good for two years.

But then, I was helping a 40-year-old stroke patient—huge guy: former Bengals linebacker with CTE—and he stumbled and I instinctively tried to catch him. Fell right on me. Fractured my L1, L2, and a couple of ribs when we hit the floor. My back was wrecked, and hands-on nursing was clearly not something I could do anymore.

My medical bills and college loans weren't going to pay themselves, so—after I could walk again, I had to find another job. I tried telemedicine for a while, but I found it super frustrating. Then a colleague told me Allfine was hiring nurses as medical claim reviewers. I thought, "Why not?" and applied.

They hired me and five other nurses, and at first it seemed ideal. The pay was amazing, and the company had great perks like Aeron chairs and a fully-equipped onsite gym. I was determined to get my mobility and function back. Being able to do my PT throughout the day was huge.

Another great thing was that I met Willow. She was one of the nurses in my training cohort. One of the smartest, kindest, most decent people I have ever known, period. And she was so much fun! Everyone loved her. I fell for her really hard, and before I knew it we had an apartment in Victorian Village together—

Yes, I'm bi.

...No, I don't do threesomes. May I finish my story? Thanks.

Willow was a shining light at that company. The others in my cohort? Not so much. The worst was a guy named Rodney. He'd been a corpsman in the Marines, and rumor was he witnessed a massacre in Iraq. Now, clearly this man had PTSD, and a lot of insecurities that he was trying to compensate for, so I tried to be patient with him.

But he was just such an *asshole*. Loud, abrasive, bragged all the time about how he was screwing people out of their benefits because he'd found some small technical problem in their claims. He took joy in keeping people from getting health care! Every day I wanted to shake him and ask, "What is *wrong* with you?"

Our six-month reviews came up. Willow and I...got mediocre scores.

Rodney, of course, couldn't keep his mouth shut about how well he'd done. So, I went to my supervisor on the QT and was like, "What gives?"

Then I find out that, contrary to *everything* in our training documentation, contrary to *everything* the company tells their customers... they really wanted us to reject as many claims as we could. Didn't matter if it was a newborn baby with a malformed heart valve. Didn't matter if it was a mother of five with cancer. Find a defect in the claim? Reject it, and don't offer advice on fixing it.

Be silent in the face of other peoples' pain and misery.

Willow and I were appalled. This was the *worst* bait-and-switch. We honestly felt like our life missions as human beings was to help people. Except that wasn't the job. We talked about walking away, but we both had mountains of debt.

And she told me, "The money shouldn't matter this much, but it does. If we quit, they'll just hire someone else to do what they say. And we won't be able talk about what Allfine is doing because of the NDAs we signed. But if we make our supervisors happy, we can get promotions and work to change the company from the inside."

So naïve, right? But she seemed so certain, and I wanted to believe it was possible.

We both stuck with it for ten years, trying to do what the company wanted while trying to help as much as we could...and it was really, really difficult. We'd turn down claims that we desperately wanted to approve, and it killed us a little each day.

In my heart, I'm convinced that's why Willow developed aggressive triple-negative breast cancer. I think working there poisoned her on a cellular level.

She worked as long as she could, then went on short-term disability. I knew what was happening, what was *going* to happen, and couldn't stop any of it. I shaved her head for her so she wouldn't have to watch it all fall out. Held her hand during chemo treatments. Rubbed her back when she was puking her guts out afterward. I watched the woman I loved more than my own life waste away and there was nothing I could do.

I got fired about a week before she died. It was because of all the leave I'd taken. Not officially, of course...I'd filled out all the FMLA forms, and nobody would find a damn technicality in *my* paperwork. But Ohio has at-will employment, so they don't need a reason to lay you off.

And it wasn't just me: they dumped about a dozen other employees. Their brass boy Rodney was one of them, probably because he said the quiet parts out loud too much. I hate to admit it, but knowing he was out of a job, too...it was a little slice of schadenfreude pie. I was so sick with grief and anger, any other emotion seemed refreshing no matter how sour.

After Willow was gone, I lost our apartment and had to sell off most of our belongings. Ended up in a crappy one-bedroom in North Columbus. Anger just built and built inside me. I needed a release valve...and I didn't have one. I couldn't afford therapy and couldn't go punch bags because of my back.

So, I bought a handgun—a Glock 19—and took up target shooting. I imagined Allfine Insurance executives' faces on every sheet of target paper I blew to bits at the range.

And that might have been enough...but the next year was Allfine's 50th anniversary. Suddenly I was seeing their ads on every station, and I couldn't open a local magazine or newspaper without finding a puff piece about all the charity work Allfine executives were doing for the Columbus community: school events, walk/run fundraisers, concerts. All a bunch of heartwarming horseshit, and at the end of every article, all I could see was Willow dying in her hospice bed.

And I thought, "How is it fair that these lying, cheating mother-fuckers are still alive and she's gone?"

And then I figured, "Well, I can't bring her back...but I sure can fix that other part."

I flexed my social engineering skills and got an appointment to see Karen, the HR director, after I spun her administrative assistant Julie a bullshit story about how I was enrolling in an actuary science program and wanted an informational interview about industry needs. Apparently, Karen had been working at the New York branch a whole bunch and had exactly one day available for interviews for like six months. Otherwise, she was booked solid. Karen's office was on the same floor as the main executives' offices. Once I was up in her area, I could just walk down the hall, shooting targets at my leisure, assuming nobody stopped me.

And honestly? I was okay knowing that I'd probably get killed by the police. I missed Willow so much, just hurt so much every day...I didn't want to live. I felt bad about what it would do to my parents, but they still had my sisters and their kids, you know? They'd get over losing their unemployed queer daughter who most certainly hadn't lived up to her potential.

That said: I was incredibly nervous the day of my "interview." Hadn't slept for like two days and had barely been able to eat. But I stayed cool. I still knew most of the people on the first floor, and so when I arrived, one lady let me in the side door, where they didn't have a metal detector. She took me to a security guard who I also knew; he gave me his condolences about Willow as he escorted me up to the top floor.

Julie met me at the elevators. I remember she was wearing this amazing blue silk dress—I never knew how she always looked so great on what couldn't have been a huge salary. I always admired how put-together she was, but also how kind she was. We were both on the company softball team, and so I'd found out she rescued feral cats and fostered kittens. She seemed like a really good-hearted person. If I hadn't been with Willow, I think Julie and I would have gotten to know each other a whole lot better.

And if Allfine's whole C-suite had been like Julie...well, I wouldn't have been there that day.

Anyway, she took me down the hall and around the corner to the waiting area, which was all done up in Grifter Grey and Beyond Boring Beige. Stare at the walls long enough, and you could feel your will to live draining away.

"Have a seat and Karen will be out to get you herself when she's ready," Julie said, and went back around the corner to her desk.

She left me alone on the uncomfortable reception sofa, my pistol-laden purse heavy against my hip, staring down at a glass bowl full of individually-wrapped wintergreen mints. I love those damn things; I always used to grab one when I was walking by.

And seeing that bowl of mints...I don't know why that was the thing, but it suddenly grounded me in the moment, and I felt the weight and sheer insane enormity of what I was about to do settle in my guts. I'd lied to Julie—a sweet girl who had never been anything but decent to me—and I was about to kill her boss. She'd hear the gunfire and probably see everyone with their brains blown out.

I was about to inflict an unspeakable amount of survivor trauma on her...and she didn't even remotely deserve that nightmare.

What the hell am I doing? I thought. *This isn't me. This isn't who I am, and it's not who Willow wanted me to be.*

And so, I stood up, slung my purse across my body and was about to get the hell out of there when I heard the elevator ding open...and then the stuck door alarm went off.

A moment later, I heard Julie gasp, "What are you doing?"

Then a pop. A gunshot. Holy shit.

The thump of someone collapsing to their knees, then moaning. Julie's voice. She was hurt.

My nurse instincts kicked in, and I hurried around the corner...and saw that she'd collapsed on her side on the floor. Facing me, her eyes shut in pain. She clutched a bloody wound in her belly. A man in a black suit with a pistol stood above her.

I finally recognized him as he took aim at her head.

Rodney. Fuckin' *Rodney.*

"No!" I shouted at him.

He fired. The 9mm hollow-point round pierced her skull near her left coronal suture and blew out the right side of her jaw. It had to have killed her instantly, but her body jerked and spasmed, and I took a couple of steps toward her, somehow thinking that maybe I could save her.

Rodney pointed the black Beretta M9 at me. I stopped and raised my hands. Everything seemed to slow way down. He moved toward me, and I finally got a good look inside the elevator behind him. He'd murdered the nice security guard, too.

"Jesus Christ, Rodney, how could you kill Julie?" I stammered.

We locked eyes. He had the proverbial thousand-yard stare. Part of Rodney was just *gone*. I don't know if it was his PTSD or if he was on drugs or both. He raised his pistol higher, moving his aim from my core to my face.

"What the hell are *you* doing here?" he demanded.

I was frankly amazed he hadn't shot me yet.

"Interview," I croaked. "Karen only had the one day for interviews."

His gun hand didn't waver. "Julie was part of it. She was *culpable*. We saved them millions, and they threw us away? They need to pay. You see that, don't you?"

I nodded. "I see it."

"You were always nice to me." He lowered his weapon and strode past me. "But don't get in my way again or I will fucking *end* you."

I cannot tell you how profoundly relieved I was. The irony of the whole thing wouldn't hit me until hours later, after I lied to the police, after I lied to the press. But my sudden, inexplicable survival in the face of that bastard wasting the second sweetest woman who ever worked at Allfine left me feeling utterly calm and focused.

When Rodney was beyond me, his back fully turned to me, I drew my weapon from my purse and shot him in the back of the head.

Let me tell you, it was *much* more satisfying than a paper target. Horrible, yes, but exhilarating. Having that kind of power in your hands...it's a little addictive, if I'm being honest.

I had arrived there that day expecting to die as one of the few female mass murderers in history...but I lived as a hero. I was nationally famous for about five minutes, as I said. The Second Amendment folks immediately latched onto me as "a good gal with a gun." Once I realized *that* was happening, I made sure to point out that Rodney had murdered two very good people before I stopped him, and everyone would have lived that day if nobody had a gun.

Well. Everyone but Willow, of course. And all the people Allfine had denied critical care to.

So, when I was lying in my bed that night, far too keyed up to sleep, I wondered if maybe I shouldn't have just let Rodney do what he'd gone there to do. They *did* deserve to die, even if he was completely wrong about the reasons.

I'm not the most religious person in the world, but I do believe in fate. I believe there are guiding forces in the universe. I believe individuals are born to do certain things, and a big part of life is figuring out what those are.

Mass murders...they're no good. That seems obvious, right? But they're blatant acts of terrorism. If your actual goal is stopping powerful people from doing more harm...well, it's like trying to do cancer surgery with a chainsaw.

That night, I realized I needed a scalpel. Maybe I needed to *be* the scalpel. Either way, I needed to be much, much smarter and deliberate about what I was doing with the unexpected gift of the rest of my life.

And that's where you come in, my dear.

I mean, you didn't think that I would flagrantly violate my Allfine non-disclosure agreement with just *anyone*, right? Surely not. I know you're a man of *supreme* discretion, and your lips are sealed.

That's a little joke. You literally can't talk right now because of the raphides I put in your martini.

I know it seems like our rendezvous at this oh-so-chic hotel suite was a random mutual swipe-right situation...but I've been planning to meet you for *months*. The policies you've implemented at your insurance company have killed over 1,000 people just this year alone. What a guy! I *had* to put you on my list.

Oh. I've hit a nerve. I can see by the look in your eye that you want to protest that you're not a murderer! You want to tell me it's just business...but I've done my research. I'd be more than happy to show it to you, but your vision is quite blurry by now, thanks to the modified digitoxin I put in the merlot.

If you don't mind, I'm going to tidy up a bit. Don't want to leave any evidence behind, just in case. But I doubt the police will think this is anything but what it appears to be: a wealthy executive with cardiovascular disease and the high-risk factor of cheating on his wife with Internet strangers had a heart attack in a hotel room. A perfectly mundane, statistically predictable cause of death. Your body will go to the county coroner for a post-mortem examination, of course...but they're a little overwhelmed by the pandemic right now. They just won't have the resources to look for something they don't suspect is there.

You're my third removal this year. I'd do more if I had some sponsorship, but that's a little tricky. For now, this has to be an avocation.

Don't worry. I won't make you die alone. Company is more than you deserve, but I need to make sure I finished the job.

And between you and me? I *really* enjoy watching the lights go out on you bastards.

ABOUT THE EDITOR

Jess Landry is a Canadian screenwriter, director, and Bram Stoker Award-winning author. Her work has appeared in numerous anthologies, including ALIENS VS PREDATORS: ULTIMATE PREY. Her collection, THE MOTHER WOUND, is set for release in 2023 from Crystal Lake Publishing and features her Shirley Jackson Award-nominated story, "I Will Find You, Even in the Dark." She co-edited the Bram Stoker Award- and British Fantasy Award-nominated anthology, THERE IS NO DEATH, THERE ARE NO DEAD, alongside Aaron J. French, and has edited novels, novellas, and collections for authors including Gwendolyn Kiste, Lisa Morton, and S.P. Miskowski, among others. Find her online at jesslandry.com.

ACKNOWLEDGMENTS

A HUGE THANKS TO ALL OF OUR BACKERS WHOSE GENEROSITY HELPED BRING THIS PROJECT TO LIFE!

Alexandra, Eric & Peggy Altherr, Todd Anello, James Aquilone, Melissa Barrett, Arnela Bektas, Rick & Bonnie Beran, Jamie Berilla-Macdonald, Priscilla Bettis, Scott Billingsley, Jon Black, Rob E. Boley, John Bowen, Megan Brandewie, BroknAngels, Courtney Brown, BuddyH, Skye Bythrow, Michele C, Megan Canada, Anton Cancre, Paul Cardullo, Michael Carter, Harley Christensen, Antonio (Tone) Collura, Bon Comics, Caroline Coriell, Todd Cox, Rachel Daugherty, Marianne H. Dean, Corinne Dee, Elena DeGarmo, Willian DeGeest, Theresa Derwin, Kenneth Dodd, M.G. Doherty, Kathryn Dokken, Laura Drum, Geoff Emberlyn, Kenny Endlich, Jessica Enfante, GCAT01, Lakyn M. Gibson, Jenni Giguere, Shawn Gilliland, Victoria L. Gilliland, Daniel Gogul, Laura Goostree, Cathy Green, Carol Gyzander, Megan Hart, Robin Harvey, Michael Haynes, Shari Heinrich, Marcelina Hernandez, Caelin Hill, Jamie Irish, Lee Jacobs, Susan Jessen, John K & Ginny G, Bunny Johnson, Tara V Johnson, Matt Jones, William Jones, TJ Kang, Steven J. Karaiskos, Tarhan Kayihan, David Lakin, Algie Lane III, Steve Leonard, Frank Lewis, Paige Lisko, Elizabeth Lyons, Christopher Mahen, Sunita Matharu, Susanne McGirr, Abigail McHie, Lauren McKay, Heidi Ruby & Jason Jack Miller, Jason Miller, Jacob Steven Mohr, Julia Morgan, Joleene Naylor, Johnnie Nemec, Hugh Newton, Ellie Nowels, Lorin Oberweger, John O'Hare, Olivier, John (JohnnyO) Orem, Richard O'Shea, Ginger Pantle, Amber Pasternak, Steve Pattee, Jeanine & Scott Pearson, Zach Pearson, Michael Jeramy Lee Perez, Charollote Platt, Rebecca Potter, Webberly Rattenkraft, Sheila Redling, Jen & Justin Reynolds, Robert Riordan,

Giusy Rippa, Nikolas P. Robinson, Tracy Robinson, Missy R. Rogers, Javier Romero, Shannan Ross, Brad Sanders, Jigo Santos, Nicole Scott, Scott W. Sheaffer, Tim Simons, A. Todd Skaggs, James Skala Jr., Lauren Sletta, James D Smith, Scott Montgomery Snider, Dawn Spengler, Paul Staples, Charlie Stark, Nicholas Stephenson, Susanne Stohr, K. Stoker, Christopher Stollar, Katrina Stonoff, Sally A. Struthers, Nita Sweeney, Ali Sweet, David Swisher, Georffrey Talarico, S. Taushanoff, Emmy Teague, Tenebrous Press, Tracey Thompson, David Tomblin, Paul & Laura Trinies, Victor Twynstra, D. Matthew Urban, Michael Jeramy Lee Vermilye, Bill & Heather Walden, Rhonda J. Watt, Graham Weaver, John Winkleman, Alex X.

CPSIA information can be obtained
at www.ICGtesting.com
Printed in the USA
LVHW100534211222
735629LV00004B/401

9 798218 052232